The Lovely One

Naemi Tiana

Cover Design: Vixen Designs
Editor: Laura MacAulay
ISBN: 978-3-00-067163-0

The Lovely One

Prologue

I FIDDLED WITH THE ENDS OF MY HAIR, WAITING FOR MY FRIENDS' reactions. Jasmin and Sophie pouted their perfectly glossed lips, and my best friend Lisa narrowed her eyes as if looking into an annoyingly bright light. Students streamed past us in the hallway, ready to call it a day. I straightened my backpack to have something to do in the uncomfortable silence.

Finally, Jasmin spoke up. "I thought you were just kidding about going abroad, Emily?" She glared at me, blonde curls falling down in waves.

Sophie hopped on the bandwagon, raising one overly plucked eyebrow. "Are you even aware of how different American culture is? It's nothing like Germany."

I tried to swallow down the lump in my throat and looked at Lisa for support, but when our eyes met I realized that even she couldn't be counted on anymore.

"Do you seriously think you can survive without us?" she said, crushing my last shred of hope. I inched back until I felt the cold wall against my shoulders.

"Guys, please . . ." I felt tears crawling into my eyes already.

"We can't protect you when you're ten thousand kilometers away. Why does it have to be an entire year?" Lisa demanded. I looked down at her hand. Her fingers were clenched around my upper arm.

"I always wanted to get to know another culture," I mumbled, giving her my standard response.

But that wasn't really why I'd signed up to be a foreign exchange student. For starters, I wanted Reason #1 on my private list: *Have an adventure.* An escape from my own life. I wanted to throw myself into a bustling, lively American city. LA, Miami? The thrill of wild parties. A rush. *Something.*

"But you're part of our group. Does that mean nothing to you?"

I avoided her stare. For the first time in four years I wasn't following orders, and I didn't know how to deal with it. "It does, but . . . I just really have to do this, okay?"

Lisa could have pierced me right through with her eyes. "You really are serious about this." She sighed and stepped away. I rubbed my arm at the spot she'd put pressure on.

My role in the group was clear: I was their *Puppe,* their "little doll." A plaything they could order around as they pleased. I had played this charade for way too long. They'd taken away my voice, my entire backbone. That's how Reason #2 made it on the list: *Find confidence.* I needed to be myself again.

"I'm sorry, guys, but I need to do this," I repeated lamely.

"What are you ladies talking about?" a male voice cut in. Michael. A tall, red-haired, average-looking guy . . . and for a reason I didn't even understand myself, my boyfriend.

"Your girlfriend is going to America for a year. Getting herself some hot football players," cooed Jasmin.

I tried not to sink too deep into the ground beneath me. This was the last way I wanted him to find out about my decision.

"You're kidding, right?" He crossed his freckled arms. I looked at my friends, hoping against hope that they'd speak for me again.

But this time I was on my own. "We'll leave you lovebirds alone," Sophie said, and the three of them giggled away, leaving a waft of way-too-sweet perfume in the air. I hadn't played by their rules, and this was my punishment. I stood still, hoping Michael would start the conversation, but he just quirked one eyebrow at me expectantly.

"Michael, you know it's my dream to see the world." My voice was cracking, so I held onto my backpack tightly for support.

"You could just travel in the summer!" His voice echoed through the school hallway and a dozen pairs of eyes landed on us.

"That's not enough." I bit my lip, gazing past Michael to the window behind him. *Why does nobody get that?*

"So I'm just a stupid boy toy for you?"

"Of course not! I just . . . I just feel like every week is the same here. And I . . ."

I'm unhappy. I'm not in control of myself. And I'm not in love with you.

My silence said what I wasn't brave enough to put into words. Michael scanned me from head to toe, shaking his head. "Fine, but I won't be waiting for you when you come back."

I stayed stiff, staring at his reflection on the window because I couldn't handle looking straight into his hardened eyes.

"Have fun with the football players," he spat before walking away without a backward glance.

I dabbed at my eyes expecting tears, but there were none. What Michael and I had wasn't real. I was just a handy boost for his reputation since I belonged to the popular clique. And now, he'd given me the freedom to start over. Maybe even with Reason #3, a reason whose existence I tried to deny. A reason that would be my downfall.

Experience real love.

I made my way to the exit, meeting Cologne's usual dark clouds. On the other side of the street, my friends were looking pleased. I was about to walk over to apologize when my phone rang.

"Mom? Yeah, I told them . . ." My mother was the hardest person to leave behind, but she was also the only one who understood why less than a year wasn't enough.

I shrugged off my backpack and felt a huge weight being lifted off my shoulders. Everyone knew. The foundation of my new life was set.

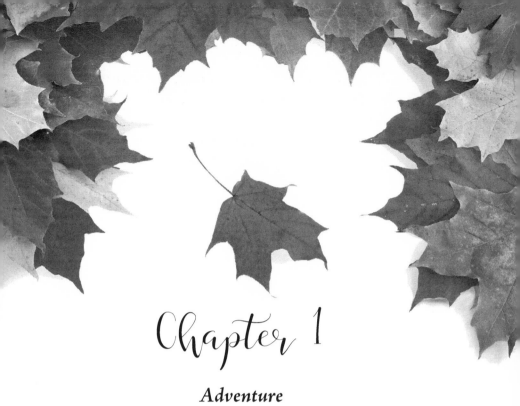

Chapter 1

Adventure

ON ALL FOURS, I CRAWLED ON THE GROUND, RIPPING OUT weeds that had grown in between the steps of the staircase from the house down to the lake. Twenty-four steps, and I was at number sixteen, obediently doing my work. My hands burned from the cold and the scraped-open skin, and my parched throat craved a glass of water. The October wind soughed through the trees, and from behind dusty clouds, I could just make out the outline of the sun. I let go of my spade and sank down onto step sixteen.

Sixteen. The number of years I've been on this earth, and the first year of my life that I was utterly alone. I thought being an exchange student would be a cure for loneliness, but instead, it had only rubbed salt into the wound.

Sighing, I straightened up and trudged down the remaining steps, stopping at number two to look out onto the placid lake in front of me. *Two.* The number of months I've been in this crap hole. I sucked in my breath to prevent tears from escaping the corners of my eyes. *Less thinking, more working.* I brushed my dirty blonde hair out of my eyes and turned around, instantly regretting the view of my Saturday afternoon. Eight steps left before I could jump into the shower and scrub my skin until it became a shade of pink again.

Eight, the number of months left until I'd be back with my family. Until this failed adventure would be over. My knees hit the concrete of the steps. Why did I think I would find my voice by coming here? "Come on, if you hurry up, you can be done in two hours, Emily," I repeated to myself, hoping to make my hands work faster. But the cold numbed them to my coaxing.

Instead of California or Florida, I'd landed in Boonville, Missouri, a town of only 8,000. The only indication that this town wasn't totally dead was that a car occasionally drove by. But apart from that . . . nothing. No thrills, no rush, no adventure. So not what I'd come here for. I punched the ground, ripping open a second layer of skin on my knuckles.

"This can't be it," I muttered, gritting my teeth. I never could've imagined that staying with a host family would mean a full-time job as a maid. While other students were hanging out with friends after school, I was busy vacuuming the living room or scouring dishes until they sparkled. And if I didn't work fast enough, I ended up with a dinner gone cold. It was the only meal I could expect to get in a day because I wasn't sure if I was allowed to take anything out of the fridge. Whenever I went for it, I felt my host mother's eyes on the back of my head as she gave a snarky comment. So I simply stopped doing it, no matter how hungry I was. School, clean, sleep, *repeat.*

When I finally finished weeding, my hands covered in dried blood, I climbed back up to the house. It looked like something out of a fairy tale, with ivy creeping up pastel yellow walls and a grandiose balcony facing the lakeside. No one could have guessed that the family living in it wasn't nearly as magnificent. I entered the house, knees trembling as if I was about to face my worst nightmare—which was actually a pretty accurate description. The living room alone was bigger than my entire apartment back home with my mom and my big brother, Lucas.

"Hello, Emily."

My entire body went stiff. *Hello, Nightmare.*

"Hi, Mrs. Stone." My voice squeaked a bit.

She gave me an approving nod and my toes curled into the carpet. At first glance, she seemed anything other than terrifying. With her natural curls, dark brown eyes, and colorful pearl necklace, she looked like a sweet lady. But the smile I once thought was friendly now gave me the chills. No matter what mood she was in, she always kept that smile glued to her face, upholding her facade for the people outside these walls.

"Have you finished the gardening work I gave you?" she asked.

I let go of the breath I was holding. "Yes, I'm finished."

"Good girl!" She picked up her wallet from a dresser that wasn't there this morning. Must have come from another one of her antique shopping sprees. "Here's ten dollars for your time."

"Thanks." I took the money and darted cautiously past her.

"Emily, wait!"

I'd tested my luck. Slowly, I turned around. "Yes?"

"I couldn't help but notice that you've been a bit distant lately. Come, let's have a chat."

She walked over to a cayenne-colored couch with too many throw pillows and arranged herself on it, patting the spot right next to her. On the mahogany coffee table were two of her best porcelain teacups, already filled—she'd been planning this attack. I sat down, scooching as far away as possible. The ticking of an old wooden clock echoed in my ears, an eternity in each second that passed by. She took her cup and nodded at me to do the same. Politely, I took a small sip. It was her "nighty-night" concoction, more bitter than sweet. Like a wicked witch, she'd once explained the powers of the herbs in her recipe. Supposedly they calmed the nerves. But they definitely weren't enough to calm mine.

"You've been here for quite some time, and I assume that you've made some friends by now."

Friends? I wish.

"I wanted to use this opportunity to remind you that in order for you to live with us, there are certain rules you must follow." Her fingers twisted the string of pearls around her neck.

"Rules?" I coughed, the bitter taste of the tea spreading down my throat.

"You're probably aware of your organization's restrictions? There's a zero tolerance policy on drugs and alcohol. Oh, and let's not forget parties."

"No parties?" I pressed my lips together so as not to lose my composure.

"Not as long as you live under my roof. Parties lead to drinking and I don't want you getting any ideas." Her lips were curled up, but her voice was sharp.

I picked at my fingertips, feeling the adventure I longed for slipping even further away from me. My throat ached from the lump forming in it.

"Your area representative is only one call away. We certainly don't want you getting sent back home to Germany so soon. Don't you think?" She smiled even more broadly and panic spread in my chest. I couldn't go back and admit to my friends that they'd been right. I couldn't make it without them.

"There won't be any need for that." I pulled at my dirty shirt with a bloody hand, hoping she would get the hint that I needed a shower. She gave a slight nod and drained her teacup. I got up and sped to the door. Today wasn't the day I was ready to confront her about how she treated me. Not today, and probably not tomorrow either.

I made it to my room and shut the door. It gave its usual loud creak that echoed through the hall. Sliding down the door onto the itchy carpet, I hugged my knees, fighting not to break down in tears. *What did you do, Emily? Why did you leave your safe cocoon?* I rocked back and forth in a motion that had become a daily habit.

After the shivers subsided and I regained control of my heartbeat, I decided that a shower and an episode of *Grey's Anatomy* would drown out my self-pity. But first, my phone. I'd left it on my dresser before the weeding. I swiped the screen, hoping to see a message from my friends in Germany, but there was nothing but my background picture of a sunset.

I threw the phone onto the bed and headed back into the hall for the bathroom. I couldn't blame them for not texting me. I'd barely sent them any messages myself thanks to the advice I'd gotten during prep week for exchange students: *If you're always on your phone talking to your friends and family back home, you'll get homesick.* Aiming for the best experience possible, I was diligently following every single recommendation they'd given me. Plus . . . my friends couldn't know that they'd been right about me all along.

I pressed my ear to the bathroom door to hear if it was occupied. To my luck, it was empty, so I slipped inside, squirmed out of my clothes and stepped into the shower. The hot water burned my scratches a little, but it was still the highlight of my day. Going on this adventure was the stupidest idea I'd ever had. Instead of starring in one of those typical high school movies, I'd ended up as Cinderella. With an abusive host mother, an absentee host father who was always at work, and a host sister who couldn't care less about me. The only difference was that there was no Prince Charming to save me from my misery. I was all on my own.

Wrapped in a towel, refreshed by the scent of green apple shampoo, I made it back into my room unseen. It wasn't only Mrs. Stone's fault that everything had gone wrong. At school, I hadn't managed to make a single friend in two months. I was too afraid to say much. Even though my friendships in Germany were based on beauty, boys and babbling about nonsense I never really cared about, I missed them.

At least I had some kind of voice with them, however small. Screw the advice.

I had just slumped into bed to text Lisa when I received what I'd least expected. A message from a moody, independent Puerto Rican girl in my Culinary Arts class. And it changed everything.

What's up, girl? Want to come over and hang out? - Breana

My breath caught as the message sank in. This was the first time I'd been asked to hang out. Why would Breana bother? We'd barely even exchanged two words in class. Guided by a spark of hope, my thumbs made themselves independent.

Sounds good. Send me your address and I'll be over in 30.

I felt my cheeks turning pink with excitement. I was going to escape this house, if only just for one evening. I was actually going to socialize with someone! When her address popped onscreen, I jumped over to my sparsely filled closet and pulled on high-waisted black jeans plus a white crop top over my red bra. I brushed out my hair, making sure it was lying over my way-too-small chest and hiding the birthmark on my left cheek I so despise. Grabbing a black cardigan and sneakers, I went down to the kitchen.

I was met by my own reflection in the shiny stainless steel of the fridge—messy waves of halfway-dry hair and red spots on my face, which I ignored—and my host sister, Madison. She was standing at the marble-topped counter, picking at a salad in her pajamas.

Doesn't a seventeen-year-old have anything else to do on a Saturday night?

One of the first and only things she told me about her was that she was vegetarian. Her deep brown hair fell straight over her shoulders, and even though she didn't wear makeup, she had perfect skin and long dark eyelashes. She was the dream daughter: good student, keen on volunteering, top in the track-and-field club. But to me, she was everything I tried not to be. A robot programmed for perfect performance.

"Hey, Madison . . . Breana invited me to hang out with her tonight."

"You scared the poop out of me!" Madison pointed her fork at me.

"The *poop*?"

There were two types of Americans: the ones who cursed like crazy and the ones who frowned on any swearing at all. The Stone family belonged to the second category. Madison was a good girl who wouldn't dare pronounce the word "shit."

"Whatever," she huffed, rolling her eyes way too far back in her head.

"Um, do I have to ask your mother for permission?"

Madison shrugged, evidently unimpressed about my going out for the first time. "She's already asleep, but if she wakes up I'll tell her you went to your girlfriend's place."

"Thanks." My shoulders instantly relaxed. That went way easier than I thought. I wouldn't have to deal with my nightmare again today. Mrs. Stone probably would've gone through all the rules again. I turned toward the door, but Madison's voice pulled me back like a lasso around my neck.

"Don't let Breana pressure you into anything."

I turned around with a frown. For the first time since I'd been here, Madison was showing an interest in me. "What are you getting at?"

"Nothing. Just be careful around her and her group of friends."

Chin held high, Madison left the kitchen, leaving her salad bowl on the table as a reminder for me to clean up.

Once I'd put fifteen meters between the house and me, I relaxed out of my slow-motion tiptoe and walked like a normal human being. The excitement of not spending another lonely night with my TV dramas, dreaming of a kind of love I don't even believe in—it was enough to quiet the alarms going off in my head. As dusk fell over the streets, I made a mental list of every way this night could possibly turn out. Breana's neighborhood was a little less upscale, but not run-down either. I met her in front of her house.

"Emily, I'm glad you made it," Breana purred.

Breana, a girl from who you never knew what to expect. Would she be as unruly as her long dark curls or as distant as the faraway look in her eyes? Or maybe she'd be grinning like this world had never once harmed her tanned skin? I'd witnessed her mood swings countless times in Culinary Arts class. Tonight she gave me a satisfied smile, and I couldn't tell if it was real or fake.

"Thanks for the invite. I needed to get out of the house," I said cautiously, still hearing Madison's warning echoing in my head. When Breana gave me a confused look, I added, "My host mother drives me insane."

"Ugh, I feel you! My mom can be so exhausting too!" She nodded knowingly.

"I wasn't used to moms being so crazy," I blurted out before I had the chance to overthink it.

"Oh really? Then you're a lucky bitch!" Breana laughed. *First category.*

"What's up with you and your mom?"

Breana jumped on the question like a dog on a bone. "I do everything wrong! The other day I made cupcakes and I thought that would make her happy! But you know what she did?"

"I—"

"She just complained about the kitchen being covered in flour! I had just finished making them, I would've cleaned up, you know? And she hasn't even tried one yet."

"Oh, um . . . I'd like to try one." I gave her a reassuring smile.

"Aw, thanks." She giggled and pulled me into a hug. "You're so sweet!"

It was my first hug since I'd said goodbye to my own mother at the airport two months ago. The moment was emblazoned in my memory. "I'll miss you so much, my lovely one," she'd sobbed, holding me as tight as she could, practically cutting off my breath.

"I'll miss you too, Mama," I said, without any tears in my eyes because I was so naively excited about what was to come. She hadn't wanted me to go to America at first, but my stubbornness had won out after months of my adding pros to the list.

"Don't forget to stay true to yourself. You're perfect exactly the way you are, lovely."

Those were the last words I heard from her face-to-face before exiling myself thousands of miles away. And I disagreed. I was anything but perfect.

I was wrenched out of my thoughts when a car zoomed up the road, going way over the speed limit. Breana pumped her fist and hollered like a cheerleader. The car squealed to a stop in front of us and honked twice. A guy leaned out of the passenger window, his face hidden in the shadow of the night.

"Hey, ladies," he called. "Tonight's gonna be one for the books. I hope you're ready for an adventure."

I stood there, paralyzed.

This night, this exact moment . . . it felt like the beginning of something huge.

Chapter 2

The Taste of Danger

"I HOPE YOU DON'T MIND," BREANA SAID. "I ASKED SOME other friends to hang out too."

I did mind, but I wasn't going to tell her that just hanging out with her was already overwhelming. She pulled me into the back seat, and I barely had time to put on my seat belt before the engine roared to a start. The wind whistling through a cracked-open window muffled Breana's greetings as she leaned toward the front to give the driver and passenger a quick peck on the cheek. Two dudes. I inhaled deeply, settling into the sweet reality that for the first time in ages, I wasn't spending the evening alone.

"*. . . Missouri Tigers better get a touchdown soon or they'll get skunked!*" the radio announcer's voice was blaring. The two guys growled.

"Mizzou's losing, huh?" Breana fell back into her seat when neither of the boys turned around to reply. The driver rolled up his window.

After a pause, the dude in the passenger seat mumbled, "Yeah, they need to get their shit together." He lit up a cigarette and the acrid smell of tobacco invaded my senses.

Suddenly aware of the driver studying me through the rearview mirror, I looked away quickly and ran my fingers through my tangled hair. When I sneaked another peek and saw his eyes still on me, I choked a little on my own spit. They were ocean blue, so luminous that I smiled in spite of myself. I dropped my gaze to my hands, but it was too late. The heat in my cheeks betrayed my blush.

The radio connection broke off and out of the corner of my eye, I watched the driver twirl a button around to find the signal. "C'mon, work!" he muttered.

Breana was chatting with the smoking guy about football plays. He had a husky voice. Probably because of the cigarettes.

I couldn't shake the feeling that I was still being watched, so I peeked at the mirror again. Yep. The driver was definitely shifting his attention between the road and me—as if he was struggling to look away too.

The radio announcer kept up his warnings. *"The Tigers have got one last chance!"*

I risked another glance at the driver. The messy cut of his light brown hair couldn't hide his high cheekbones. His heart-shaped lips had a natural reddish tinge. And he wasn't trying to hide his well-toned arms, considering he was wearing just a tank top. *An athlete?*

A loud cheer erupted out of the radio, and the driver slammed his fist onto the steering wheel. "Fuck!"

"I told you they stand no chance, man," remarked the guy in the passenger seat.

"God, it's just a football game." Breana rolled her eyes and pulled out her phone. The driver just grunted and turned his attention back to the road.

"You heard that, dude? It's just a game, so chill," teased the passenger. In the reflection on the windshield, I saw that his eyes were the color of dark chocolate, almost black. His hair, perfectly disheveled, was darker still. He was casually slumped in his seat, his nearly finished cigarette neatly perched on his lower lip. He tossed the butt out the window and turned to face me. When my eyes locked with his, I recognized him. This was the guy from my US History class.

I remembered it clearly. I was a little late for that class since it was my first day at Boonville High and I couldn't find the room. The teacher, Mr. Harrison, told me to sit wherever I wanted, not an easy choice considering that half the room was empty. *How do you decide where to sit when you don't know a single soul?* I scanned the rows of students staring at me. He was the only one who kept his head down. That was why he grabbed my attention—because he wasn't giving me his.

When Mr. Harrison noticed my discomfort, he said, "You can sit next to Hannah Brown, in front of Jon Denson."

And that's when he looked up, only for a short second, but long enough for me to remember those dark chocolate-brown eyes filled with so much pain.

The same eyes were staring at me now. This time they looked curious, almost impatient.

"Do I know you, Little One?" Jon's lips turned up in a cocky smirk and mine tightened.

What an idiot! I'd come to America so I wouldn't be anybody's "little one" anymore, a fragile girl people thought needed protecting because she was made of glass. *I'm not weak, I'm brave.* At least, I wanted to be brave . . . I wanted to cross out Reason #2 for coming here. *Find Confidence.* Which is why I responded like I had nothing to lose.

"I'm not your little one."

It was supposed to sound confident, but my voice shook at the edges, exposing me for a fraud. My stomach felt like it was about to twist 180 degrees. I caught a glimpse of Breana trying to hold back a laugh while Jon . . . Jon didn't even try to hide his mirth. "You're cute, *Little One,*" he said, cracking up.

I could have tried to throw another wannabe-sassy line at him, but I made myself small in the back seat, regretting my words. He leaned over and reached out his hand.

"I'm Jon. Jon Denson."

I hesitated, then put my hand into his. His eyes were smiling along with his mouth now.

"I'm Emily Klein." I tried to move my hand up and down for a handshake, but he held it still.

"Do I recognize an accent? Italian? Dutch? French?" His hand was still holding mine in his, his thumb slowly caressing my skin. A sharp shiver ran up my arm and up the back of my neck.

"N-no, I'm from Germany."

"So what they say is true."

"W-what?" I said a little louder, curiosity piqued.

"German girls really are beautiful."

A thrill ran through me. I loved how straightforward and bold he was. Something about that cocky smirk was exhilarating.

"*Touchdown for the Jayhawks!*" shouted the announcer. Jon whipped around and yelled at the radio, and the driver gave a bitter laugh. The Tigers were clearly lost. I pressed back into the seat. *What on earth was that?*

"Don't take his flirting too seriously," Breana whispered, her eyes glued to her phone.

"I didn't—" I began, but seeing her scroll through her feed on Instagram, I realized that she wasn't listening.

I was debating whether getting into the car had been a good idea after all when the driver remarked, "We're here." We had stopped in the completely empty parking lot of a grocery store. There was nobody in sight. In a town that was dead at the best of times, this place was deader. The lights were flickering like they were fighting not to go out. *What did Madison mean by not letting Breana pressure me into anything?*

"Don't get caught!" the driver said as Jon pulled on the door handle.

"Dude, you know I'm capable." Jon's eyes found mine again. "See you in a sec, Little German," he said with a mocking smile.

"I—" But he'd already slammed the door and walked away, hands slung in his pockets. *Great, I got myself a nickname.*

So that was Jon Denson. But why hadn't the other guy introduced himself? Gathering up all the courage I had left after my encounter with Jon, I called to the driver, "Hey, I think we probably haven't been introduced yet. I'm Emily, it's nice to meet you."

I'd learned that "It's nice to meet you" was how you started a conversation with a stranger in America. Everyone said it. "*It's nice to meet you. We should hang out soon.*" At first I took it at face value. "*Oh, that would be lovely!*" But now that I knew better, I just smiled politely. No one really meant it—but I still did.

"Yeah, I heard your name," the driver replied with an edge of annoyance.

"And what's your name, then?" I pressed. There was no hint of a shake in my voice this time and I gave myself an imaginary pat on the shoulder.

"Paul Shields." He shrugged and turned up the volume of the radio, I suppose as a signal for me to shut up.

Breana started a conversation I thought we had finished already. "You said your host mother drives you crazy. Why is that?"

"Um, yeah . . . she's . . ."

"That bad, hm?" Breana placed her hand on mine and gave it a squeeze. I almost flinched at the warmth of this little gesture.

"It's just . . . I'm used to my mother trusting me. Mrs. Stone thinks the worst of me. If she knew I was in a car with strangers tonight, she'd lock me in for the rest of the year. And I always have to do chores even though her daughter doesn't lift a finger. I didn't come here to be a maid . . . I . . ." I looked up and bit my lower lip. I didn't want to scare Breana away.

The sound of an ad on the radio filled the car as Breana let the news sink in. Paul turned around to look at me, his expression indifferent.

"I just don't know what to do. I don't want to talk back and risk getting kicked out." My voice cracked again. I expected to hear that I was overreacting. Their silence made the entire situation feel even more real.

"Maybe try talking to her about this again? I get your struggle, but you can't let her treat you like that," Breana said with a shrug. It wasn't like I hadn't heard this advice before—it's what people had been telling me my entire life.

"Breana, if talking to her worked, don't you think she would've tried it already?" Paul had put my thoughts into words. I guess he cared to be part of this conversation after all.

"Well, do you have any better suggestions?" Breana shot back. Paul was quiet.

I knew that I could call my area rep to request a new host family, but finding one in the same tiny town was really unlikely. I didn't want to completely start over again.

"So . . . what's the most shocking thing about America for you? Apart from your evil host mother," Breana joked. I smiled gratefully and wiped away the tears in the corners of my eyes.

"Hmm . . . I'm still processing that you guys are allowed to drive at sixteen!" I gestured to Paul, who was smiling too. I couldn't help but admire his cute dimples.

"How old do you have to be to drive in Germany?" he asked.

"Eighteen."

"Wait, you can drive at eighteen, but drink at sixteen?" said Breana. "I remember reading something about that on the internet. So unfair. We're supposed to wait till we're twenty-one."

"Yep. But only wine and beer. For hard liquor, you have to be eighteen," I said.

"Then I hope you have an eighteen-year-old friend." Breana giggled and exchanged a look with Paul. He turned back to the front.

"I do, but what are you—"

The revving of the engine swallowed the rest of my words. In the side-view mirror, I saw Jon sprint out of the store with something bulky under his black leather jacket. Paul opened the passenger door with a soft push of the wrist like it was second nature. The second Jon jumped into the passenger seat, he hit the gas and drove out of the parking lot, tires squealing. The blood froze in my veins. Jon was definitely not twenty-one.

"I hope you all like rum?" Jon smirked in triumph, holding up a bottle of white liquor. I held on tightly to my seat belt as Paul picked up speed. My brain should have been screaming to stop the car, but I suddenly smiled. This rush. It made my chest heat up from the blood pounding through it. It was ... different.

We got onto the highway and Paul let off a little. Jon tilted his head and grinned at me, the bottle still raised in his fist. I couldn't help but grin back, shaking my head with my hand over my mouth. He definitely had guts. Yet it was kind of troubling to see that this was totally normal for him. As a goody-two-shoes, I'd never done anything illegal. Heck, I was too scared to swipe even a pack of gum with my friends back in the 7th grade.

But now, I'd tasted danger, and I liked its sharp flavor.

"It was a close one this time." Jon knocked another cigarette out of an almost empty packet of Newports. *Lighting it. Inhaling.* "They hired another security guard." *Exhaling.*

Breana grabbed the bottle and read the label. "Yes! You got the good stuff too!" she shrieked like a kid at Christmas. Clearly she didn't mind that they'd broken the law.

So this was how they spent their weekends. Stealing and getting drunk. Now I knew what Madison was talking about. I frowned as I realized what I was getting myself into. I was literally breaking all the rules Mrs. Stone had just laid out.

"Why the spooked look, Little German? Too much for you to handle?" Jon said, his cig hanging off his dry lip. He'd read my face like an open book. Anger hit me with an unfamiliar fire.

"If I get caught being an accomplice to a crime, I'll get kicked out of the country," I snapped.

"I don't see any handcuffs around our wrists," he fired back.

"Well, no, but we could've—"

"But we didn't! Relax. Life is too short to worry all the time."

I didn't reply.

On the tips of our toes, yet less cautiously than the type of sneaking I did at the Stone house, we crept into Paul's place. It was drop-dead quiet and dark inside. His parents were probably already asleep. We rushed down to the basement, which turned out to be Paul's bedroom. It looked comfy, a little messy, but tonight I didn't mind. A small window invited moonlight into the room. A king-sized bed occupied the far end, and a worn-out couch sat across from a fireplace that looked like it hadn't been used in ages. But what really caught my eye was the chalk scrawled on the walls. I wandered over to take a closer look at the quirky drawings, the writing with slang words I didn't understand, and best of all, the sketches of sunsets. I loved sunsets. I let out my breath. I felt safe here.

While I'd been checking out my surroundings, everybody had flopped down on the couch. Judging by the bottle's contents, it was already making its second round. The three of them were drinking the rum straight without any soda. The way they slugged it down pained me. They didn't drink for the pleasure of it—they drank to get their demons out, to stop feeling anything.

"Little German, we all have something to drink for. Unless your life is too perfect?" Jon said with a twinkle in his eye, offering me the bottle.

It wasn't that he was forcing me into it; it was more like he could tell I had demons too and just needed a little push to let go. I nodded shyly and grabbed the bottle. Letting my heart show me the way, I joined in the numbing and drank. Drank to forget, just like them.

Chapter 3

Main Character

"**D**O YOU SEE YOURSELF AS A MAIN CHARACTER, A supporting actor or an extra?" Jon asked as the low pulse of the music died away.

We'd been listening to rap, aggressive and angry as if the mic was being attacked. Not really my style, but the three of them had bobbed their heads to the beat, clearly into it.

"Man, that's a difficult question. Why do you ask?" Paul took a gulp of the half-empty bottle and passed it to Breana.

I was curled up on the edge of the couch, feeling my head spin already. I couldn't even remember when was the last time I'd had so much to drink.

"Random thought . . ." Jon shrugged, but a flicker in his eyes said otherwise. "What about you, Little German?"

He caught my eye, and I chewed the inside of my cheek. Boys had always made me feel ordinary, like a side character. No, less—a background character. A little doll on the shelf of my friend group.

"Not sure," I hedged. I didn't feel ready to open up to them like that.

"For me it's easy: main character!" Breana declared, striking a pose. I smiled. The easy way she held herself up to the world—it's how I wanted to be too.

"You gotta keep up, German!" Breana passed me the bottle. She was already so intoxicated that she started jumping on the couch like she was trying to reach the clouds.

"Fine!" I snatched the bottle from her. Tonight was my escape. I was free to think my own thoughts, make my own decisions. I'd live like there was no tomorrow. I was already in deep trouble anyway. I tipped back the bottle for a swig.

Breana knocked into me as she landed and the rum spilled over the front of my shirt, soaking it through.

"Bre!" Paul chided, sliding over to me.

I noticed his stare and looked down. My red bra showed clearly under the white fabric of my shirt. I quickly crossed my arms over my chest.

"It wasn't her fault. I had an accident," I mumbled, then snorted with laughter. Either this situation was suddenly twice as funny as it actually was, or the alcohol had made me loosen up.

"An *accident*, huh?" Jon smirked at me as he slumped deeper into the couch. Breana was laughing hysterically.

I looked at Paul. "What's so funny?"

"An accident means that you peed yourself," he explained with a chuckle.

"Oh!" I joined in Breana's laughing fit with a full heart. Gosh, it felt so good to laugh like this again. *Thank you, dear alcohol, for keeping me from overthinking.* When the giggles petered out, I looked down at myself. I couldn't go back to the Stones' place smelling like this.

Paul went to get something out of the closet. "Here." He handed me a jersey of the Mizzou Tigers.

"Aw, don't you have a better jersey to lend me? I don't want to wear the shirt of the losing team," I said teasingly, powered by the booze pulsing in my veins. He quirked an eyebrow and I started backing away.

Paul sprinted after me, out of the room and down the hall, calling, "You take that back!"

"Never!" I screeched. I dashed into the bathroom and tried to close the door behind me, but he was too quick. I jumped into the bathtub and hid behind the shower curtain, peeking out first left and then right, almost meeting his face each time. He latched his arms around my middle so that I was wrapped in the curtains like a burrito. "Ahhhh!" I tried to wiggle out of his grip, but he held on tightly and managed to climb into the bathtub.

"Say: The Mizzou Tigers are the best team!" His voice was so playful and precious.

"Never!" This playfight was the new highlight of my trip.

He picked me up bridal-style and in retaliation, I reached down and turned on the tap. The cold water engulfed all my senses, and since I knew it was coming, it was nice and refreshing.

Paul, on the other hand, accidentally swallowed some. "I'm gonna let you win this round just this once," he said, coughing, and suddenly we were lost in each other's eyes. Water dripped down his face, and his damp hair glittered. His gaze landed on my lips and—

"What the fuck are you doing?" Breana gasped from the doorframe, staring at the two of us in the bathtub, soaking wet.

Quickly I jumped out of Paul's arms and climbed out. "N-nothing . . ." I could feel the ground trembling beneath me, my heart racing along with my breath. Would he have kissed me if Breana hadn't walked in?

"Mm, right." Her eyes wandered all over me before landing on Paul. "Can you come outside with me? There's something I have to talk to you about."

"Sure." Paul walked over to her, his features calm. I couldn't tell if he wanted to talk to her or not.

I changed into Paul's jersey and headed back into the bedroom. Jon was sitting there, staring out the window. The couch creaked as I sat down next to him, and he passed me the bottle with a cheeky smile. "So you don't see yourself as a main character, huh?" he said.

Stalling for time, I took a huge gulp of rum and let the burn spread through my chest.

Then I opened my mouth, and we talked about anything and everything.

Later, after we'd discussed . . . already forgot . . . Paul and Breana were back and joined us on the couch. I barely knew these people, but I felt oddly comfortable around them. Breana put on another rap album, and we were so smashed that we all started dancing to the music, jumping up and down like kids at a sleepover party. We threw our poisoned bodies on the carpet and rolled around on it for no reason, sometimes ending up on top of each other but never for too long. Laughing, crying, and feeling every little impulse of joy in our bodies. Forgetting all our problems, all our pain. Forgetting it all.

"What made you come to America?" Paul asked.

We'd ended up back on the couch together while Breana and Jon made their way to the back of the room and onto Paul's bed for a private conversation. I could hear Breana give a high-pitched giggle after Jon said something, but I couldn't make out what they were talking about. All I could see were Paul's brilliant blue eyes focusing on mine. Even though the lights were dim, I still caught their sparkle.

"Emily?" he said again.

I could've given the same long, tedious answer about experiencing another culture, meeting new people and improving my English skills, but this time I went for honesty. It was like an instinct that this boy could be so much more than a drunken encounter on a Saturday night.

"I have three reasons," I said shyly.

"And those reasons are?" Paul gave a playful smile, revealing those dimples. His eyes were slightly red and his words a little slurred, but other than that, he was handling the rum pretty well.

"Basically, there were things missing in my life in Germany, and I was hoping to find them here." I moved my hair out of my face. It felt tremendously good to tell him this.

"It's really brave to leave your home like that, you know?"

"Maybe."

"Maybe?"

"I don't think my coming here has anything to do with bravery. I ran away. When I go back, my issues will still be there." My chest suddenly flooded with warmth. Paul was looking at me with so much interest—he actually wanted to hear my story.

"Maybe coming here will help you solve those issues," he said.

"I hope so." I cocked my head to one side and gave him a coy smile. "So, I told you about my issues. What are yours?"

"My issues?"

"Yeah, what are you drinking for?" I raised my glass.

"I don't know, just for fun, I guess." He fidgeted with his cup before putting it on the shelf above him.

"Oh, so your life is all sunshine and rainbows then?"

"No . . ." Paul sighed. "I guess I'm like you." He ran his fingers through his messy hair.

"Like me?"

"Yeah. Searching for something that's been missing in my life."

Paul's tired smile was replaced with a snort when kissing sounds came from the other side of the room. I turned and saw Breana's mouth crushed onto Jon's. Her body was glued on top of his. My stomach dropped. Something about it made me feel queasy, but I couldn't put my finger on what exactly.

Paul looked at me quizzically and I had to smile again. Inspired by Jon and Breana, I imagined what it would feel like to have Paul's lips on mine. Feeling my cheeks flare up, I let my hair fall back over my face.

But he reached out and tucked it behind my ear, caressing my cheek. "I really like this little birthmark," he whispered, scooching a little closer.

My heartbeat sped up and I quickly looked away, grabbing the nearly-empty rum bottle off the table and taking another sip—regretting it immediately. Paul's hand dropped away, and my stomach turned from the revolting smell and taste of the liquor. I tried desperately to hold it in, but I had to resign myself to the bile crawling up my throat. The taste of acid spread in my mouth as a puddle of vomit formed on the carpet in front of me. *Why do I have to be such a lightweight?*

Paul jumped up in shock, then carefully held me by the waist as he pulled me up. I threw up all the way to the bathroom.

"I got you. It's okay," he whispered, holding me until I felt the cold surface of the toilet seat against my chin.

"G-Go . . ." I begged.

The last thing I wanted was a guy I barely knew holding my hair back while I upchucked. But he simply brushed back a few loose strands from my face and kept his warm hands on my back while my body dispensed of the rum I'd chugged. I suddenly realized that I hadn't eaten anything since breakfast.

"Everything okay in there?" Jon's voice came out of nowhere, making my embarrassment climb to an even higher level.

"I got this, man. Go back to Breana."

The sound of footsteps signaled that he was gone. He wasn't the caring type, I guess. But Paul was. We had just met, and already he was holding my hair like it was nothing. My body forced against my pride, pushing out everything I had left in my stomach. Hot tears burned my eyes and coursed down my cheeks. I had to give in to those too.

"I'm really alone," I moaned in between sobs. "Since I got here, I've been alone. I'm not used to being alone . . ."

"I'm sorry, Emily." Paul sighed. "But you know what?" I looked up at him, my arms still hugging the toilet seat. "You have us now. We had a really great time with you tonight."

"I'm sorry about the carpet," I mumbled.

"Don't worry about it. I understand why you drank so much." He threw me a soft smile.

"Paul . . . Can I ask you something?" I looked at him pleadingly.

"Anything."

"Am I a main character?"

He sat down on the floor next to me and took my face in his hands, cupping my cheeks. "To me, you are."

I looked down, trying to hide my blush. "Oh . . ." Why did I even ask that? But he'd given me the perfect reply, and with that—*hope.* I tilted my head back up to him. Partly because of the nasty smell of the toilet, but mostly because I wanted to look into the eyes that had brought me so much in just one night.

I closed the toilet lid and tried to get up.

"So, what's the missing link in your life?" I asked, going back to our earlier conversation. Paul snorted with laughter, getting up as well and helping me stay on my feet. I was still dizzy.

"You really are a curious one, aren't you?" he said.

I shrugged. Paul searched for something in the cabinet before turning toward me. "I'll keep that story for another time—when you'll actually remember it." He held up a bottle of green liquid. "Mouthwash?"

After I'd freshened up, we went back to the bedroom. Breana and Jon had fallen silent. They were probably passed out. I let myself drop into the middle of the couch and stared at the ceiling, watching a bird Paul had drawn there. I could have sworn its wings were moving.

Paul turned on the TV and sat down right next to me, a blanket in his arms. He spread it on top of us and opened his arms, offering me his chest. Without hesitation I accepted his invitation. I snuggled against his body, listening to his heartbeat and inhaling his comforting scent. Fitting right in with his ocean eyes, it was like a fresh breeze, clean and addictive.

A horror flick was playing, but I can't handle them, so I concentrated on Paul. The way he'd wrapped his arms around me. How gently he was caressing my hair. How intently his light blue eyes were now looking into mine—how crazily my heart thumped in my chest.

"It was really nice to meet you tonight, Emily," he whispered, tugging a strand of hair behind my ear, looking at my lips.

"Are you just saying that, or do you actually mean it?" The question came out before I could really think about it.

Paul grinned, looking up to my eyes again. "I wouldn't say it if I didn't mean it." He brushed his lips against the birthmark on my cheek and my skin tingled. I believed him. Back in the car, he hadn't bothered to say it because he wasn't sure about me, but now, I'd managed to change his mind. I didn't dare move an inch. "You're different," he murmured.

Maybe I was just being naive, but I was really savoring the way Paul was treating me tonight. Even though I'd been gardening all day, I wasn't the least bit tired. I felt electrified. And I wanted more of it. More of *him.*

"I'm really glad we met tonight too."

An indescribable smile lit up his face and he let out a long breath. Gently, he took me by the hips and pulled me onto him so that I was kneeling in his lap. I interlaced my hands behind his neck to support myself as he drew me closer to him. There wasn't even a centimeter—or what he'd call an inch—between us. It was like our hearts were beating in sync. He dragged his hand up my shoulder to my neck. The tremendous desire I felt—it was something I'd never experienced before.

Is this really happening? It feels like a dream. I bit down on my lip as a test and pain radiated through it. *It's real.*

"Emily, I really want to kiss you right now." Paul lightly touched his nose to mine. But something held him back.

"Then why don't you?" My voice came out insecure.

"A first drunk kiss? Is that really what you want?"

I had paused my life in Germany because I was done catering to what other people wanted. Done being the doll of my friend group, the trophy girlfriend for Michael, the obedient daughter to my mother. I wanted that kick—the adrenaline rush that would show me that I was more than a robot that had to function. Because that's what I did: I functioned. Forced smiles and fake hugs, acquiescent on the surface but wanting more inside. In Germany, I was liked by everyone but myself. I felt like I couldn't breathe, stifled by what society expected of me. And tonight, I finally did it—I breathed. All thanks to Paul and his ocean-blue eyes.

"I've never been more sure of anything."

He gave me an astonished grin before closing the remaining space between us and pressing his lips to mine. *Mmm* . . . His lips were ul-tra-soft, the taste of him bitter from the alcohol. But gosh, he tasted so good. I held tightly onto him so he wouldn't back away. He kissed me like I'd never been kissed before, with an intense longing that fed on our proximity. I felt safe, like nothing could take away this moment. I parted my lips to deepen the kiss, but the sound of a cough behind me made me jump and turn around.

Jon was standing right in front of us, his hair mussed up. "Sorry to interrupt, man," he said to Paul. "We have to go."

I quickly got off Paul's lap and Paul let out a little chuckle, his eyes still fixed on me. I peeked into Jon's eyes and saw something I hadn't seen before. His gaze was even darker than usual.

Breana was next to break up the party. "Come on! Right now!" she said directly to me, like it was my fault we hadn't left yet. "My mother will kill me if she notices that I'm still out at four in the morning."

With that, she stormed past us to the door.

Chapter 4

Like Blood from a Stone

ONLY FOUR HOURS AFTER I HAD CLIMBED UP A TREE, SNUCK over the roof and slid through the window into my room, my alarm went off. It was 8 am on a Sunday morning. Church time for the Stone family.

On any other Sunday, I would've had to go to church with them, but today I'd been instructed to prepare a typical German dish for lunch. "We're so fascinated by German culture," Mrs. Stone would gush, but whenever I started telling her about it, the topic got changed abruptly. I didn't mind cooking though. I liked spending time in the kitchen, especially when my other option was to go to church and pretend to pray. I told Mrs. Stone that I didn't believe in God, and her only reply was: "Good thing we have some time to fix that."

I forced myself out of bed, ignoring my heavy eyelids and oily, blotchy skin in the mirror's reflection. I had to get to the grocery store and go through the motions, or Mrs. Stone would find out that I'd gotten drunk last night. Which, right after her discourse on the consequences of drinking, wouldn't be exactly ideal.

To my luck, it was milder out than yesterday, and the fresh air on the walk over helped to soothe my hangover. When I stumbled into the grocery store, my stomach almost turned again as the stench of sweaty blue cheese hit me. I made a face and clutched my belly. *I hate cheese.* A woman nearby wrinkled her nose at me before taking a huge detour around me so I wouldn't puke on her precious Prada bag. I wandered around the store like a lost zombie, trying to find the ingredients I needed.

The food here was different than in Germany. Meat tasted like chewy cardboard, and vegetables were large but bland, like they got treated with way too many chemicals. I missed real German bread, hearty brown loaves that were baked from sourdough and actually had flavor. I was tired of eating wishy-washy white toast all the time.

After wobbling my way down almost every aisle, I'd finally found everything I needed to prepare a German-ish dish. By 10 am, I was back in the Stones' kitchen with a dizzy head and a gross empty feeling in my stomach.

I started peeling and slicing carrots while my mind wandered to the events of the night before. I had finally escaped the house, but then I'd also destroyed a pretty carpet and kissed a guy I just met. I'd never done that before . . . Hell, I'd only kissed two people in my life so far. One was just a little peck while playing truth or dare in the 7th grade, and the other was with Michael.

I sighed and threw the peels into the trash. Next on the chopping board was the watery zucchini for Madison's veggie stew. The way Michael kissed me was nothing like Paul's kiss last night. It had taken three dates with Michael before I let him anywhere near my lips. My friends didn't understand why I was so closed off, but to me it didn't make sense to exchange spit with someone whose mouth had been god knows where. Oddly, none of that mattered when I'd tasted Paul's tongue on mine. He could have kissed thousands of girls before me, but I didn't care.

My gaze landed on my reflection on the stainless steel of the fridge.

I looked different. Exhausted, but excited for what would come next. *How come I suddenly forgot all my rules when I looked into his eyes?*

"Ouch!"

I had cut the side of my thumb while thinking about that incredible kiss. A kiss with a guy I knew literally nothing about. Blood dripped from the wound, narrowly missing the fresh-cut vegetables. I quickly put my hand under the tap to let water rush over it. It burned a little, but it helped. *The water stops the bleeding . . . maybe Paul Shields is the hot water for my frozen heart?*

What shook me even more than breaking my own rules was that I didn't mind that I'd done it. On the contrary, I wanted nothing more than to stamp all over them again. Who knows, maybe if I overcame my fear, he could help me fulfill #3 on my list. *Experience real love.* I was burning to know what it was like to be truly in love with someone.

The sound of footsteps came down the staircase, followed by the voice I feared most. "Madison, eat whenever you like," Mrs. Stone called. "I'm meeting Ophelia for lunch."

I jumped when the front door banged shut, but then my shoulders relaxed. I turned off the water. I wouldn't have to face her. *Is her not catching me hungover a sign that I'm supposed to stay in the US?*

Madison came into the kitchen and went straight for the stove, ignoring my greeting. She curled her lip at one of the pots. "Ew, you made pork? I'm vegetarian!"

Mentally rolling my eyes, I answered with a saccharine smile, "I made mashed potatoes and sauerkraut too. Oh, and the veggies you—"

"Sounds even worse." She was typing like mad on her phone.

I gritted my teeth, trying as hard as I could to not freak out on her. Staying on Madison's good side was the only thing that would get me through the next seven months and twenty-nine days.

"Where's your dad?" I asked to change the subject.

"He's at work." She paused her typing and bit her lip. Mr. Stone was always gone, even at noon on a Sunday. I couldn't blame him. I'd spend every minute away from the devil he called his wife too.

Before I had the chance to reply, Madison had disappeared from the kitchen. I guess I'd gone to all this trouble making a meal only for myself.

The next day, I woke up extra early for a long hot shower while Mrs. Stone was still asleep to avoid getting nagged about the water bill. After my shower, I picked out a ripped black high-waisted skirt with a simple blue top and boots, going for sexy yet classy. I didn't want to look like I was trying too hard, even though I obviously was. I applied a touch of mascara and draped my hair over my chest as usual—covering up my insecurities, hoping that in a sober state I would still be enough for him.

When I came down into the kitchen, Mrs. Stone and Madison were already sitting at the spotless table. Madison gave me a brief glance before turning her attention back to her bowl of oatmeal. Outside, the birds were chirping cheerfully, but Mrs. Stone narrowed her eyes at me even as she presented me with her signature smile. *How can someone look so evil and smile at the same time?*

"Good morning, Emily. I didn't see you yesterday."

"After I finished cooking, I cleaned the kitchen and—"

"And you forgot to vacuum the living room," she interjected with her sharp, pointy voice.

"I did that on Friday, so I thought it would be fine if—"

"We can't afford a maid because we put food on your plate. You should show more gratitude that we let you live here for free."

I was stunned into defenselessness. How come I didn't see it sooner? She'd never wanted for me to be a part of her family or learn about another culture. My only purpose was to make sure this house was correctly sanitized. Nothing more. I wasn't being spoiled or delusional.

Not even realizing what she had just thrown in my face, Mrs. Stone flew past me to give Madison a goodbye kiss on the forehead. "Bye, dear, see you later," she said, her voice as sweet as honey.

When the exchange program organization had told us that host families didn't get paid, my mother had expressed concern. But I didn't—I never imagined that people could take advantage of me like this. I was so naive.

I watched Mrs. Stone leave the kitchen. The vibration of the door closing brought back my ability to speak.

"In your mother's eyes, I'm like a maid?" I said quietly to Madison, hoping that she would support me on this.

She shrugged as if the matter was inconsequential. "She didn't mean it like that."

I crossed my arms fiercely, but I could feel my lower lip trembling.

"How was it with Breana?" Madison mumbled into her oatmeal, cleverly changing the subject.

I fell right into her trap. "We hung out with some friends of hers. You might know them—Paul and Jon?"

Madison choked on her cereal, and for a second it looked like I was going to have to do the Heimlich maneuver. "Paul, the football player?" she coughed out.

"Um, maybe? He didn't mention whether he played football."

But that would explain why he was so buff. It seemed like Jasmin had been right after all . . . I *was* getting myself a hot football player in America. *Maybe.*

"Ah, he's okay, I guess." She put down her spoon and folded her hands in front of her. For the first time since I'd got here, I had her undivided attention. "Did Jon hit on you?"

"Why on earth would he hit me?" I said, startled.

Madison laughed hysterically. "Not if he *hit* you! If he hit *on* you!"

I rubbed the side of my arm and looked at the ground. All the confidence I'd tried to gather this morning had vanished in the blink of an eye. I was still getting used to the English language, and not understanding what people were saying made me even more insecure. All I wanted was to crawl back under my cozy blanket and hide from this world I had no clue about.

"Gosh, you really are a German exchange student." Madison sighed. "It means if he tried to have sex with you, obviously."

Was it really that obvious? No matter how hard I studied English at school, I still needed time to get familiar with the slang.

"My friend told me Jon wants to sleep with you." She giggled.

Blood rushed into my ears. If her friend knew about this, who else did? Had Jon known who I was all along, then? But why was he hooking up with Breana if he liked me? Not that I was complaining, but—

"Earth to Emily!"

I jumped. "Nothing like that happened . . ."

I was regretting telling her anything about that night. But her eyes were giving me a doubtful look, and I knew she wouldn't let off until I spilled more tea.

After a pause that should have signaled that I didn't want to talk about it anymore, I finally added, "I actually got closer with Paul."

"*Did you have sex with him?*" she literally screamed.

"Gosh, no!" I cringed. "We just talked."

The kiss Paul and I had shared was my one happy moment in America. I wouldn't let her steal it away.

"Welp, keep me updated."

She left the kitchen and went into the hall, her hair fluttering behind her.

Madison always drove to school early to meet up with her study group, leaving me to take the yellow school bus. I didn't mind it though. It was a break from all the craziness surrounding me: sitting there, listening to music, watching the streets of Boonville roll by. Around here, it was as close as I could get to peace.

Chapter 5

166

I WANDERED THROUGH THE BLUE AND WHITE HALLS, TAKING the long route to class and keeping my eyes open for Paul. The school's pirate mascot peered at me from his stencil on the wall, and so did other friendly or not-so-friendly faces I didn't know. Every day I saw different people, rarely the same ones. A girl's heels echoed through the hallway while a dude smashed his locker shut before striding past me. From hippies to rockers to jocks, you could find every type of person in this school. Yet I didn't feel like I fit in with any of them. I was just lost in the crowd.

But today . . . today there was a face I needed to find. A face I'd recognize in the masses of people. A face I somehow knew I belonged with. At this rate, I was going to be late for class. But there was no sign of Paul anywhere. Of course not. This was a school with over two thousand students.

First period was Sophomore English. Our task was to write an essay about our current life situation. With a blank sheet of paper in front of me, a pen stalled in my hand, and a perfectly empty mind, I fidgeted in my chair. No one else seemed to mind this task. Their pens flew over their paper while mine remained in neutral. The time on the clockface seemed to have forgotten how to move forward. What an irony that I'd been asked to write about the disappointment I'd felt ever since I arrived in this country. Two months of fear, hard work and loneliness—except for last Saturday night. The night I'd felt less alone than I did in my entire life. Paul had given me so much hope that this year could still blossom into the adventure I was looking for.

After eighty-five minutes of staring at my blank page, it was time for Algebra. I can't say I understood a single thing—math terms in English are like Chinese to me. Anyhow, I was busy daydreaming about what I'd say to Paul when I saw him again. By the end of the class, I still hadn't found the perfect line.

I headed for my locker in front of the huge industrial kitchen we used as a classroom for Culinary Arts. It was my favorite class. I'd chosen it expecting it to be a breeze, but I couldn't have been more wrong. From culinary history to cutting techniques to the terminology for every piece of cooking equipment, it wasn't easy for someone who wasn't used to the English language. "Not one of you is going to make a single dish in here until you master the basics," thundered our teacher, Chef Sayle, on our first day of class. We all thought he was joking, but it turned out that he was dead serious about it.

The locker area was bustling with students grabbing their cooking uniforms. I hadn't even put down my bag in front of my locker when I was confronted about the weekend.

"We heard you got really wasted, girl!" a voice sang out.

It was Danielle, one of my classmates. Her roundish face was framed by straightened dirty blonde hair, and her baby blues were highlighted with a flawless lid line.

Great, I guess everybody knows about my failed attempt at a good time.

Danielle giggled when I hesitated, and I suddenly felt more at ease.

She didn't limit herself to small talk—she brought smiles to people's faces. As much as I admired her for it, I felt smaller in comparison. I couldn't make people laugh by simply being me.

"Yeah, about that. Emily, we have to talk."

One eyebrow lifted, arms crossed, Breana was standing next to me. Apparently, her mood today wasn't in my favor. There was a weird twist in my stomach. Danielle shot me a concerned look but gave us space.

When Breana didn't start talking right away, I twirled my combination lock: 166, the 16th of June, the day of my return to Germany. With a click, the lock opened.

"What's going on between you and Paul?" she said finally, her voice sharp. All our classmates had disappeared into the kitchen.

I slipped out of my shoes and climbed into my cooking pants. "Nothing," I replied, trying to sound unimpressed. "We were drunk, we kissed. That's about it."

Something in her facial expression changed. The crease in her brow was making her look more worried than furious now. "You sure?" she pressed. "I mean, he kissed you goodbye too."

I decided to keep my feelings about Paul to myself. Mainly because I wasn't even sure about them yet.

"I don't want to get into a relationship while I'm here because I have to leave in eight months," I said, taking out my chef jacket.

Seven months and twenty-eight days to be exact.

Breana gave me a piercing look. She didn't believe me.

"Also, he isn't my type."

Oh, he so is.

I tied my hair into a bun and placed the ridiculous-looking chef hat on my head. My mom said I looked like I'd jumped straight out of *Ratatouille* in this outfit.

"I think he's a good catch. He's practically a pro football player. And really hot." Breana wiggled her eyebrows in mock flirtation.

I pretended I was looking for something in my locker to hide the warmth in my face. "I guess . . ." I was feeling more and more unsure about this newly built friendship. "So are you and Jon a thing?" If I had to reveal my feelings about Saturday night, I had every right to ask her the same question.

"Yeah, we have something going on," she exclaimed as if it was the most obvious thing in the world. "We'll be official . . . soon." She bit her lip and started playing with her bracelets.

I don't think I can trust her.

"Yet another day of cutting carrots, celery and onions. What a surprise," Danielle said jokingly, carving her carrot into a heart shape and holding it up to her chest with a smile.

This was our fourth straight week of prepping—and smelling like—vegetable stock. Breana giggled when Chef Sayle walked up to our table.

"That's a cutting style I haven't seen before, Danielle. What's the name of it?" He grinned, flashing his pearly whites. With his three-day beard and ice-blue eyes tipped with crow's feet, he was a really sweet man.

"This, Chef Sayle . . ." Danielle paused for dramatic effect before holding up her heart carrot to him. "Is the Heartiette."

Breana burst out laughing and I couldn't help but chuckle too.

"Julienne, Batonnet, Allumette . . . I guess Heartiette fits the pattern," Chef Sayle said, grabbing Danielle's creation and popping it in his mouth.

She pouted, then chopped an onion with a flourish. Onion juice splashed into Breana's eyes and mine.

"Fuck, Danielle!" said Breana. She wiped her eyes carefully, trying not to ruin her mascara.

For me it was too late. The burning made tears run down my cheeks.

"Ah, watch out Emily!" Chef Sayle gave me a broad smile. "I don't want any crybabies in here." I laughed, but it didn't really help get my tears under control.

"How come you don't cry from onions anymore?" Danielle asked our teacher.

"Years of practice, Danielle."

"Oh, so you were a crybaby once too, huh? Interesting." Danielle winked at him, totally unafraid of his reaction.

"You—" he started. He shook his head and the corners of his mouth shot up. "You got me, Danielle. You got me." Still grinning, he walked away, and we cry-laughed for the rest of the period.

I dreaded my next class. US History with Jon Denson. I tried for what seemed like forever to wash the pungent smell of onions off my hands before realizing that it was senseless to keep scrubbing. I was rushing to get to US History when I saw him.

Paul.

Leaning against a red brick wall, eyes on his phone. Crowds of people were between us, forcing me to slow down. He put his phone into his pocket and started walking off. I zig-zagged through the remaining people over to him.

"Hey, Paul," I said. After all the overthinking, I'd settled for the casual approach. I hoped he wouldn't smell the onions on me.

He spun around, rubbing his neck. His eyes landed briefly on me before continuing to scan the crowd flowing past us. My smile faded as he followed after them like I hadn't just spoken to him. My mind raced with sudden anxiety, connecting the dots that were forming in front of me.

I was just a game to him.

I was so naive to think that someone like Paul would even be interested in me. Clearly, I wasn't a main character to him after all.

With a lump in my throat, I arrived at US History. The class hadn't started yet. My table was the one right before Jon's in the back. Jon noticed me and threw me a cocky grin, but it left me cold. *I'm Jon Denson and I can have every girl I want*, it practically screamed.

Madison's words from earlier this morning floated through the mist of my thoughts. Jon wanted me . . . More specifically, he wanted to have sex with me? But I was a nobody. What just happened with Paul was living proof. I slid down into my chair, feeling his eyes plastered on the back of my head.

"Recovered, Little German?"

I turned around in my seat. His eyebrow was raised provocatively as if he looked forward to witnessing my embarrassment. My blood boiled.

"Obviously," I spat. The last thing I needed right now was for him to put me down too. The veil had fallen. I was nothing to Paul and nothing to Jon either, and I hated myself for being played.

"Did I miss out on something?" a male voice interjected.

It was Brandon, an African American dude who sat with Jon in the last row. He was the opposite of Jon, always smiling, and his brown eyes were warm and welcoming. The first time we talked, he'd given me his Superman cape when I hadn't gotten the memo that we were supposed to dress up as superheroes for theme week. He'd noticed my disappointment and made my day with his kindness.

"Nah, I met her last weekend. She and Paul had *something* going on," Jon said, throwing air quotes.

Before I could get a word in, my seatmate Hannah joined in the conversation. "You're the girl Paul talked about?" she exclaimed.

Like Brandon, Hannah gave off a positive vibe. She had ginger hair and dimples on her cheeks, and her light blue eyes had something so friendly about them.

"Depends on what he told you," I said. I pulled my bottom lip between my teeth, picturing him proudly announcing to Hannah that he'd tricked me.

"Oh, we've all said a lot of things about you, Little German," Jon mocked.

And then I snapped. *Nobody's going to interrupt me anymore!*

"Stop calling me *Little German!* I have a name!" I barked, probably with the eyes of the entire class on me.

Jon shrugged. "Everybody has a name."

English was just too draining right now. "Immerhin werde ich nicht als Arschloch in Erinnerung bleiben, nicht so wie du!" *At least I won't be remembered as an asshole, unlike you!*

It was probably the first time in my life that I'd dared to express so much fury.

"German, you do know that insulting me in a language I don't un-derstand will get you nowhere? It's stupid," Jon scowled, but his eyes had twitched to the ground and back.

"Then why do you look so nervous, huh?" I said, convinced that I'd found his weakness. I turned back to my table and concentrated on getting out my supplies for class. Hannah and Brandon were both laughing, pretty sure because of Jon's stunned face and not me.

Mr. Harrison arrived. With a quick "Good morning, class," he got right into his lecture. I could barely focus on what he was saying. Jon and Brandon were whispering to each other behind me, but I couldn't make sense of the slang they were using.

"The Boston Tea Party happened when . . ."

It took me a second to realize that Mr. Harrison didn't mean a party where you served tea. My mind kept wandering to Paul. I didn't care that Jon had made fun of me—well, I did care, but what unset-tled me even more was Paul. I had actually considered dating him, but he'd just proved that I'd better stay away from boys while I was here. I doubted #3 on my list would ever come true. Hot tears swelled in the corners of my eyes, and I looked up at the ceiling to keep them from escaping. *I am so stupid.*

When the bell rang, I got a text message.

Hey, Emily! Can we talk? I'll wait for you at the main entrance
of the school - Paul

My heart started crashing dangerously hard against my ribs, not
sure whether out of anger, fear or hope. Where had he even gotten my
number? I jumped out of my chair. I couldn't wait another second to hear
Paul's side of the story. Maybe it was all just a big misunderstanding.

Naivete returned.

Chapter 6

Game Plan

PAUL WAS ALREADY AT THE SCHOOL ENTRANCE, SLOUCHING against the brick wall and looking intently at his phone, his tousled almond-colored hair falling over his forehead. When I was just three steps away, his ocean-blue eyes met mine and he straightened up nervously. I tried to suppress the stupid grin I always got when I looked at him.

"Hi . . ." I croaked.

"Hi, Em . . . Thanks for coming." He looked down at his sneakers.

"I don't have much time. My bus . . ." I gestured to the exit.

He nodded and took two steps toward me. "I didn't mean to ignore you earlier."

Then he drew me into a tight, unexpected embrace.

My first instinct was to fight him, but surprising myself, I pressed my forehead onto his chest, letting the fresh scent of his cologne wash over me. My anger vanished. There was something about his gentle touch that made me feel secure. As I returned his hug, his muscles relaxed and he sighed into my ear. I suddenly felt like kissing him again. *Ugh, stupid hormones.*

"I need to go," I mumbled, pulling away. I couldn't let him off the hook so easily or he'd think he could play games like this with me all the time.

"Let me take you home?" he suggested.

I dared to look up, and his magnetic gaze weakened my resolve. If I wanted to catch my bus I'd have to sprint for it, and I wasn't in the mood for running. Or maybe it was just an excuse to say, "Okay."

Another decision I'd made with my heart instead of my brain.

A broad grin formed on Paul's face, illuminating his eyes. It was like they shone a trillion times brighter. I beamed at him in spite of myself. Maybe earlier really had been a misunderstanding and I shouldn't sweat it.

His eyes darted to a girl who'd just come out of the main doors. She had wavy strawberry-blonde hair and a tight skirt showing off a figure that was curvy in all the right places, so unlike mine. She was glaring at Paul like she was about to scratch out his eyes with her manicured fingernails. When her toffee-colored eyes shot over to me, I could practically see the vein in her neck pulsing in anger.

"Come on, let's go before we get stuck in traffic," Paul said lightly, as if he hadn't noticed the girl glowering at me with clenched fists.

The car ride started out in an awkward silence. Letting my fingers glide over the grey fabric of my seat, I coaxed myself to say my piece. But when I opened my mouth to speak, my foot spasmed and knocked an empty plastic bottle, and I closed my mouth again. Instead I focused on the air freshener dangling from the rearview mirror—green apple, the same scent as my shampoo.

"It smells like your hair," said Paul, noticing where I was looking.

"Uh-huh."

I gulped. He remembered the smell of my hair. And he'd basically apologized for ignoring me. He would've told me why if he wanted to. Maybe there wasn't any special reason after all.

"So . . . it's nice out again," Paul remarked.

"Yeah, um . . . it was so cold on Saturday." *So much to talk about and we discuss the weather?*

"Yeah. What's the weather in Germany like?"

"Cloudy, rainy. It's nicer here."

"You get a lot of storms?" He smiled widely, as if eager to hear more.

"The weather isn't really extreme," I said, my tense shoulders relaxing a little. "The winter gets cold but never that cold. The summer's warm but not too hot. We don't have as many tornadoes either."

Paul nodded. "What else is there to know about Germany? I always wanted to go there one day. It sounds like an amazing country."

The awkwardness quickly evolved into an easy conversation. You couldn't have guessed that minutes before, we'd been sitting in dead silence. Looking out the window, I saw someone wearing the same skirt as the girl who'd glared at me at school.

"Who was she, Paul?" I asked, realizing too late that I sounded like a jealous girlfriend.

"Who?" he repeated. His hand wandered up to scratch the back of his head. I recognized the nervous gesture from last Saturday night, when I'd asked him what he was drinking for. He knew exactly who I meant.

"That girl with the strawberry-blonde hair, she looked like she wanted to kill me." I didn't want to feel naive again.

He sucked in his breath sharply. "That was Jamie . . . my ex-girlfriend."

"Oh . . ."

There was no explanation needed. Obviously, it hadn't been long since they'd broken up. Catching sight of Paul's muscular arms, I remembered what Madison had said about him. "So, um, you play football?"

"I do, but I'm thinking of quitting."

"Why? Aren't you any good?" I teased, poking his bicep. *Ouch, it's hard.*

"Ah, it's a long story. I'll tell you when we have more time."

Paul switched off the ignition. We were already at the Stones' house. Just looking at it made an ice-cold shiver run down my spine. I didn't want to go in there yet. I opened the passenger door slowly, but when I was about to get out, my mouth suddenly disconnected from my brain.

"Can we go to your place?" I almost cried out.

"Yeah—sure!" he stammered.

I closed the door again and sank back into the seat, letting out the breath I'd been holding. Paul hit the gas, saving me from this moment. I opened the window a bit and breathed in deeply. The wind caressed my skin and blew my hair off my chest. Something had changed in me today. I stood up to Jon, I gave Paul a second chance, I took risks. My chest felt warm and . . . *light.*

Paul's place was a white two-story house with an old oak tree standing guard on the lawn. Fallen yellow and orange leaves surrounded the four steps up to the front door. Paul opened the car door for me like a gentleman, and I suddenly realized that coming here would have way more of an impact than simply avoiding the Stones' place for an afternoon. There'd be no way to get through the year without losing myself in those ocean-blue eyes.

We walked up the steps and into a sun-dappled hall decorated in warm fall tones, yellow, orange, and brown. Cheerful family photos hung on the walls. One picture caught my attention immediately: a young Paul holding up a fish with a proud grin on his face. He looked so blissful, so at peace with himself.

Paul stuck his head into an adjoining room and called out that he was home. I pulled my gaze away from the picture and followed him into the doorframe. A middle-aged couple was lounging on a couch, watching the news.

"Hey there!" the man said to me, his voice deep. He had a head of dark curls, and his smile revealed the same dimples as Paul's. He and the red-haired woman sitting next to him looked just like in the pictures—friendly and kind.

Paul gave me a confused look. "Come on, let's just go into my room."

How rude. Ignoring his request, I moved closer to his parents.

"Hi, I'm Emily. I'm . . ." I hesitated. *What am I to Paul?* "A friend of Paul's."

"How sweet of you to introduce yourself to us, honey!" said the woman on the couch. "I'm Gena, Paul's mother."

She got up and pulled me into a hug. She smelled like lavender, and to my surprise, her proximity didn't make me uncomfortable. Gena didn't look like Paul at all. Her fair skin was lightly dusted with freckles, and her bob cut suited her perfectly. But then I noticed that Paul had her eyes. The same ocean-blue brilliance that made you smile instantly.

"She's a good one!" Paul's dad chuckled. "I'm Mr. Shields, but please call me Henry." He took a nacho chip from a bowl on the couch and popped it in his mouth.

"Yeah, she's great." Paul scratched his head, and a little giggle escaped my lips. Nervous Paul was so adorable.

"Will you join us for dinner tonight, honey?" Gena asked me.

I didn't give it a second thought. "I'd love to." Dinner would take a while, so I'd have an extra couple of hours before going back to the crap hole, aka the Stones' place.

Paul and I went down to the messy basement where everything had begun on Saturday night. We flopped down on the couch.

"Nobody has ever introduced themselves to my parents before," Paul said, turning on the TV and flipping to the sports channel.

"Didn't you want them to meet me?"

"No, I actually like that you did it."

His eyes were beautiful. The corners of my mouth twitched up and I looked away to keep my smile from getting too big.

For the next little while, we just sat there and talked, keeping a respectable distance between us. The space containing our unspoken kiss. Neither of us dared to go there just yet.

"So, uh, what's your favorite class?" Paul asked.

"Um, I really like Culinary Arts. I have it with Bre and Danielle." My heart was pounding way too hard for a simple question like that.

"That's cool. I thought of taking it too, but cooking just isn't my thing." Paul turned his gaze to the football game that was playing on the TV.

I wanted to say that cooking was easy if you knew the basics, but decided against it. I cleared my throat and tried to get my breathing under control. I missed how easygoing the alcohol had made me.

"Yours?" I said after a long moment of silence.

"My what?"

"Um, your favorite class?"

"Oh! Biology. I'm a big fan of nature so it's cool to get more into the deets of how it works."

The sparkle returned, the one he got whenever something excited him, and he leaned a little closer toward me. His fingertips were almost touching the side of my thigh. My breath hitched again so I quickly looked back at the TV. A player in blue tried to catch the ball but was thrown to the ground by a man in red. I didn't get the rules of football—something every exchange student should read up on before coming to America.

"It looks like people crashing together to hurt each other," I commented. This was not a game for my little body.

"It's actually a good game if you understand the rules." Paul laughed, relaxing some of the tension between us.

"And what are the rules?" I dared to look at him again.

"Okay, so you gotta run or pass the ball to score or get a first down. Play defense to tackle dudes and make sure they don't score," he explained, as if it was the easiest game to understand in the entire world.

"Oh yeah, I totally get it now."

"I can teach you how to play if you want?"

And end up in the hospital? *No thank you.*

"C'mon, don't look so afraid," he said, jumping off the couch. "I won't hurt you."

Maybe not physically, but I had a feeling that he'd own my heart way too soon.

Paul offered me his hand and I took it without hesitation. Just one little touch sent blood into my cheeks and made my skin tingle. Once I was on my feet, he let go of my hand and backed up two steps.

"All right, tackle me!" he instructed, taking an athletic stance and bouncing lightly on his feet.

I pretended like I was thinking about how to attack him. He threw me a mischievous grin and my heart started going double-time. I felt like collapsing into Paul was meant to be. That there was a reason why I'd kissed him on Saturday night. I wasn't scared to fall for him anymore. I was ready to let him in, no matter how vulnerable that would make me. I'd gotten a taste of happiness, and a little nibble wasn't enough. I longed for a mouthful of this flavor.

"Are you afraid—"

Before Paul could finish his taunt, I jumped on him like a lunatic, using the full weight of my body to make him fall backward. Luckily, we landed on the carpet, which was now perfectly clean. A warmth spread through my whole body as our chests connected.

"Never underestimate my height," I said teasingly, lying on top of him almost nose-to-nose.

Within a mood-shattering second, Paul's look sparked up, and he picked me up off the ground and threw me over his shoulder like a towel.

"Ahhhh, let me down!" I screeched, trying to catch my breath, scared he would drop me.

"Try to get down, Princess!" he exclaimed, starting to turn in circles. I kicked my feet, hit his back with my fists, tried to squirm out of his grip, but I stood no chance. He burst out laughing as his muscular arms held me steady.

"Paul, stop, I'm gonna feel sick!" I giggled, laugh-tears in the corners of my eyes.

He stopped turning and dropped me softly onto his bed, hovering over me, his eyes attached to mine. He was darn good at giving me those meaningful looks. Those looks that made me forget my rules, that hypnotized my soul. He held my head with one hand and supported himself with the other as he moved only inches above me. Anticipation heated up inside me as if in a sauna.

I was about to pucker my lips when he suddenly stiffened. Before I could say anything, he shook his head and lifted himself up to return to the couch, leaving me there on the bed.

"Dinner's ready!" yelled Gena from upstairs.

"You hungry?" Paul asked, barely looking at me.

I got off the bed. I wouldn't let him play this game. With every ounce of confidence I'd gathered from being with him, I strode over to him, swung my arms around his neck and planted a brief kiss on his mouth. *No tongue though.*

"I . . ." He stroked my cheek.

I turned around and sashayed out of his room like I was on a runway, satisfied with my new self. If this was a game, I was in it to win.

Chapter 7

All in the Family

MY MIND STILL ON PAUL, I HEADED UP TO THE KITCHEN. On the counter sat a stack of dinner plates along with large yellow crackers, freshly cooked minced meat, grated cheese, a plain salad and tubs of sauces.

"Grab a plate and fill it up, honey," Gena said, gesturing at the setup.

"Oh, it's okay, you go—"

"Hush, c'mon. You're our guest."

I took a plate and put a few crackers on it. Next to those, I added meat and salad, skipping the cheese. I stared at the containers of sauces, lost.

"You need to put the beef and lettuce in the taco shell, hon. Oh, and try it with sour cream!" Gena suggested, pointing at a little white bucket.

"Oh . . ."

I had never eaten tacos before. They were nothing like what we usually ate in Germany. I probably looked like a fool putting them together.

Henry walked in with a wide grin. "Your first time eating tacos?"
I nodded.

"You'll love it! Gena makes the best tacos on the planet."

"Oh, Henry, all I do is to cook the meat."

"Which you do perfectly." He gave Gena a gentle kiss on the cheek.

They looked so happy, and they'd probably been together forever.
My parents got divorced when I was twelve, and ever since, I doubted
that love was everlasting. But seeing how affectionate Gena and Henry
were gave me a hint of an idea that love wasn't always just a fairy tale.

Spotting a table on the other side of the room, I took my plate
over and sat down on a wooden bench. Paul came up the stairs and
just stared at me. Gena and Henry followed, looking at me in a way I
couldn't put into words.

"Did I do something wrong?" I said hesitantly, accidentally bumping my hand against my plate.

"Oh, it's nothing, honey! C'mon, Paul, grab your food before it gets
cold."

Paul nodded. His cheeks were still slightly red from the play fight
we'd just had. *Or maybe from the kiss I gave him?*

Carrying a plateful, Paul sat next to me on the bench, and after a
moment's hesitation, Henry and Gena took chairs across from us. The
TV was still on in the living room. It was weird that they hadn't turned
it off.

"You didn't have to wait for us, Emily," said Henry, taking a first bite
of his taco.

"Food doesn't taste good if you start before everyone has theirs."

I tried mine and most of the sour cream ended up on my cheeks.
Paul chuckled as I wiped it away with the back of my hand. *Gosh, this is
really good.*

"If you see it like that, you're totally right," Paul said, leaning over
to rub a dab of sour cream off my face with his thumb when his parents
weren't looking. I blushed from his little gesture.

"So you're from Germany?" Gena asked me curiously.

"Yes. How did you know?"

"Well, first of all, no American hasn't had a hard-shell taco in their life—" Henry started.

"And you have that accent." Gena completed kindly, shushing her husband.

"Oh yeah, I don't really hear my accent myself."

"It's adorable." Paul winked at me, and I almost choked on my food. But Gena and Henry didn't blink at his obvious flirting.

A phone rang and Gena rushed out of the kitchen. "Sorry, I've got to take this," she called.

Henry watched her go with a proud smile. "She's the principal at an elementary school," he explained. "Always hard at work taking care of things, even at night."

"That's amazing," I said. "How about you? What do you do?" I quickly put my napkin to my face, unsure if my question was too nosy.

"I'm a teacher too! But for the big kids." He laughed and I let out my breath in relief.

"So you're a high school teacher?"

"Nope. College professor." He took a sip of water. "I teach geography and environmental science. A really interesting field." Henry continued telling me about his profession. I was pleased that he cared enough to fill me in on what his work was all about.

Gena returned to the table, concern etched on her face. "I'm sorry about that, Emily. I didn't mean to be rude."

"Oh, it's fine. Is everything okay?" Again, I'd spoken without thinking. *Ugh, Emily, it's her personal business.*

Gena smiled. "Yes, don't worry. It was about a student who's having problems at home. The poor boy isn't safe there." She massaged the side of her neck. "I just wish I could do more to help."

"Mom, you're doing your best, okay?" Paul looked at her pleadingly, and Henry placed his hand on hers. She took it and squeezed it.

"You're right. What would I do without the two of you?" She gave them each a warm smile—and then to me.

I wished the Shields were my host family instead of the Stones. Paul gave me one of his looks and took the last bite of his taco. The fire in my chest heated up and I couldn't help but giggle into my hand.

After dinner, I said my goodbyes. The sun was already setting and I didn't want to risk angering Mrs. Stone.

The minute Paul and I were in his car I asked him, "Why did your parents look so confused when I sat down at the table?"

"We normally eat on the couch and watch TV," he said as he backed out of the driveway.

"Oh . . ." In my family, dinnertime was when we talked about how our day went and shared advice or comfort. I couldn't picture my day without it.

"But I think they really enjoyed eating at the table tonight. We haven't talked that much in a long time." Paul said, throwing me one of his handsome smiles. "And I liked it too."

For the first half of the ride we barely said anything. I just looked out of the window and admired Boonville, probably for the first time since I'd gotten here. I always complained about how quiet and boring it was, but now I saw it from a different perspective. Squirrels were jumping from tree to tree and a deer peeked out from behind a bush. The American flag waved from multiple houses we passed. At a park a group of teenagers was just hanging out, enjoying each other's company.

It wasn't about parties, clubs and bars. What was important was that you were with friends. No matter what you did together. I couldn't see it at first because I didn't have any, but I suddenly felt like that was about to change.

My thoughts were interrupted by Paul's uncertain voice. "Why did you kiss me today?"

I opened my mouth but no words came out.

"Breana said you don't want to have a relationship while you're here," he added. "And that I wasn't your type . . ."

She said what?!

"But you kissed me and . . . you're not the type to play around.

Right?" His hands were wrapped tightly around the steering wheel, and his eyes were focused a little too intensely on the street.

I looked down at my hands. He was right.

"I like you, Paul, you make me smile." I took a deep breath, gathering my thoughts. "But I have to go back to Germany in eight months."

"I understand . . ." he said quietly. My heart started pounding, sending tingling sensations down my arms.

"I don't want you to stay away though!" I burst out, ignoring my brain's protests. I couldn't go back to how it was before him. Not after I knew what it was like.

Paul cocked his head at me, rescuing his gaze from the street, and his eyes sparkled again.

We arrived at the Stones' house and my hope deflated.

"I wish you didn't have to go in there right now," Paul said, his voice husky, sending butterflies rippling through my belly. He leaned over to me and cupped my cheeks in his broad hands. His touch was a shot of courage to my fears. "In case you ever need me to pick you up, text me, okay?"

"About that . . . how did you get my number?"

"I asked Danielle for it. We have Chemistry together."

Thank you, Danielle.

Paul looked me deep in the eye. That intense stare of his made my legs turn to mush. Then he pressed his lips on mine. I responded to his kiss openly as a way of saying thank you. This wasn't the kiss he'd given me on Saturday night. It contained even more emotion. More longing. It was like Paul was sending me strength through his kiss.

I sneaked into my room, feeling energized. My cheeks were so warm and red, you probably could've cooked an egg on them. My phone displayed one missed call from my mom. I couldn't wait to finally tell her some good news.

I jumped into bed and stretched out on my back, a massive grin on my face. *Is this what it feels like to fall in love?*

Chapter 8

Head Up, Chest Up

"**W**HAT DID YOU TELL MRS. STONE THIS TIME?**"
Breana's voice echoed off the mossy walls of the cave as she jumped from one rock to the other, trying not to fall into the water. She'd convinced Paul, me, Danielle and, to my annoyance, Jon to drive out to the cave outside of town to take pictures for her photography class.

"She's at church. I told her I still had a cold and didn't want to give it to anyone in the congregation." I squatted down on a rock to watch Breana's balancing act. She took a final leap, an easy task for her long legs.

"Still? Your cold is lasting awfully long, don't you think?" she joked, raising her camera. The flash lit up the cave as she captured a thin stream of water trickling through a patch of moss and down the dark rock face.

"I know . . ." I sighed. "I'll need to come up with a new excuse soon." The last two weeks had flown by in what felt like minutes—I was having so much fun hanging out with these folks.

"Hey, Jon! Come over here, I want a picture with you in it!" Breana called to the other side of the cave where Jon, Paul and Danielle were crouched, smoking weed.

Jon just shrugged and took another drag of the joint. Breana's shoulders sagged a little, and I wasn't sure if it was the water reflected in her eyes or if those were tears welling in them. Jon had barely given her any attention since the night they'd kissed.

"I want to be in the pictures!" Danielle said, clearly noticing the tension, and jumped as light as a feather over the rocks to Breana to cheer her up. Paul waved at me to come over to him and I got up to go join him. As I analyzed the gap between us, a weird taste filled my mouth. My old Chucks hadn't exactly been the best choice for this slippery field trip. I took three big steps onto the rocks and—

Just as I was about to fall, Paul grabbed my hips and held me in place, saving me from smashing my head on the rock face. "Watch out, Princess, you don't want to get soaked," he said.

I beamed at him. "Thank you, Paul."

Seeing Danielle busy posing and Breana peering into her camera, Paul leaned in and placed a lovely kiss on my lips, still holding onto my hips. I couldn't get enough. I kissed him back, then pulled him into a close hug, closing my eyes and inhaling his scent. Like the breeze blowing over the pools of water in the cave, it was fresh and invigorating.

When I opened my eyes again, it was to Jon's dark glare, tinted red from the weed. "I guess you still gotta grow up some more before you can take a bigger step," he said mockingly.

I rolled my eyes at him and pulled myself out of Paul's arms, focusing on the cute little dimples on his cheeks. Next to his 1.85 meters in height—6 feet in American terms—I looked like a midget with my 1.6 meters—5 foot 2. But when Paul wrapped me in his arms, I appreciated our height difference. I felt so safe in them.

Paul was studying my face, not breaking eye contact.

"What?" I bit my lip and looked down.

He put his thumb under my chin and lifted it up softly. "Can I not look at you?" The blood rocketed into my ears.

Paul and I texted 24/7. Countless times I'd told Mrs. Stone I'd be late because of a school project when I was actually watching his football practice from the bleachers. Whenever he could, Paul sneaked away from the bench to plant soft kisses all over my face. We spent every free second we had together, and it was still never enough.

"Hey, man. We gotta go, Ted's waiting for us." Jon said to Paul. He left the cave without looking back.

"Ted?" I asked.

"He's our plug . . . We ran out of weed, you know?" Paul kissed me on the cheek and whispered into my ear, "I won't be gone long." I nodded and watched him navigate the rocks, a slight hobble in his step.

"Wait, what's wrong with your foot?" I called after him.

He turned around and threw me a smile. "Nothing to worry about."

I frowned into the darkness. Even though we spent so much time together, Paul remained a mystery to me. I knew all of these little things about him, but I was still missing the big picture.

"Hey, girl!" Danielle waved at me. "Come here, we're taking group selfies!" I found another safer path around the rocks, no Paul to catch me.

Overall, things were great. Even at the Stones' place, I was managing not to get sucked in by the grey clouds of the Nightmare. I did my chores and gave her no further reason to approach me. It still wasn't perfect, but it was better than before because I had something—or rather, someone—to look forward to. Paul was my adventure, and I wouldn't have wanted it any other way.

On Friday morning, I was woken up by the vibration of my phone. One eye still closed, I swiped the screen to accept a call from my mom.

"Good morning, my lovely one!" she said, a little too enthusiastically for my ear. "Any new gossip about Paul?"

"Mom, I haven't even gotten up yet," I mumbled, sitting up in bed and rubbing my eyes to get the sleep out.

"You didn't answer my question."

I sighed loud enough for her to hear it, but she didn't let it go. "He's still a real gentleman," I said.

"Keep my advice in mind, okay?"

Her serious tone made me giggle. "I know, Mom. 'Find yourself a man you feel comfortable, beautiful and worthy with,'" I trilled.

"I just want you to be careful. You can't stay in America forever," she reminded me. I pulled in my lower lip.

"I know, Mom . . . I wouldn't want to stay in this place forever anyway."

"Mrs. Stone?"

My mother knew exactly who I'd hinted at. I'd told her bits about how Mrs. Stone treated me, but not everything. It would be too much for her to handle. My current silence exposed me.

"Head up, chest up, lovely. We'll figure this out. And if it's unbearable, you can always call your area representative to get you to another family."

But going to another family would mean going to another town, and that wasn't an option anymore. Not after *him*.

"I'm actually going to Breana's place tonight. Remember the party I told you about?" I said, changing the subject.

"Of course, lovely. You mention it every call we have." She laughed. "And I'm looking forward to hearing about how it went."

I headed down into the kitchen, filled with renewed confidence. Even though Mrs. Stone was there, making a sandwich at the counter, I didn't make myself small. *Chest up, head up*—just like my Mom said.

"Good morning, Mrs. Stone," I said brightly. I wouldn't offer her a single thing to complain about.

She jumped as if I'd screamed in her ear. "Don't sneak up on me like that, Emily!" she said accusingly, her hand on her chest.

No matter what I did, I did it wrong. I started playing with the ribbon on my sweater, my head doing its telltale droop again.

"Where have you been the last couple of days? I've barely seen you around the house." She examined me from head to toe like she was searching for a tattoo or a hickey. When she couldn't find anything, she fell back on her creepy smile.

"I was hanging out with friends, Mrs. Stone," I said carefully.

"I've noticed. The house is so dirty lately." She tucked her sandwich into a plastic bag.

My mouth twitched angrily, but I was silent.

"And you didn't ask for my approval," she continued. "If you're planning a visit with friends, I want to know who, when and where." She looked gravely pleased with her pronouncement.

I felt like she was trying to ruin my life on purpose but I had no other choice than to play along. I had to tell her about my plans. The ones I'd been looking forward to all week.

"If that's the case . . . I wanted to go to Breana's place tonight." My voice shook to the rhythm of my heartbeat.

"Hmm . . . Who's going to be there, and what are you doing together?"

Something inside me told me to keep my lip zipped, but I had already started the conversation. There was no turning back now.

"Breana, Danielle, Paul, um—probably Jon."

Mrs. Stone gasped in shock. "Boys too?" Her eyes seemed to have doubled in size. "You're not going if boys are going to be there!"

"But—" I squeezed my eyes shut, then opened them again. "We're only watching a movie!"

"A no is a no, Emily." She turned to her lunch again. "And that's final. You're not going out tonight."

My hands clenched into fists. I was so done with her. I had to see Paul and nothing would stop me.

"You're not my mother!" The sentence shot out of my mouth like a bullet.

Mrs. Stone's ever so perfectly carved smile vanished. I was suddenly light-headed. Now I'd done it. I'd spoken up, and the consequences would follow.

"You live under my roof, so you follow my rules," she snarled, planting her hands on her hips.

"I understand that, Mrs. Stone, but it's not fair if I can't go out," I replied meekly.

"You *can* go out. As long as it's only with girls." Mrs. Stone said with finality. There was only one possible way left for me to go.

"Um, okay . . . I'll um . . . ask Breana if it can be a girls' night." I rubbed my cheek like it was itchy to hide my lying face.

Mrs. Stone raised her eyebrow, but then her carved-in smile returned. "Okay then. Give me the number of Breana's mother in case of an emergency."

I let out a long-held breath and agreed.

"Oh, and Emily? I need you to clean the house more often, and the silverware needs polishing."

"Sure," I mumbled.

I retreated from the kitchen. *So much for being in control.*

Yet I was proud. I had finally *somehow* spoken up for myself. I hadn't let the Nightmare snatch away my plans.

Even though the only thing standing between us was a bald-faced lie.

Chapter 9

Diving In

I N CULINARY ARTS, WE'D MOVED ON FROM CUTTING VEGETABLES to cooking risotto. Still not terribly exciting because all you do is stir, add soup stock, and stir some more. But it wasn't too shabby all the same because Danielle and Breana were there with me.

"Here," said Danielle, pouring some of her stock into my pot. Before I could thank her, Breana playfully nudged her hip into mine.

"I'm so excited! And I just can't hide it!" she sang, using her spoon as a microphone and spinning in a circle.

"It's just a party, Bre." Danielle turned down the heat on her stove.

"Just a party?" Breana dropped the spoon and bent down to pick it up again. "I've been planning this on the sly for weeks. Picture it: parents out of town, dressing up, talking to boys!" She held up her spoon in triumph. "This is gonna be the night of the year! Or the month at least!"

I stirred my risotto one last time, deciding it was done. I doubted Breana's party would be the night of the month. Nothing could top the night I'd met Paul. But who knows, it would probably come in second if everything went as planned.

"By talking to boys, you mean talking to Jon, don't you?" Danielle gave me a look while Breana spun around again.

"Well, duh!" Breana said. "He won't be able to resist me in the dress I'm gonna wear." She glided her fingers down her body seductively. "You're coming too, right, Em?"

"Yeah, I am. But can I get your mom's phone number? Mrs. Stone wants it, you know, just in case of an emergency," I said, trying to make it sound like a minor detail. There was no need to tell Breana that I'd lied about the guest list. *Right?*

"Sure, but she won't call, right?"

"I doubt it."

Breana raised an eyebrow, but I assured her that she had nothing to worry about and she gave me the number. I really hoped lying wouldn't become a habit for me. I wasn't a fan of the queasy knot it was twisting in the pit of my stomach.

After a long and uneventful day, I headed for the bus, taking my time in the hopes that Paul would see me and offer me a ride, just like he had for the last ten days.

"Emily, wait!"

Bingo.

I turned around slowly while shaking my hair out of my face, trying to look like one of those slow-motion girls in movies. And there he was, looking at me brightly in a red flannel button-down, a white shirt peeking out underneath. The afternoon sun reflected on his hair, lending it extra shine. All day I'd looked forward to those eyes, that charming smile. They were the reason I tolerated my own twisted truths.

"Can I take you home again?" Paul asked.

I nodded, my legs feeling like noodles under me. Just the sight of him made me high on happiness. That he managed to find me in the crowd each day after school reassured me that we belonged together.

"If we keep going like this, I should start giving you gas money," I said, giggling as I leaned against his chest. *Mm, straight off the ocean. Heaven.*

"Oh heck no! Your company is enough." He planted a kiss on my cheek.

I looked around for Paul's gym bag, but it wasn't there. "Are you skipping football practice today?"

"Dropped out." He shrugged nonchalantly, as if it was normal to quit something you'd been doing your entire life.

"You dropped out?" My voice was a notch louder than usual.

"It just . . . wasn't for me, I guess. It was missing something."

I tilted my chin up to look at him more closely. *Will he finally tell me what's been missing in his life?*

"It's not what I'm passionate about . . . aaand this way, I get to spend more time with my Princess."

He leaned in for a kiss. Hesitantly I got on the tips of my toes to meet him halfway. My longing to feel his perfect lips on mine was stronger than my curiosity.

"Really, dude?" said a voice behind me, just as I was getting pulled into the sweetness of his tongue. *Jon.* I spun around. He was standing there with his arms crossed over his chest, decked out in his usual leather jacket over a dark blue shirt. He looked tired, his eyes a little swollen and his hair a perfectly arranged mess.

Paul shrugged. "Get over it, man."

"I ain't getting over it. You said you'd drive me," Jon said belligerently, pretending that I wasn't standing a meter away.

"It's fine," I interjected. "He'll take you where you want to go first, then drop me off."

Paul gave me a questioning look, but he knew I took every opportunity to delay going back to the Stones' place.

"What she said, man. So let's go."

Paul gestured for Jon to go ahead, but before I could follow, he grabbed me gently by the shoulder. "Emily, Jon and I are going to get weed. Are you sure you want to come with us?"

I took a deep breath, debating my options, not really separating right from wrong. "Will it get me in trouble?"

"Those dudes are okay, but do you feel comfortable getting involved?" He didn't like risking my stay here in America. Ever since that Saturday night, he'd made sure I was somewhere safe before he and Jon did their business. *Aka stealing alcohol or getting weed.*

"Guys! What are we waiting for?" Jon called from Paul's grey Fiat.

I took Paul's hand and laced his fingers through mine. Though I appreciated his concern, I didn't want to hide behind closed doors anymore. I wanted to know all about his world, even if it meant trouble.

Jon was quicker to call shotgun, so I got the back seat. He gave me an exasperated look through the rearview mirror, then lit up a cigarette.

"Square?" He held out the pack to Paul.

"Nah, I'm good."

The car was quiet apart from the same rap music we'd listened to the night we met. At least I thought it was the same—rap was still pretty new to me. I started playing with the ends of my hair.

"Where are we going exactly?" I said finally to break the uncomfortable silence.

"German!" Jon barked, turning around to scowl at me. "Stop questioning every damn thing. Can't you just live without being in such a hurry to know everything?"

"Hey, calm down, man! No need to bite her head off," Paul quickly put in.

"You know it's not a good idea to bring along your *princess*," Jon retorted.

He must have heard Paul call me that. When Paul said it, it was cute and loving, but the way Jon sneered the word, making it sound like I thought myself high and mighty, destroyed the innocence of the nickname.

I'm not anyone's princess.

"We'll just go in and out, no harm done," Paul said placatingly. "What's up with you, Jon?"

Jon ignored him. "Have you ever smoked weed, Little German?"

"N-no," I stammered, unsure about the outcome of my answer.

Jon turned around, satisfied. "See?" he said to Paul. "She's a good girl. She doesn't belong with us."

I felt my pulse quickening in my palms. Who was he to tell Paul who he should hang out with? "You don't know a damn thing about me, Jon!" I snapped, my face burning.

He let that comment pass, and in the reflection of the windshield, I could see the amused look on his face. He wasn't impressed—yet. *Screw getting along with Jon. I'm not gonna let him treat me like this!*

"I left Germany! I'm brave, okay!" I huffed. "I'm in a country that speaks a language I barely know, in a culture I have no clue about, and on top of that I have to deal with idiots like you! Just let me be me, and don't put me in a fucking box!"

Jon winced. By the end, I was pretty much screaming. For the first time, I'd yelled at someone full on, no holding back. Plus I now officially belonged to the category of Americans who cursed. I felt a wave of relief roll through me.

For a couple of seconds, everybody in the car was quiet. Then Jon sighed extra loud and cocked his head at me.

"Will you look at that. She has a voice."

"Jon!" I protested, but he just rolled his eyes.

I realized that there was nothing I could do to stop his constant heckling. He would always have the upper hand on me.

"It's fine, geez, you can come with us," Jon said. "But if we get caught and you're sent back to Germany, it'll be your own damn fault."

"Like you'd care."

But he was right. I hadn't exactly won this fight.

A little while later, we pulled into a side street lined with modest single-story houses. Our destination had a low fence you could easily jump over. A dog barked at us from the other side of the street as we parked the car and got out. The smell of rotting food made my stomach turn as we walked past an overflowing garbage can.

Paul stopped when his phone buzzed. "You guys go ahead, I'm coming after this. It's my coach." He picked up the call and went back to the car. "I've made up my mind, Coach . . ." he was saying. But the wind rustling through the trees and the dry leaves crunching under our feet muffled the rest.

Jon jerked his head for me to follow him. We skirted around the house and he opened a rusty gate into the backyard. It shrieked just like in those horror movies I hated watching with Michael. We were approaching a weather-beaten door in the back of the house. I guess the guys had been told not to go to the front.

Jon suddenly stopped in his tracks. "I'm sorry I put you in a box. I hate it when people do that to me," he said without looking at me.

I realized that back in the car, he hadn't winced at my use of the word "fuck"—it was "box" that had thrown him.

"Jon?"

"Yeah, I apologized. Take it or leave it," he snapped.

"And you say *I'm* impatient," I said, emboldened by his confession.

Jon did his typical eye roll and went to open the door. Within a split second, I'd grabbed his wrist in a panic. Going into a drug dealer's place affected me more than I cared to admit.

He froze, his gaze traveling from my hand clenching his arm up to my eyes. I was about to back off when his expression transitioned into something I hadn't seen before. *Appreciation?*

"You really don't have to worry. You're safe with me, Little German."

"I am?"

"Of course."

I felt my shoulders ease up. I smiled.

There was a low flame in his iris fighting not to burn out. It was small, but it was there. Maybe we could be friends after all. Even if it was a friendship based on fighting and screaming at each other.

"You know, it's high time you called me by my real name and not by my height and nationality," I remarked with my version of a cocky smirk.

"Maybe in another life, Little German," he replied, sarcasm at full bloom. He squeezed my shoulder with a dry smile. Then he opened the door, and I dived into a new world.

Chapter 10

Reckless

THE ROOM WAS FILLED WITH SMOKE. PILES OF CLOTHES AND odds were strewn about everywhere you looked, and the floor apparently served as an ashtray. The minimal furniture had seen better days—except for a brand new flat-screen TV hung on the wall across from me. When Jon closed the door behind us, it was as if most of the oxygen had been sucked out.

"Who's the twelve-year-old?" a guy with long dark dreadlocks inquired. He was smoking a cig as he reclined in a chair.

I looked at Jon for help. The way the guy had singled me out didn't make me feel any braver.

"This is Emily, she's cool," Jon commented briefly.

"Hi," I said meekly, and a trashy-looking girl on a ratty couch snickered. Two steps ahead, four steps back. I still had a long way to go.

"Hi, sweetie, I'm Ted," the guy said, throwing me a little wink. Jon gave him a venomous look.

"Coming for the usual, Jon?" Ted asked.

"Yep, the same as always."

Ted nodded and gestured for Jon to follow him into the next room. Jon leaned down toward me until his lips nearly brushed my earlobe.

"I know you're scared but it's okay. I'm not far, Little German."

A shiver ran down my spine. But before I could beg him to stay, he'd already left me alone with the girl. Her greasy hair was scraped back in a ponytail and her mascara had wandered out of place, giving her a panda look.

"And who are you exactly?" she said, standing up and crossing her arms protectively over her territory.

"I'm Jon's friend," I mumbled. *At least, I think we're friends now?*

"Jon never brings friends. At least not girls." She was checking me out from head to toe.

I didn't know what to say, so I just shrugged. *Where the hell is Paul?*

"Want a Xanax? You look kind of uptight. It'll relax you a little." She held out a small white pill.

"What's Xanax?" I said timidly.

She burst into laughter, making me look like an idiot when Jon and Ted reemerged. I bit my lip and sought out Jon's eyes. He was the only person I wanted to see in this room.

Jon gave me a reassuring look and explained, "It's medication pre-scribed for panic attacks and depression."

Judging by what I'd seen so far, the prescription was liberal. I was about to ask about the side effects when Paul finally came in through the back door.

"What's up, Ted?" he said. They clasped hands briefly, then Paul turned to the girl. "Marna."

"Oh, Paul, it's nice to see you too," she exclaimed sarcastically.

"All right my dudes, we gonna smoke one now or what?" said Ted.

My stomach clenched. I didn't think we'd be staying here.

Paul took a seat on the couch and gestured for me to sit on his lap. I didn't want to look like a little girl who needed protection, so I perched on the armrest instead. Marna was watching my every move, and she seemed relieved to see that I was closer to Paul than to Jon.

Jon pulled out a little plastic bag, and within two minutes he'd rolled a perfectly shaped blunt and started passing it around. I was already woozy from the lack of oxygen in here, and now it was like a hot box. I started feeling nauseous. I'd pretty much stink of weed and cigarettes when I got out of here.

I couldn't follow what the others were talking about, so I just sat there quietly. I'd never smoked weed before. I'd never even smoked *cigarettes* before. And now I was in the living room of a drug dealer. It was exciting, stupidly exciting. I checked my phone for the time. I still had to do my chores before I could go out tonight.

Paul hit the blunt and held it out for Marna.

"She didn't get it yet." Marna pointed right at me.

Everyone stared at me, waiting for my decision. Jon's words from earlier were stuck in my head. *See? She's a good girl, she doesn't belong with us.* Maybe it was just to provoke him, but I grabbed the blunt.

Paul looked shocked. "Emily, you don't have to do this," he whispered so only I could hear it.

"I know." I gave him an even gaze.

He sighed and relit the blunt for me. My hand was unsteady as I brought it to my lips. I took a long, shaky drag, pretending I knew what I was doing. The herbal taste made my throat itch, and I hacked out dry coughs I fought to suppress. Tears formed in the corners of my eyes and warmth bloomed through my chest. Still coughing, I passed the blunt to Marna, my face assuredly crimson.

She laughed, satisfied. "That one hit you good."

It was a stupid decision, but at least it was my own. I peeked at Jon. The expression on his face was hard to interpret.

Marna was right. It did hit me good. All the way to the Stones' house I had a broad grin on my face. The fabric of the car seats felt as soft as cotton balls. Every time I felt the urge to talk, I giggled and said something about Mario Kart, and Paul would look at me with a tired smile. He held my hand tightly as he drove through the empty streets. This time I was sitting shotgun. Take that, Jon! *Hehe.*

I didn't feel tense at all when I walked through the doors of the Stones' house—just relaxed and especially hungry. As I passed by a mirror in the hall, I started at the person in the reflection. There was a reddish mask over her eyes. I looked away rather slowly and went into the living room. Madison was sitting on the carpet in front of the couch, surrounded by schoolwork.

"Hey, Madison. What's up?" I giggled for no reason.

"Just doing homework. What about you?" She didn't look up.

"On a Friday afternoon?" I burst out laughing.

Her head shot up and I saw her puffy, bloodshot eyes. She'd been crying.

"Geez, you look wasted," she said. "What's wrong with you? Oh. My. Gosh. Are you *high?*"

I shushed her. "I don't want your mother to hear!" I looked around frantically, suddenly aware of how much trouble this could bring me.

Madison rolled her eyes. *I wonder if she's smoked weed too.*

"Why were you crying?" I said gently. I placed my hand on her shoulder and stroked it with my thumb. I had no clue where this affection for her was coming from, but I sincerely felt sorry for her. "I've only been here for a couple of months and your mom's already messed with my head. You can talk to me, I know what you must be going through."

Madison winced. "There's leftover pizza in the fridge," she said shortly. She started gathering up her stuff.

"Thanks," I mumbled as she left the room. This time I didn't giggle. *Why is it so hard for her to let me in?*

I headed for the kitchen and yanked open the door of the fridge to look for the promised goods. I was so hungry, I didn't care that Mrs.

Stone would kill me if she saw me plundering. I pulled the coat of cheese off a slice and rearranged the veggies on the dough. It felt too good when a juicy bite finally hit my mouth.

"I'm home early!" a voice echoed from down the hall.

Mrs. Stone was here.

I hadn't even started cleaning.

And I was high.

It was a wake-up slap in the face. Quickly, I stuffed as much pizza in my mouth as possible—only chewed it halfway—and ran the tap for the dirty dishes in the sink. I splashed water on my face and rubbed my skin, hoping to wash off some of the smell. *Let's pray she won't sniff it on me.* I focused hard on scrubbing the plates clean just as footsteps sounded at the doorframe behind me.

"It's still a pigsty in here!" Mrs. Stone said. "Finish those dishes and wipe down the counters or you can't go out tonight." I swear I could feel her breath on my neck even though she was a couple meters away.

"I will," I replied obediently, though with a huge grin on my face. Footsteps. She was gone again.

I let out the breath I was holding and the dirty dishes glided back into the sink with a subtle splash. Today was my lucky day. She hadn't caught me. This was probably the most reckless thing I'd ever done, but it was surprisingly exhilarating. And I was ready to dive right back in.

In my room, I put on a crimson V-neck dress with closed black pumps and applied a hint of red lipstick to my dry lips. Breana had insisted on us dressing up. Not fun when you have five minutes to get ready, but I had no other choice.

I turned to the mirror to check if I looked presentable. The dress I'd chosen hung unpleasantly off my body. When I'd packed it back in Germany it charmed my figure, but I'd lost a lot of weight in the past two months. *Great, of course, mostly off my boobs.* They were already small, a little A cup. Now I might as well not wear a bra anymore at all. I sighed as I settled my wavy hair in front of my chest, hiding both the loose fit of the neckline and the beauty mark on my cheek. *There, not bad.*

As if on cue, my phone screen lit up with a message from Paul.

Hey, beautiful. I'm down the street. Are you ready?

So ready.

Chapter 11

The Wrong Girl

TODAY REALLY WAS MY LUCKY DAY BECAUSE NO ONE CROSSED my path in the corridor, down the stairs, through the living room or out the door. I hurried away from the property as fast as I could in my heels.

Paul was leaning against his grey Fiat with a cigarette hanging out of his mouth. When he saw me, he smiled and threw the unfinished cig on the ground.

"I didn't know you smoked," I said.

"Only at parties." His eyes widened as they ran over my body. "You look . . . wow." I flushed and patted my hair down, making sure it was still in place.

"What's wrong?" he asked, noticing my anxious vibes.

"Oh, nothing!"

I jumped into his arms and hugged him tightly. The second I was in his embrace, my worries about Mrs. Stone melted away. All that mattered was inhaling his scent and savoring his tender touch.

"Oh no, she fell into a bowl of makeup," someone exclaimed in mock woe from the other side of the car. None other than Jon. Why did they always have to be together?

Letting go of Paul, I prepared to fire off one of the comebacks I'd found online one night when replays of Jon's insults were keeping me awake.

"Your ass must be pretty jealous of all the shit that comes out of your mouth!" The sentence came out sounding less impressive than I'd hoped.

"Oh, did someone use the internet?" Jon sniggered.

"You're such an ass, Jon!" I snapped.

"Yes, that's coming from the heart." He winked at me, enjoying my pouting face.

"Don't listen to him," Paul said. "You look gorgeous."

He went over to the passenger seat and opened the car door for me. Jon rolled his eyes and got in the back, defeated. Looks like I'd laid claim on shotgun.

Breana's place was booming with drunk people shouting over the music. I had gotten used to rap by now, but it was cranked up to the point of being deafening. People were yelling to each other and singing, holding red plastic cups I recognized from the movies. Some were filled to the brim, some were already empty. Joints got passed around like candy bars and smoke hung in the air above us. I followed Paul and Jon through to one corner of a jam-packed living room, where Jon greeted Brandon, the nice guy from my US History class, with a complicated handshake.

"Paul, my dude. I see you brought Emily. Looking good, German!" Brandon beamed at me and treated me to a hug.

"Thank you, Brandon, you too!" I squeezed him back, thankful to see another friendly face. When I let go, Jon was bolting into the mass of people, leaving us behind without another word.

"Have we missed out on any fun yet?" Paul asked Brandon.

"Nope. Just the usual drunk people doing their usual crazy shit."

The two of them entered slang mode and I lost the thread of the conversation. *So, this is the usual, huh?* Maybe for them, but for me, it was my first American high school party.

"Let's go grab some drinks." Brandon nodded toward the open-concept kitchen and we followed him there, Paul holding my hand tightly as he pushed a path through the crowd. He looked back at me and I swooned over his adorable dimples.

When we got to the counter Paul poured me a drink and I accepted, resolving that I wouldn't have as much as last time. I lifted the cup to my lips and almost sighed in relief when I realized it was only beer.

Gosh, this tastes like pee! I pulled back with a shudder and cleared my throat.

"That bad, really?" Paul laughed.

"You have no idea." I shook my head incredulously. "This stuff doesn't hold a candle to German beer." He and Brandon were in stitches as I took another tentative sip.

"One day I want to try German beer." Paul winked at me.

"You'll never be able to drink pee again." I held up my cup.

"But aren't you drinking it right now?" Brandon pointed out with a tremendous smirk.

"Crap." Now we were all laughing.

A few minutes later, Brandon placed his hand on my shoulder gently. "Emily, is it okay if I steal your man for a minute?"

"Um, I guess so . . ." I wasn't exactly thrilled at the idea of being at this party on my own.

"If you don't want me to go, I can stay," Paul said, stroking my cheek softly.

I bit my lip. "No, it's fine. Go ahead." I didn't want to hog all of his attention. He had other people to hang out with too. And I wasn't his girlfriend after all . . .

But when he left, I realized that it did bother me. When had I become such a hypocrite? I leaned against the counter awkwardly, searching the crowd for people I might know. A couple of guys gave me thirsty looks that I didn't return. And I got sidelong glances from some of the girls, probably because I was still the new one. They looked hungry for me to do something strange that they could judge—or worse.

As I surveyed the room, more and more twisted thoughts tangled themselves in my head. I ended up chugging my drink instead of sipping it. *Crap, just go talk to someone, Emily.*

And then I saw her. *Jamie.* Paul's ex-girlfriend. She wore a skintight navy blue dress, and her strawberry blonde hair was straightened so that it almost reached her belly button.

Jamie stalked toward me, her brow knitted in anger. "What are you doing here?" Her red cup made a little cracking noise as she tightened her hold on it.

My mouth went dry. This was unexpected. Only a weird gurgling sound came out of my throat.

"You have some nerve showing up here!" Her voice contained so much hatred that for a moment, I wanted to apologize.

"I, um—" I pressed back against the counter until my skin started pounding from the pressure.

A hand pulled at Jamie's shoulder, not hard, but authoritative nonetheless.

"What do you want?!" She spun around, making most of her drink slosh onto the ground.

"I suggest you leave her alone."

I'd hoped it was Paul returning to defend me, but the husky voice was Jon's. I let out the breath that had been trapped in my throat.

"Mind your own business," Jamie snapped.

"Emily's my friend. If you have a problem with her, you have a problem with me," Jon retorted. He looked hard at Jamie, his dark eyes lit by a flickering flame.

"And if you have a problem with Jon, I'll have you on my hit list too," chimed in a melodic voice I'd never heard before.

Standing right behind Jon, the girl took my breath away. Everything about her was flawless. Tall, but not too tall. Shiny dark hair, ivory skin contrasting with cherry-red lips. She reminded me a little of Snow White.

"I can't believe you two are sticking up for her instead of me!" Jamie mewed, then rushed out of sight.

"Are you okay?" Jon asked me, softly touching my shoulder.

I nodded, still a little shell-shocked.

"Jamie doesn't like it when new people join the group, but she'll get over it." The girl smiled warmly and came closer, and Jon's hand jumped away from my skin. "I'm sorry about that," she said, drawing me in with a single breath. "You must be Emily. I've heard a lot about you."

Jon laid an arm around her shoulder with a grin. *Who is she?*

"It's okay." My jaw cracked as the tension released. "Thank you for standing up for me. Um . . ."

"Katherine, but everyone calls me Kiki," she filled in. Her silvery voice raised goosebumps on my skin.

Behind her, I saw Hannah, the ginger-haired girl from my US History class, waving at me from a couch on the other side of the room. She beckoned for me to come over.

"I think Hannah wants me to—" I began, but Jon was whispering something in Kiki's ear which made a little giggle escape her perfectly shaped lips. They were clearly in their own world, so I carefully squeezed myself through the mass of people to the couch and sat down next to Hannah. Danielle was there too. She threw me an infectious smile.

"Guys, this is Emily," Hannah shouted to the people around her. "The German exchange student I told you about."

Multiple pairs of eyes landed on me like I was a piece of fresh meat.

"Hi." I squirmed, waiting for someone to call the spotlight away from me.

"Finally, someone else from another country! I'm Marcos, from

Spain," said a guy with jet-black hair, leaning over and giving me kisses on both cheeks. His emerald green eyes shone brightly against his deeply tanned skin.

"*Thank you*," I said under my breath, glad that he'd broken the silence.

"What's up, German? I'm Leni," another dude said. His look was quite average—blond hair, brown eyes, bad skin. Not one I'd notice in a crowd. "Welcome to the best country on earth." He raised his cup.

I put my hands in my lap. I didn't understand all this national pride. In Germany, it would be odd to praise our country or hang our black, red and gold flag in front of our houses. The only time we did this was during the World Cup.

"I guess 'German' is your new nickname, Emily." Danielle giggled.

I gave her a wry smile. Among my very first days at Boonville High, when I was introduced by my math teacher as the German exchange student, nasty whispers filled the room. I heard things like "*Hitler girl*." Yet I didn't say anything. Back then I only knew basic English. "Yes, no, I don't know, what does this mean?" and the like.

The introductions were interrupted by the sight of Breana running past us with her face in her hands, almost stumbling over some empty cups on the ground. Tears were streaming down her cheeks, but nobody attempted to go after her as she wrenched open the front door and dashed out of the house.

"What's wrong with Breana?" I asked Danielle since they seemed close.

"We should give her space," she replied in a serious tone I'd never heard from her before.

"She's a temperamental person, German," threw in Leni.

"Exactly. She needs time to cool down," Hannah concluded.

But it didn't look to me like Breana wanted to be left alone. Running through the room, crying—she'd basically screamed for help, and I couldn't just ignore it.

"I'll go check on her." I stood up, fixing the hem of my dress.

"She'll just send you away," Marcos said, shrugging and taking a gulp of brown liquor. "We've all tried it before."

Ignoring his comment, I started squeezing my way through the people to the exit. And that was when I saw the reason she was crying.

Jon's tongue was all up in someone else's throat—*Kiki's throat.*

Chapter 12

False Illusions

JON AND KIKI WERE KISSING EACH OTHER PASSIONATELY, oblivious to the people around them cheering them on. Jon had tangled his fingers into Kiki's hair and pressed her up against a kitchen cupboard. The sight of their dancing tongues made a spasm of disgust shoot through me. Breana thought she and Jon stood a chance. I understood why she was crying now. Gritting my teeth, I tore my gaze away from the couple and raced after Breana.

Outside, I nearly ran right into Paul and Brandon on the pathway to the front gate, smoking cigarettes and talking earnestly. Their conversation came to an abrupt stop when they saw me. Brandon looked at me wide-eyed, but then swung his gaze up to the night sky when Paul nudged him.

"What were you talking about?" I asked Paul, raising my eyebrows expectantly.

He took the cigarette out from between his lips. "Nothing much," he said. "Why are you out here?"

"Breana ran off crying. I want to check on her," I replied before continuing down to the gateway. I was annoyed that he'd brushed off my question. They had clearly been talking about me.

"Emily," Paul yelled after me. "She probably wants to be alone!" But I didn't care. He was wrong.

I stumbled down the street searching for a sign of her, hoping I was going in the right direction. My eyes stung from all the smoke in the air at the party. And even though I'd only had one beer, it was a struggle to walk in a straight line.

A couple houses down the road, I spotted her sitting on a swing at a playground, her shoulders hunched over. As I came near her, she tilted her face up. It was covered in tears and smudged mascara.

"Breana?" I almost whispered, now unsure if the others had been right.

"Emily, why did you follow me?" She looked up at me, her brow furrowed in confusion.

I sat down on the swing next to her. "You're upset, so I wanted to see if you were okay."

Breana's sniffling turned into full-fledged sobbing. Her whole body shook uncontrollably and tears dripped down from her chin.

"Emily, I . . . I'm fine, you should lea—" she started, but her voice was cracking too hard to continue.

"You don't look fine." I picked up her hand to show her that she wasn't alone. It could've easily been me bawling on the swing right now. Breana tried to pull away, but I laced my fingers with hers and she held on.

I slowly slid off the swing, not letting my grip loosen, and kneeled on the sand to hug her tightly. She responded in kind, not softly, no, she squeezed my body like it had been a while since she'd been held. She buried her head in my neck and her tears wet my shoulder.

"Every guy turns away from me eventually. I'm never good enough," she moaned in between sobs. "It's never me . . ."

Breana always acted so dauntless, so indestructible. But in the end, she was just like every other girl, dealing with heartache, worried that she was falling short.

"I really thought Jon was serious about me. But no, he didn't even bother telling me that he wasn't interested. And he isn't the first guy who's done that to me . . ."

"Breana?" called a voice I knew darn well by now.

Paul. He must have decided to follow us after all. Breana jerked out of the hug and jumped away from the swing defensively.

"P-Paul, what are you doing here?" she croaked.

"Emily was looking for you and—"

"And then you came because you're worried about *her!* Because it's never me!" Breana spat the words in his face.

Paul took a deep breath and backed up a step. "Breana," he said, his voice quiet but firm. "I heard what you said and I'm sorry for not wanting more than friendship with you. It was never my intention to hurt you." It sounded like they'd had this conversation before.

For a moment, Breana didn't say anything. She just picked at her nails. "I can never make a guy stay with me . . . No one likes me the way I like them."

"Bre—" Paul began, but I interrupted, feeling like he might accidentally make things worse.

"You'll find the right guy, Bre. You just can't force somebody to be 'the one.' It has to come naturally."

Breana sat still for a moment.

"You could be right . . ." she finally replied, a bit calmer. "Look at you two. You were doomed to fall for each other right from the beginning."

My mouth fell open. Paul and I had hit it off straight away, it was true, but I couldn't let myself fall for him. I mean, I wanted to, but I knew it was wrong. It would only end up in broken hearts.

Paul grinned widely at me, obviously not feeling as intimidated as I was. "Let's go inside," he said to Breana. "I'm sure you don't want to miss your own party."

He took the lead, but when I went to follow him Breana grabbed my hand.

"Thank you, Emily."

"Don't mention it."

We walked back to Breana's in silence. The party was still going strong. To my surprise, Kiki and Jon were leaning against the kitchen counter, casually chatting like their lips hadn't been crushed together just before. The way they interacted looked so natural, so easy—the opposite of how Jon and I were. Kiki wasn't constantly hitting her head against a brick wall.

"Hey, Paul, I'll be back in a second, okay?" I said in Paul's ear. He gave me a questioning look and I motioned toward Jon.

Paul rubbed the back of his head. "Sure thing."

Still kind of peeved at him for acting shady, I didn't bother reassuring him before making my way over to Jon and Kiki.

"Hey, Kiki," I shouted over the music. "Is it okay if you give Jon and I a minute?"

She gave me a friendly look before floating off like she didn't need to touch the ground. *How can someone walk so darn good in heels?*

When I didn't speak right away, Jon raised his eyebrows. "What do you want, Little German?"

"We need to talk." I gestured for him to come away from the kitchen with me. There were too many ears around us and I didn't want them listening in.

He gave me his trademark look of annoyance, but followed me past all the drunk people up the stairs into an unoccupied room.

It was evidently Breana's—I recognized her stuff. And there were paintings too, everywhere I looked. The floor was littered with brushes and canvases. I hadn't known she was so into art.

I sat down on the small bed and motioned for Jon to close the door. It dampened the sound of the music and I sighed in relief. I wouldn't have to keep yelling.

Jon jumped onto the bed and made himself comfortable against the wall, crossing his legs.

"Not gonna lie, I'm wondering why *the* Little German wants to talk to me in private," he said, his tone lazily confident.

I ignored this. "Listen, Jon . . . Gosh, I can't believe I even have to talk to you about this."

But like he'd said himself, we were friends now. *Friends are supposed to tell each other if they're acting ridiculous, right?*

"We don't have to talk, you know?" He gave me an impish smile and leaned closer to me, his gaze flickering to my lips. For an endless second, our eyes connected.

Then I shook my head no. He'd *just* made out with Kiki. And I wasn't going to be one of his trophies.

"Stop being an ass for just one minute, please!" I said. Why did I think talking to him would be a good idea?

Jon gave an exaggerated roll of his eyes and rested back against the wall. "Fine, what do you want to talk about then?"

I took a deep breath and looked up at the ceiling. Then I launched into the monologue I'd prepared for myself on the way over. "You're not looking for commitment. You just want to have fun. I get it."

"Are you asking me to make out with you?" He sniggered, leaning in again.

He was enjoying this way too much. I gave him an evil glare.

"Sorry, it was too good to let slip. I'll stop being an *ass* now."

I hit his shoulder in a sudden surge of frustration, making him topple back.

"You're blushing—aren't you!" Jon's eyes glinted with excitement.

"This is about Breana." I looked down, letting my hair fall over my face to hide the flood of color in my cheeks. Because he was right—I *was* blushing. Why? I didn't even know myself.

"Breana and I are only friends!" he protested, the mocking tone leaving his voice. I had clearly thrown him for a loop.

"Did you ever actually say that to her?" I said, more confident now.

"Not exactly, but . . . she knows that—" He paused. "She saw me making out with Kiki, huh?"

I raised my eyebrows and gave him a look that said, *do you really have to ask?*

For a moment, Jon stared at the bedspread, a hint of shame in the crease of his brow.

"Thanks for telling me this, Little German."

Surprised at his being friendly for a change, I gave him an encouraging nod as he got off the bed.

He suddenly reached over and tousled my hair, his usual self again.

"Ugh, seriously, Jon?"

He chuckled and cocked his head at me before making his way back to the door. He put his hand on the doorknob, but paused and said in a low voice, "So, you and Paul, huh?"

"Me and Paul?" I repeated, even though I knew exactly what he meant. I didn't have an answer to his question, and I doubted I'd have one any time soon.

"Ugh, never mind," Jon growled and swung the door open.

I brought my hands to my mouth when I saw Paul standing there, one fist lifted in the air like he was about to knock.

"Oh, sorry, man," Paul said to Jon. "I didn't want to disturb your booty call," he joked.

Then his eyes landed on me, my mussed-up hair. His smile vanished.

Jon didn't even blink. "Not a booty call," he said with a shrug as he walked past him.

Paul stared after him angrily. Then he strode into the room and closed the door.

Chapter 13

Guilty, Not Guilty

"WHAT HAPPENED IN HERE?" PAUL ASKED, SPREADING his arms out between me and the door.

I smoothed my hair down quickly. "I was just talking to Jon about Breana."

Paul drew in a breath and let it out slowly. "Yeah, sure." He pressed his lips together.

My mouth fell open. "Don't you believe me?"

He ran his fingers through his hair and turned to stare at a painting of a thunderstorm that hung across from him. The bold strokes of black and blue dashed together a beautiful yet terrifying landscape.

"Ah, I don't know. Jon knows how to . . . Forget about it." His voice was quiet, just above a whisper.

"That's not fair. I've never given you any reason to doubt me." I pulled my lower lip between my teeth.

Paul suddenly turned back toward me. "I know, I'm sorry." He let out another long sigh and pressed the bridge of his nose between his fingertips.

The Lovely One

Now I was the one looking away. A fire was spreading through my chest.

"I just didn't see you anywhere for so long and I got worried," he said. But the fire was already overtaking my mind.

"Oh, so *now* you care about me being alone at the party?"

He was doubting me when I was the one who should be suspicious! I was being naive as usual. I hid my face in my hands. The veins in my palms were pulsing with questions. *Why would you think that I'm interested in Jon? What were you talking about with Brandon? Why are you always so secretive?*

"Fuck, I knew you would get mad that I left with Brandon."

I let my hands fall into my lap and glared at him. "Then why did you?"

"Emily." Paul came closer and sat down next to me on the bed, covering my hand with his.

I turned my gaze to the wall.

"Brandon wanted to talk about Hannah." Paul squeezed my hand. "He's got the biggest crush on her and he wanted me to help him approach her."

"Oh . . ." The fire in me sputtered. "You weren't bad-mouthing me when I saw you outside?"

He smiled shyly and shook his head. "I would never say anything bad about you, Emily."

I allowed myself to look into his ocean eyes again and my heart started thumping in my chest.

"I told him to be himself. Because whenever I'm with you . . ." He grinned nervously. "I'm truly me, and it just feels right."

My heart soared. Just like that, he'd found exactly the right words to calm my fears.

"I'm sorry for doubting you." I leaned my head against his chest.

"Don't apologize. I shouldn't have assumed that something was going on with Jon."

I chewed on the inside of my cheek as he reached for my face.

"I really like you, Emily." Paul's hot breath caressed my skin, and his words, my soul. Within a split second he'd pressed his lips to mine, as if wanting to seal his confession with a kiss. It was filled with so much heat that I felt like my head was about to explode. I kissed him back, overflowing with gratitude that he truly cared about me. I parted my lips and granted admittance to his tongue.

Keeping his mouth to mine, he guided me to lie down on the bed and hovered over me, not breaking contact for even a second. He explored my skin with his hands, electrifying me with every caress. No one had ever touched me like that before. His lips traveled down to my belly, planting soft kisses onto every inch of his path and making my back arch up in an unfamiliar motion.

"Gosh, you drive me crazy," he whispered. "Emily . . ." The way he breathed my name made my heart race even faster. I pulled him back up to kiss his face and rolled him onto the bed so I could sit on top of him. I caught my breath for a moment and crashed my lips onto his again. He tasted of cigarettes and cheap beer, yet I craved more. *What am I doing here?*

I lifted Paul's shirt over his head and ran my index fingers over his bare torso. Craning his neck up, he kissed the soft spot behind my ear, and a moan escaped my lips.

I was losing control, but I didn't care. It was oddly comfortable. A new part of me was awake and it wanted to explore all the pleasures life had to offer. Our bodies moved to the rhythm of the music blasting on the other side of the door. This was my adventure.

Paul swung me around again and continued to kiss me with everything he had. He gently bit the skin above my collarbone and I tilted my neck back, rewarding him with another moan. With a satisfied smile, he glided his hands over my thighs, underneath my dress and up to my panties—

"What on earth!?" The door had swung open and Breana was there. In her voice was an edge of panic. I pushed Paul off me and jumped up off the bed, suddenly aware that the music had stopped.

"Paul, you have to leave right now!" Breana said urgently, her face as red as a tomato.

"Chill, Breana—" Paul began, pulling his shirt over his head, but she tugged him by the arm toward the door.

"You don't understand! Mrs. Stone is coming over!"

Mrs. Stone is coming?! I stood there, stiff, unable to move. I should've known that she'd call Breana's mother. I had too much faith in her.

I drank beer, I partied with boys, and I was about to do more than kiss one of them.

If Mrs. Stone found out, it would confirm all her suspicions about me. I'd be the hormone-ridden teenager she thought I was. And worse, she'd be right—and I would have to say goodbye to America. Goodbye to Paul, goodbye to Breana and Danielle, goodbye to my dream of completing my list.

We hurtled down the stairs and into the living room. People were chugging their drinks, grabbing their bags and dashing out the door in droves like sheep from a wolf. I flattened myself against a wall to avoid getting trampled.

"Didn't she know you were going to a party?" Paul asked, puffing.

"S-She didn't . . . She—" I was short of breath and my voice was failing me. "I lied and told her it was only Danielle, Breana and me. If she finds out . . ." I burst into tears and put my face in my hands.

Paul quickly pulled me into a hug, and I felt myself being infused with strength and calm. The tears in the corners of my eyes melted away. I could handle this. *How does he have such an effect on me?*

"You'll be fine. You were with Breana and Danielle all night. Ask Breana for some pajamas to change into. Then go outside with them and wait for Mrs. Stone. That way, she won't suspect a thing."

Paul was taking charge. But not like my friends in Germany did, to control me. No, he stepped in when he felt the fear overwhelm me, when I couldn't finish a single thought without panicking.

I nodded and buried my face deeper in his chest, trying to get rid of the sickening feeling that had settled within me. This party was getting crashed because of me. I had ruined the fun for everybody.

"Paul!" I heard Jon shout. "We have to get out of here, now."

I pulled back. Jon was waiting by the front door. "You should go," I told Paul. "I'll be all right."

"You're really fine with me leaving, though?"

His double-checking made me laugh. *He's perfect.* "Yes, this time is different."

He gave me a sweet and caring kiss on the forehead before tearing off after Jon. Now it was only Breana, Danielle and me left in the living room.

Breana laid into me. "Mrs. Stone told my mom I was throwing a party!" She put her hands to her head. "*Fuck.* Do you know how much trouble I'm in?" she shouted.

"I'm so sorry, Breana . . . Mrs. Stone said I wasn't allowed to go if boys were going to be there, but I really wanted to come."

Breana took a deep breath, trying to contain her anger. "Shit, I understand why you lied."

It was a good thing I'd decided to follow her out to the swing set earlier. Otherwise she probably would've been harsher on me.

Mrs. Stone's car was perfectly clean. I shifted on the passenger seat in a horrid nightgown plastered with pink and purple cupcakes, my confidence level close to zero. "Laundry day," Breana had explained. *Great.*

"I'm sorry for interrupting your movie night, girls," Mrs. Stone said, her hands stern on the wheel, "but I'll feel more comfortable knowing you're not home alone."

"Of course," Breana muttered in the back seat. The hint of sarcasm in her voice made Mrs. Stone look at me suspiciously, and I held my breath.

"You're right, Mrs. Stone," Danielle piped up. "We can watch a movie anywhere."

Mrs. Stone's face relaxed and she gave Danielle a sweet smile. *Thank you, Danielle.*

The rest of the drive was pretty much silent. Mrs. Stone pulled into the driveway of her pastel yellow house and led the way in.

"Could you go ahead to the living room, girls?" she chirped to Breana and Danielle, ushering them into the kitchen. "I need to talk with Emily about something for a moment."

My friends gave me worried looks before nodding and leaving me with my own personal nightmare.

Mrs. Stone walked over to the table and rested her hands on the back of a chair.

"Is there anything you would like to tell me, Emily?" she asked with a saccharine smile the second Danielle and Breana were out of earshot.

I stared at the ground. "I don't know what you're talking about," I mumbled.

She straightened up, her lips turning down. "I wanted to give you the chance to be honest with me, Emily. But you're leaving me with no other alternative."

I clenched a corner of Breana's nightgown, my breath trapped in my throat again.

Mrs. Stone dropped the bomb. "I know there were boys there too. I saw them outside with bottles of beer. Are you drunk?" Her voice was getting shrill.

I froze, trying to find something to look at so my eyes wouldn't cross hers.

"Because if you are, I'll have to report it to your area representative."

With this statement, she'd cornered me. I had do what I hated most: *lying.*

"No! I didn't drink any alcohol a-and I don't know which boys you're talking about," I stammered, accidentally biting down on my lip.

"Don't lie to me!" She suddenly slammed her palm against the wall.

I jumped half a mile, leaving my stomach down below. I'd never seen her face so contorted. I actually missed her usual smile.

"Even if there were boys, they aren't poison, Mrs. Stone," I said desperately. The first tear of the evening escaped my eye. I'd have to leave America. The fear took over my entire body, and I trembled as if the temperature had dropped below freezing.

"In my household, you're not allowed to run around with boys or drink, not even a single drop!" she bellowed, totally ignoring that I was breaking down in front of her. "If you want to keep on living here, then you have to follow my rules, and not getting pregnant is one of them!"

The tears were coursing down my cheeks at full speed now. This couldn't be the end yet . . . *My adventure only just started!*

I had nothing left to lose so I let my anger explode out of me. "I'm a virgin, Mrs. Stone! I didn't plan on changing that at a stupid party!"

But I was madder at myself than her, because I did do something inappropriate with Paul tonight. Maybe we wouldn't have gone all the way, but he made me forget my rules. I'd surrendered to his touch.

"You're a sixteen-year-old girl who evidently doesn't have a problem with lying," Mrs. Stone sniped.

"I had n-no other choice!" I cried out before running out of the room. I couldn't take this cross-examination for one more second.

"Don't you run away from me!" she warned, but that made my legs move even faster.

I stumbled past the living room where Breana and Danielle were standing with stunned looks on their faces. I didn't have to say anything. They followed me up the stairs into my bedroom.

"Emily, she's crazy!" Danielle whispered the second my door was closed. "She enjoyed seeing you suffer . . ."

"And I thought my mother didn't trust me," Breana said in disbelief.

I grabbed a tissue and concentrated on wiping off my smudged mascara.

"I'm sorry for yelling at you, Emily," Breana added. "I had no clue how bad your host mother actually is."

I inhaled as much air as possible to get my voice under control. "Thanks, Breana. I just hope she won't call my area rep."

"She will, no doubt." Danielle shrugged.

"Danielle, this is not the time for candor," Breana whispered in her ear.

"No, she's right," I cut in. "I'll have to call her myself. Tomorrow."

"You can't tell her that you drank, Emily!" Breana protested.

I dropped the tissues into the trash can. "Don't worry, I won't."

"Then what will you tell her?" Danielle asked, looking at me with a frown.

I let out a long breath. "That Mrs. Stone abuses me. That she treats me like a maid." I hated saying it. But after all, it was the truth.

"She does what?!" Danielle put her hands to her mouth, her face turning pale.

"Fuck, Emily, I thought it got better?" Breana sat down on the bed, and I joined her.

"I tried to tell myself that it did . . . but the only difference was that I figured out how to escape the house more often. I can't keep doing this anymore. Especially if she starts ruining your nights too."

My sobbing had stopped and my thoughts were clear. I wasn't in denial anymore. It was time to confront Mrs. Stone about how she treated me.

For the rest of the evening, we just chatted about all sorts of things. My virginity was something my friends didn't neglect to ask me about. I admitted that I had never had sex with anyone, and they warned me to not let any boys know because it would make me a target at Boonville High. We had a pretty good time, but everybody from the party kept sending us voice messages and pictures of them hanging out at the park near Breana's place. It was like we'd gotten kidnapped. It wasn't a sleepover party. This place felt like a prison. And I could tell that Danielle and Breana felt it too.

Chapter 14

Last Chance

BREANA AND DANIELLE LEFT EARLY IN THE MORNING, without even a bite to eat for breakfast. They'd been released, but I was still stuck here. The minutes dragged on until I got a call from my mother. I answered the phone while opening my closet to pick an outfit for the day.

"Hi, Mom, isn't it late at night for you?"

"Yes, but this couldn't wait. Mrs. Stone called to tell me you misbehaved!" she said angrily. "You drank alcohol. Are you out of your mind?"

I sighed and sat cross-legged on the carpet. "She's overreacting. I had one beer, and that was the very first party I went to," I explained, rubbing my feet.

"Oh, overreacting, is she. You know you'll get sent back to Germany for underage drinking!" There was something in my mother's voice I didn't hear often. Pure rage. And I didn't enjoy being its target.

"Mom, I was careful, really." I hadn't planned on drinking, but there was no way to explain to her that it felt like I had no other choice. That I was controlled by anxiety.

"Careful? Mrs. Stone caught you! You know how much we paid for this program, so don't mess it up just because you're in the mood for a drink!"

Guilt washed over me. She was right. Being an exchange student was anything but cheap. Savings my mother had been putting aside for me since I was little, plus a student loan and financial aid—all of that added up to almost 10,000 euros, about 11,000 US dollars. I swallowed my instinct to defend myself and went into defeat mode.

"I'm sorry, Mom, I won't let it happen again."

"Good." Her tone softened. "I told her that I'm fine with you hanging out with boys and she started crying! How emotionally unstable is this woman?"

"She started crying?" I was so surprised that I almost dropped the phone.

"Yes, she said she's worried that you're getting out of control and she feels overwhelmed. I asked her if she was sure she was talking about you because you're an easy teenager compared to others." My mom chuckled.

It was true that I'd never been a troublemaker, but I also didn't have a lot of exciting stories to tell. I was the lovely one in everybody's eyes, and I hated that.

I wrapped up the call quickly after that. There was another conversation that urgently needed attending to. I put on some sweats and went down to the lake to make sure Mrs. Stone wouldn't overhear anything.

Sitting down on the stairs, I brushed my fingers over some stray pebbles. It felt like a century ago that I'd pulled out those weeds. They were already growing back.

I took out my phone and stared at the screen. I had to make this call now before it was too late. With an unsteady finger I searched my contacts for Mrs. Jonson, my area rep. I put the phone up to my ear and took one last deep breath.

"Hello, Emily!" her kind voice answered after the third ring. "Everything okay?"

"No—I have to talk to you, Mrs. Jonson." My heart was hammering so loud against my chest that she could probably hear it.

"I'm all ears," she said, sounding concerned.

"I tried—I really tried to make it work, but . . ."

I told her about the never-ending chores. The epic weeding, the daily cleaning, the silly tasks like polishing the silverware. And the rules.

For a moment, all I could hear was the sound of cars whizzing by the house and the wind blowing through the trees. Mrs. Jonson cleared her throat. I held my breath.

"Emily, it's been over two months. Why haven't you said anything earlier to me?"

That's when I realized that my face was covered with tears. I'd been crying while making my confession.

"I didn't want to cause any trouble"—I gasped for air between words—"and I thought it was my fault."

"We'll get you out of there as soon as possible, okay?" I exhaled in relief. Mrs. Jonson explained what would happen next. "Finding a new host family isn't a process that happens overnight. To speed it up, could you ask a friend if their parents might like to take you in?"

Paul's face popped into my head, but I quickly banished it. That would be too crazy.

"Oh, and I'll have to talk to Mrs. Stone about this."

"Please . . . can you wait till I'm gone?" My lower lip was still trembling.

"I'm sorry, Emily, but I can't let her continue to treat you like this." Mrs. Jonson's voice was full of pity.

I'd expected that answer. The nightmare wasn't over yet.

Over a week had passed since Mrs. Stone started avoiding me and I basically did the same. She'd slipped a sheet under the door to my bedroom that listed the new rules: *Come home straight after school, No hanging out with friends,* and so on. It was her way of punishing me for what happened. When we saw each other in the hall, we turned and went opposite ways. At the dinner table, we ate in silence, letting Madison brag about her current successes. I didn't mind Mrs. Stone acting like a child—it was better than a confrontation.

I assumed that Mrs. Jonson had called her and told her what we'd discussed. But I wondered if my area rep knew that I'd been drinking. So far, she hadn't asked me about it. She hadn't found a new host family for me either.

But today is a new day, I told myself as I got dressed in something black and simple. I'd asked every person I knew if I could move in with them—everyone except for Paul and Jon. But I'd given Paul the lowdown on my situation one night as we talked on the phone until sunrise.

I sneaked down to the kitchen, where I found Madison putting her empty cereal bowl in the sink.

"Hey, Madison. Has your mother left already?" I asked quietly, peeking over her shoulder.

"Yeah, don't worry, the coast is clear." She smiled at me.

That was the first moment I felt like Madison was on my side in this—a moment where she seemed to be aware that her mother wasn't the easiest person to get along with. But why was she still so distant with me? We saw each other every day, but I knew nothing about her. I still didn't know why she'd bawled her eyes out in the afternoon of the party. I was considering asking her about it, but I was too late. She waved goodbye and stepped out the door.

"Whoa there, German. How's life?"

I'd almost crashed into Brandon in the crowded school hall.

"Still looking for a new home," I replied wearily, straightening my backpack after our near-collision.

"Sorry, that must suck." He rubbed the side of his arm. "Have you asked Paul yet?" I started at the mention of Paul. Brandon had asked the question as if it was the obvious choice.

For the past week, Paul and I had spent as much time together as possible, but only at school. Due to my new rules, I couldn't hang out with him after the bell rang. And a question like "Can I move in with you?" couldn't just casually be dropped while walking to our next class, right?

"I haven't had the chance yet," I mumbled. A lousy excuse.

"Well, he's over there. Go ask him now." Brandon pointed down the hall. Paul was standing at his locker, searching through it for something and talking to . . . Jon. *Who else?*

Hannah's voice behind my shoulder surprised me. "Emily, hi," she called out, and I turned around to see her looking sheepish. "I talked to my parents, and they said that we don't have enough space for another person to live with us," she said apologetically.

"Oh, that's okay. Thanks for asking though."

Another name I could scratch off my list of potential new homes. The list was now officially down to zilch. Hannah slid her eyes toward Brandon before lifting her hand at me to say goodbye and heading for a nearby exit.

"See you in US History, German," Brandon said quickly and hurried after her. "Hannah, wait!"

My throat suddenly tight, I marched myself over to Paul. *You can do this, Emily. It's just a simple question.* I wasn't sure if I wanted to live with him. Deep down, I wished I could be close to him every second of the day. Fall asleep in his arms, make his favorite chicken recipe with him, even just sit together and do homework. But in my head, I knew that if we lived together, I would lose my heart entirely to those ocean-blue eyes.

"H-Hey, Paul, can we talk?" I stuttered.

"See you later, man," Jon muttered, walking away without giving me a single glance. For some odd reason, he was back to ignoring me again.

"Hey, Emily." Paul gave me a cute kiss on the cheek. "How's it going?"

"I probably won't be all right until I find a new host family," I blurted out.

He closed his locker and gestured for me to follow him. We walked down the hall for a bit, Paul with his brow furrowed.

Suddenly he turned to me and said, "What if I ask my parents if you can move in with us?"

I almost tripped over someone's school bag on the ground.

"You want me to live with you?" I scream-cried.

"Yes, I want you to live with me."

He must be joking, right?

"We could finally spend more time together." He took a step closer to me and poked my nose with his finger, smiling like he just got a Christmas gift handed to him.

Blood rushed into my cheeks as I got lost in his eyes. They were filled with gleeful anticipation, with love. Not a shadow of a doubt in them. This wasn't a joke.

"Soooo . . . what do you think?"

"I, um . . . yes!" The school bell went off, harmonizing with my shriek of delight.

Paul laughed sweetly and gave me a kiss on the cheek. "See you soon, Babycakes." He turned right down the hall.

Astonished, I stood there, watching him go. It was a typical heart move of mine. I was helpless—so helpless that I'd accepted an offer to live with the guy I had a crush on, without a second thought. Paul was my only hope now, my last chance, and truthfully, I didn't mind anymore. I should stop being scared . . . *Everything happens for a reason, right?*

All day my mind was fixated on whether Paul's parents would say yes. My veins were pulsing with excitement. I could barely focus on my schoolwork.

My nerves were still on fire as I made my way to my last class of the day, US History. I even looked forward to Jon's pestering. It would be fun to tease him back today. But when I took my seat, he was nowhere to be seen.

Class began and Mr. Harrison announced our new project: a presentation on one of the most influential people in the United States in the 1960s. As he was wrapping up his intro, Jon shuffled into the classroom, looking exhausted. His eyes were only half-open and his face was red. *Is he high on something?*

"Well hello, Mr. Denson. So nice of you to join us," said Mr. Harrison sarcastically. "As you're already up here, you can be first to pick your partner for the new assignment."

"I'll work with Brandon." Jon shrugged, unimpressed.

Mr. Harrison laughed evilly and dangled a bucket of folded-up pieces of paper in Jon's face. "You really think I'll let you guys pick your own partners after the last presentations?" He was enjoying this way too much.

Jon shrugged again, put his hand in the bucket and pulled out a slip. When he read it, his eyes widened to the size of healthy ones.

"Who is it?" asked Mr. Harrison, pen poised.

"Emily Klein."

Jon turned to look at me as my name echoed in my eardrums. I held tightly onto my chair. Occasional teasing, sure, I didn't mind that anymore. But spending hours together working on a project? *I don't think that's a good idea.*

After everyone was partnered up, Mr. Harrison instructed us to go to the library in pairs to start our research.

I was going to be spending a lot of time with Jon . . . alone.

Chapter 15

In Jon's Brain

"**A**RE YOU SURE MR. HARRISON IS FINE WITH US LEAVING the library?"

Jon had dragged me out to his car. A black BMW. I was surprised that he even had a car, considering that Paul drove him around pretty much every single day.

"He said to grab some books and get started on the project," Jon replied, backing out of the parking lot and driving away. "As long as we do the work, it doesn't matter where." He lifted his knee up to the wheel to steer while he took a pack of cigarettes out of his jacket and lit up.

The car was super tidy, with glossy leather seats and a spotless floor. The only thing out of place was an empty energy drink can in the cup holder.

"I didn't know you had a car," I said, my voice too loud in the awkward silence hanging in the air.

"It's my dad's." Jon took a drag of his cig and blew the smoke against the windshield. "I can only get it when he doesn't need it."

I started drumming my fingers on the leather armrest. My attempts at small talk were going nowhere. Jon fiddled with the stereo and rap streamed through the car, the volume cranked up high. I was actually starting to like it now. Aside from the anger, it carried so many emotions I could make out when I listened closely enough.

A few songs down the line, the silent treatment from Jon was starting to make my chest feel tight. When he flipped his stub out the window, I changed my mind and went in for another shot at breaking the silence.

"You know, we don't have to work together, Jon. We can each do our own part." Collaborating would probably never work out anyway.

He turned the music down. "Don't be stupid, Little German. We're doing it together." His tone was hard to interpret. Was he annoyed? Or happy? *I don't know.*

"Stop calling me stupid or I'm leaving," I huffed, crossing my arms.

"You want to jump out of a moving car? I'd like to see you try." Jon hit the gas pedal and merged onto the highway.

"You're a jerk." I tightened my arms against my chest. He chuckled, but didn't add anything more.

Silence reigned between us once again as we drove down the highway. We exited at the posher part of town the Stones lived in. I wished we could have a normal conversation. Even if it was just small talk. At least then I'd know that he didn't despise me.

I was still breaking my head over what Jon's issue with me was when he pulled into the driveway of a brick house with a nicely landscaped front yard. I realized that Jon's home wasn't far from the Stones', probably only a ten-minute walk.

"I'll just finish this square before we head in." Jon rested his back against the car.

"Why do you call a cigarette a 'square'?" I asked. "It's not even square." Not that I was still trying to start a conversation—I'd given up on that—but I was sincerely curious.

"For some reason, we do. You want one?" He raised his eyebrows and offered me the pack, its top open a crack.

"I don't smoke." I bit my lip, ready to hear what a *good girl* I was, that I didn't belong with his group of friends.

"That's good," Jon replied sincerely instead. "Never start smoking." He slid the pack into his back pocket and took a long drag, then exhaled the smoke in the air. He was staring at a point somewhere behind me. "You're better than that," he added, his voice husky.

I choked on my own spit and started coughing. *I'm better than that?* I leaned against the BMW to catch my breath and croaked, "I won't."

Jon cocked his head at me, suddenly looking at me intently.

I chewed on the inside of my cheek for a moment. His stare was unsettling, but for some reason, I didn't look away. "Jon, can I ask you something?"

"Sure," he said cautiously. His eyes were haunted with so many emotions, like they didn't even know themselves what they were supposed to reflect. They were captivating.

"Why do you make it so hard for people to like you?"

His look changed from inscrutable to defensive. I had hit a nerve.

"That way, I see their true colors."

"You think driving people crazy exposes their true colors?"

"Emily, just let it go. We aren't friends." He let his cigarette stub fall to the pavement and ground it out with his heel, looking away.

Now he'd hit a nerve of mine. "No? A week ago, you said we were!" I snapped. "You and I hang out all the time with Paul. You spend more time with me than with the other people you call your friends! What is so terrible about me, huh?" I jerked my chin up. If he was up for a fight, I wouldn't back down now. It was time to have *that* conversation. "C'mon! Talk!"

He just rolled his eyes, so I shoved him.

"Fuck, I actually like you, okay?" He shoved me back. Not hard, but combined with his words, I was hit at full force.

"You . . . like me?" I put my palms up, dazzled. I had expected him to tell me off.

"You're not bad, Little German. You happy now?" His face turned crimson, but his tone was menacing.

"Wow, really convincing, Jon." I gritted my teeth.

"I'm not a sappy person, all right? I don't mind having you around. Accept it and stop looking for my approval. It's pissing me off!"

"I'm not looking for your approval." I winced. Another nerve hit.

"You're not?" He took a step closer to me. "Then why is it so important to know what I think of you"—another step—"huh?" He was coming dangerously close.

I backed away, but he cornered me against the car. "Why do you care so much?"

"I-I . . ." *I don't know, I just do.* I looked down at the ground, feeling his breath tickle my neck.

He lifted my chin with his thumb, giving me no other choice than to return his gaze. He was so close . . . too close. My first instinct was to shove him again, but strangely, I didn't. He'd never looked at me like this before. *What if I push him away—he'll go back to ignoring me?*

I stared at the fire in Jon's eyes, flickering wildly between my eyes and my lips. His forehead creased as he focused on my face. His hand wandered up to my left ear and tugged a strand of hair behind it softly, grazing my cheekbone. I sucked in my breath at his touch. Resting his thumb on my cheek, Jon moved even closer, and I closed my eyes.

Then he backed off abruptly. "See," he scoffed. "Stop always giving people the chance to hurt you."

I jumped and banged my hip against the car. *Ouch.* "You—" I tried to fire something back, but I was still frozen. Like a deer, trapped in his spotlight.

Shakily, I found my breath again. "Why did you do that . . .?"

"To prove a fucking point!"

I looked at him with lost eyes, and he gave a loud sigh.

"You were obviously uncomfortable with me being so close, but you didn't shove me away like a normal person would have." He paced around the driveway. "Just because you want to make sure that I like you!" He threw his hands up. "Learn how to say no!"

I gulped. "Fine. You're right."

"You—" Jon stopped mid-sentence. I guess he hadn't expected me to admit my biggest flaw.

"I agree to everything. I never say what I really think. I want other people to like me. You happy now?" I sat down on the pavement at the end of the driveway, turning my back to him. His bluntness infuriated me. That, or I'd needed someone to tell me off to realize what I truly was.

"Not really." Jon's voice was quiet, like a whisper of wind through the trees.

I'd almost made a terrible mistake—a mistake he'd provoked on purpose, just to show me how easy it was to manipulate me. How small my voice was. How little control I had over my own actions. I'd always claimed that I was a control freak, but it was the opposite. I was a pushover. I cared too much. And Jon cared too little.

He offered me his hand to help me up, as if he was sorry for messing with my head. I ignored it and got up on my own.

"And you're Paul's girlfriend," he said suddenly. "It doesn't matter what I think of you anyway." He turned and walked toward the house.

"But I'm not his girlfriend . . ." I mumbled, but he was too far away to hear it.

We went through a little kitchen and down a wooden staircase into the basement. A funny coincidence that both Paul and Jon had their rooms underground. On the last step I looked around. Jon's room wasn't what I'd expected. A few mismatched couches sagged in one corner, looking like they'd already been sat on all day. Posters of jazz musicians, rock bands and rappers covered the walls. A punching bag hung on the far right, and in the center sat a double bed, welcoming and soft-looking with grey sheets. The ground was littered with dirty clothes. Nothing in this room really fit together—yet it looked complete.

"Sorry for the mess, I wasn't expecting company," Jon said, snatching something off a table.

"What's that?"

"I let you into my room, but I won't let you into my brain," he replied, effectively dodging my question as he threw whatever it was in a drawer.

I rolled my eyes but didn't push further. Just by being in Jon's room, I felt like I was getting to know him a little more. We sat down on his bed and started working on our school project. I couldn't really focus on my book about Malcolm X though. Everything Jon had thrown at me was still too present. He wanted to show what a pushover I was, but there were less intense ways to make a point. He didn't have to test my boundaries by touching my face. *What if . . .* No, I couldn't ask him that. I buried my nose back in my book.

Jon put down his pencil and turned to me with a determined look in his eye.

"Listen, I'm sorry if I confused you. I didn't mean to. Can we just forget about it?"

My muscles relaxed gratefully. "Sure."

But could I forget it? *I doubt it.*

The air lighter, we got back to work and started talking about Malcolm X. I'd finished a chapter about Malcolm's house being burned down by the Ku Klux Klan.

"Wow, his childhood was terrible," I said. His father was killed by a similar organization and his mother ended up in a mental health institution.

Jon was lying on his back with another book. He rolled himself up to a seated position on his side of the bed.

"People who never experience real trauma never make it big either," he said, smiling even though his words carried so much pain.

I raised an eyebrow. "People without a horrible past can do great things too!"

"There, you said it: great. Not world-changing." He winked at me and I couldn't help but laugh.

Jon reached for a piece of paper and started sketching out a mind map. "I was thinking that we could focus on the earlier parts of his life ... Maybe something like, how did he come to be the man we know him as?" Jon drew some bubbles and labeled them with traumatic events from Malcolm X's life, then added a few more bubbles with conclusions.

"It's all connected," I remarked, looking over the mind map.

"Exactly."

Jon was on to something. Everyone is the way they are for a reason. *So what's my reason for wanting so badly to be liked?*

My phone vibrated on the bed next to me. I reached for my backpack and threw the phone inside without checking who was calling. I was enjoying spending time with this kind of Jon.

"You don't want to take it? Could be important." He chewed on the end of his pencil, still absorbed in the words on the paper, connecting the dots.

"No." I shrugged my shoulders. "Right now I'm here, working on a school project with you."

His eyes shot up to stare at me, an exaggerated expression of amazement on his face. "You said no!" he exclaimed, covering his mouth in mock astonishment.

I closed my book and whacked him with it for making fun of me.

"*Nooo!*" Jon protested, imitating my German accent. We both broke out laughing and Jon fell back onto the bed, chuckling at the ceiling.

"You're such an idiot!" I let myself drop onto the bed next to him.

"An idiot who made you smile." He tilted his head to look at me. His laughing had faded and his mouth had turned serious. I held his gaze as his hand glided over the bedsheets. When it reached my neck, I quickly sat back up and cleared my throat.

"We should keep working."

I hadn't failed his second test. I'd pulled away. Even though there was a part of me that wished I hadn't.

"I think that's enough for today," Jon said. A little over two hours had passed.

"I agree. We're almost finished the entire project. My head needs a break."

Jon was intelligent. Smarter than he knew. It was hard for me to keep up with his brain.

"Oh, Little German, exhausted so quickly?" He gave me his usual cocky look.

"It's not that easy, considering that I have to keep up with your comments about my accent every two seconds."

"Your accent *is* very entertaining, though. And cute." He rested his chin on his hand.

When I objected to something, people called it being *cute*. But I was through with being the cute little girl. *Remember?*

"Arschloch!" I said under my breath. *Asshole!*

Jon's mask of easy arrogance gave way to a purely innocent look of confusion. But he quickly recovered. "You like talking to me in German, don't you?" he said with a smirk.

I took a chance. "Es ist lustiger als du denkst. Dein Blick ist Gold wert!" *The look on your face is priceless!*

Jon was caught off guard again. His brow furrowed in bewilderment. Then he rolled his eyes as if he didn't care, but I could tell he was miffed. I laughed so hard that tears sprang to my eyes. Everyone had their weakness—his was not to understand what I said.

Jon pushed the books off the bed and slid down to rest his head on a pillow.

"Sleep, here I come."

"You do know I'm still here, right?" I said, my mirth vanishing.

"I know, I won't actually fall asleep."

He closed his eyes. Perched at the edge of the bed, I watched the rise and fall of his chest slow down a bit. Jon wasn't the tallest, probably only around 1.78 meters, something like 5 foot 8. I didn't have to dislocate my neck to look at his face. I roamed my eyes freely over his features. The stubble on his chin—it looked like he hadn't shaved for a couple days. This one curl of hair on his head sticking up in the opposite direction to all the others. The slight smile on his face, like he was at peace with the world. Yes, in this moment, Jon looked happy. Happy and like he was about to drift off to sleep.

"The bed is big. If you want to rest too, feel free to lie down. I don't bite," Jon mumbled, as if he'd felt my stare.

"Just a few minutes, though. I need to get back to the Stones' place soon." Carefully, I positioned my body as far away from Jon's as possible on the other side of the bed. When my head hit the soft fabric, I realized how exhausted I was from all the facts Jon had taught me. *And I don't mean about Malcolm X.*

Chapter 16

The Rebellious, Sneaky Type

A HARD KNOCK CAME AT THE DOOR. A MAN'S VOICE CALLED
out, "Get this girl home! It's late!"

My eyes flew open to find myself only centimeters away
from Jon, his arm wrapped gently around my waist.

"Oh, fuck!" he yelled. He jumped out of bed and rubbed his face
with his palms.

Baffled, I looked at the spot his arm had been clinging to just before. The skin he'd touched still prickled. It took a couple more seconds
to fully realize what had just happened. I stumbled over to my backpack
to check the time on my phone and found multiple messages from Paul.

Hey Emily, I'm waiting for you at the school entrance

Where are you? I want to give you a ride home . . .

Are you okay?

My stomach twisted into an uncomfortable knot. An image flashed in my mind of Paul waiting for me by his car while the parking lot slowly emptied. It gave me goosebumps.

I pulled my eyes away from the messages. Time: 8:15 pm.

I'm in huge trouble.

"Mrs. Stone is going to kill me!" I said in a panic. Making a mental note to reply to Paul when I got home, I started gathering my things together.

"Don't worry, Little German," Jon told me. "I'll drive you."

It was already dark when we arrived in front of the Stone house. The entire car ride had been silent. I was confused that we'd slept so comfortably next to each other—that we'd snuggled. I hadn't slept that well in weeks. With his arms wrapped around me, I'd found a respite from the anxious thoughts that hounded me.

I got out of the car, and to my surprise, Jon did too.

"Thanks for driving me home," I said.

He leaned against the hood of the BMW and sucked in his lower lip, looking as if he was fighting to say something.

"Little German, you are—"

"Please don't tell me what I am."

He quirked an eyebrow.

"You were right. I care too much about what other people think, and I want to change that." I smiled in thanks and his lips curved into a broad grin—a different type of grin than his usual bad boy one.

"If you ever need the help of an expert, you know where to find me."

He gave a cheeky click of the tongue. I clicked mine right back to show him how fast I learned, and his expression softened. Lifting himself off the hood, he latched his arm around my shoulder and pulled me into a goodbye hug. I wrapped my arms around him and breathed in his aftershave.

With a sigh, he pulled back and put his palms on my shoulders to look at me. His eyes weren't flickering right now. He looked calm as he tucked my hair behind my ear again.

"You look prettier without the hair in your face." His voice was scratchy.

My heart did a backflip as I met his gaze, and a trillion thoughts raced through my mind. *He's Paul's best friend!* I moved his hand away from my face and took a step back.

"Jon, we—"

His eye caught something behind me and he stepped back quickly too.

"Hey, Paul, what's up?" he said.

I spun around and gulped as I took in the sight of a desperate-looking Paul, his hands in his pockets, his shoulders pulled up slightly. He was standing just a couple meters away. *How much did he see?*

"Jon, what are you doing here?" said Paul.

"Little German and I worked on our differences. We can hang out normally now. Right, friend?" Jon said in his usual cocky tone, nudging my arm with his fist.

Paul didn't comment. "Were you together all evening?" he asked me. "I couldn't find you after school."

"Um, y-yes," I stammered, avoiding his gaze. "We got paired up for a US History project." I felt guilty for not checking my phone. Guilty because for a couple of hours, Paul wasn't on my mind.

"We had to draw lots. Don't worry, I wouldn't have chosen to work with your girl otherwise," Jon said snidely.

I knew he was putting me down so Paul wouldn't get the wrong impression, but it was annoying nonetheless.

"Ditto, I would have preferred to work with someone who doesn't act like an ass," I fired back, crossing my arms to hide my bitterness.

Jon rolled his eyes and Paul chuckled. We were back to normal.

"I'm glad that you get along now," Paul said. He swung his arm around my shoulder and gave Jon a you-better-not-try-anything kind of look. Jon stared at the ground and didn't say a word.

I let my crossed arms drop back down to my sides and changed the topic. "Why did you come to the Stones' place, Paul?"

"I have great news that couldn't wait till tomorrow."

"Oh my gosh!" I covered my squeal with my hands, hoping it was what I thought it was.

He nodded. "Yes. My parents agreed!" His smile that was brighter than I thought possible.

I stared at him, lost for words. Then I jumped into his arms, shouting for joy. "I can't believe it! You're saving me!" I wrapped my legs around his body and crushed him in a massive hug. He pressed me tight before spinning me around in the air.

Paul was rescuing me from the Stones' place. I had a new home, a refuge. A place I could walk in and out of normally instead of sneaking around. He was giving me the chance to live my adventure.

"You're such a blessing!" I said, pressing my lips to his cheek.

Jon asked, "What did your parents agree to?" My smile faded when I saw his expression.

Paul let me back down to the ground. "Emily's moving in with me!"

Jon's jaw dropped. "What?" He looked at me, stunned.

But our conversation ended there. "Emily," called a man's voice, "would you please come inside?"

Mr. Stone was standing by the front door. And judging by his narrowed eyes, he wasn't happy about me being there with two boys.

Mr. Stone led the way into his office. I'd never been in there before; the door was always closed and it screamed *Enter at your own risk.* He kept the room tidy and well organized. Old bookshelves lined three of the walls, and a picture-perfect family portrait hung right above his desk, presenting a fake image of domestic happiness. Forced smiles, tense muscles.

"Take a seat, Emily," Mr. Stone said, sitting in a large office chair behind the desk. "Let's talk for a bit." For a man his age, his grey hair was full. Sharp black glasses perched neatly on his arrow-tipped nose.

I nodded awkwardly, staring into my lap. I wasn't sure if I was in trouble or if he just wanted to have a friendly chat about life.

"It's been a long time. How have you been?" he asked, a bit awkward himself.

"I'm okay." I ran my nails over my fingertips.

A silence.

"I've actually been waiting for you all day," he went on. My first guess was right—I was in trouble.

"I'm sorry, I was working on a school project with a friend," I explained, happy that it wasn't a lie this time.

"I can see that." His eyes shifted to the window, which opened onto the spot I'd been standing with Paul and Jon minutes before.

It must have sounded like a lie after all. I curled back in my chair, making myself small.

"I heard about the incident with my wife," Mr. Stone continued evenly. My heartbeat picked up and I felt the blood pump through my entire body up to my ears. "I know she can be fairly strict and unconventional."

I hazarded a glance at him. "You're not mad?"

He took a deep breath and straightened his glasses on his nose. "I considered notifying your area representative about your drinking." He paused. "But then Madison approached me."

"Madison?" I realized I was pushing my nails into my palms. It hurt a little when I released the pressure.

"Yes, she reminded me of what it was like to be a teenager . . . and that you haven't had it easy here."

This conversation was getting crazier by the second. *How did Madison even know about this?*

"Do you think you'd be happier with another host family?" Mr. Stone looked at me with tired eyes.

"Um . . . I appreciate your taking me into your home, but I think that I'm just not the right fit."

He nodded with understanding. "Thank you for your honesty, Emily. The last thing I want is for you to feel uncomfortable."

"Thank you, Mr. Stone." I pressed out a grateful smile. He'd been nothing but nice to me during my stay.

He gestured at the door and I got up.

"Oh, and Emily? Ignore those new rules my wife gave you. You can hang out with your friends."

With a real smile now, I left his office and headed up to my room. Once the door was shut, I spun on the spot and let myself drop onto the bed.

"I'm moving in with Paul . . ."

The next day, I got up half dead after pressing snooze four times. All night long I'd been turning the news over and over in my head. My mind was electrified with twin currents of excitement and nervousness. I was moving in with a guy that I liked more than I probably should.

I put on some comfortable jeggings and an oversized sweatshirt, trying not to be intimidated by the situation and to welcome it with open arms. I started placing my hair over my chest, but on impulse, I grabbed a hair tie instead. With a quick move I pulled my hair back into a ponytail. I barely recognized myself with that style.

Madison was down in the kitchen as usual. "Hey, Madison," I said, loud and clear. Knowing that she'd stood up for me gave me hope that we could be friends after all.

She shrugged one shoulder. "Um, girl, the bus left already, do you know that?"

"Crap, what time is it?" I whirled around to look at the clock, answering my own question. I had lost track of time today, something that normally never happened to me.

"Don't worry, you can come in the car with me," she offered.

I exhaled in relief. I was lucky that she was still here today. We grabbed our school bags and headed outside.

"How come you're going to school later today?" I asked as we got into the car.

"Jackson is sick, so no need for me to be at school early." Madison pulled out of the driveway.

"Jackson?"

"Oh, Jackson's my boyfriend. We meet up before school so we can hang out without my mom finding out about it. She thinks I go to a study group." She hit the gas pedal and I held tightly onto my seatbelt. *Madison has a boyfriend?*

"I don't expect your mother approves of you having a boyfriend," I said.

"She doesn't. But just like you, I'm not following her rules." She snickered.

"You fooled us both."

"I didn't know if I could trust you. Now I know that we're so much alike—so I can." She stopped at a red light and gave me a conspiratorial smile.

"Took you long enough to realize it." I swatted her shoulder and she squealed in protest.

I leaned back into my seat and watched Madison nonchalantly apply lip gloss while waiting for the light to turn green. *But are we really that much alike?* I'd never seen myself as the rebellious, sneaky type . . . I guess I'd changed already. Just not the way I'd expected.

"Madison, why did you stand up for me with your father?" I knew that she wouldn't dodge my questions anymore.

"Breana came and talked to me. I was so touched by how much she cared about you that I felt guilty for just looking on without doing anything about it."

Breana? I shook my head. I knew we were friends, but I never would have thought she'd be the reason that I'd be allowed to stay in America.

Chapter 17

Flying, Falling

AFTER A BORING MATH CLASS, I HURRIED OUT OF THE classroom straight to the cafeteria. And I was lucky. Paul was standing there at a vending machine, punching buttons for a protein bar. I tapped him on the shoulder and he turned around abruptly.

"Oh, it's you," he said, not coldly, but not warmly either.

"Can we talk?"

"Sure. Let's get out of here." He grabbed his protein bar and led the way.

We walked over to a park three minutes away from school and sat down on a bench. Except for two kids playing on the swings, no one was around. It was the height of fall. The path was littered with yellow and orange leaves. A few stragglers in the trees clung on to their branches.

I jumped right in. "Soo . . . your parents really agreed to have me move in?"

Paul nodded. "It was actually really easy to convince them." He took a bite of his protein bar.

"Easy?" I repeated. Taking in an exchange student shouldn't be a decision people make lightly.

He put down the bar. "I told them about your situation and how your host mother treats you. My dad got all angry, and my mom said yes too." Paul threw me an adorable smile. The sun reflected in his eyes, giving them extra sparkle.

It finally kicked in. Henry and Gena meant it. They actually wanted to help me. This wasn't some kind of weird dream—it was my reality.

"I'm really moving in!" I said, awestruck. I jumped up and planted myself firmly on Paul's lap.

"You are, Babycakes!"

I kissed him with such force that it seemed to lift us off the ground and send us flying. Paul responded to my lips and I tasted the sweet chocolate on his tongue. Butterflies exploded in my stomach and fluttered through my veins.

Slowly, we drifted back down and alighted on the bench. "You're really willing to change your entire life for me?" I said, running my fingers over a strand of hair on Paul's forehead. In return he cupped my cheeks and tilted my head up to look at me with clear eyes.

"You already changed my entire life, Babycakes." He leaned in again and pressed his lips to mine, feeding me kisses I couldn't get enough of.

"Why do you call me Babycakes?" I giggled in between kisses.

"Because you've got those adorable baby cheeks—" He started caressing them with his thumbs.

"Hey!" I hit my fist against his muscular chest.

"What?" He grinned at me. "I love those cheeks."

"Hmph, fine. But why 'cakes'?" I looked straight into his eyes.

"I don't know . . . Cake is tasty." He gave each side of my face a sweet kiss.

It was a strange nickname, sure, but to me, it was heavenly.

Breana nearly screamed when I dropped the news to her and Danielle. We were standing by our stoves in Culinary. Chef Sayle had allowed us to move on to soups. I'd almost been late to class because Paul and I couldn't pull away from each other.

"This is so great!" Danielle said. "From now on, we can have girls-plus-Paul nights."

I joined in the giggling, then cleared my throat. "I'm not totally sure yet, actually. I assume my area rep has to talk to his parents first."

Breana hugged me from behind. I laid my head on her shoulder and squeezed her upper arm.

"Thank you for talking to Madison, Bre," I whispered so only she could hear it.

"No problem," she whispered back.

"Does that mean you'll be able to come to Jamie's party?" Danielle asked me, stirring her soup.

"Jamie's throwing a party?"

"Yep. Tomorrow. Her usual Halloween party," Breana chimed in. She tasted her tomato soup and some of it spilled on her white apron. She rolled her eyes at her spoon.

"I'm not invited, so I don't think I can come," I said, putting all my focus on stewing my mushrooms. I hated missing out.

"Girl, half the school will be there, I doubt she'd care." Breana tugged down my chef hat playfully so that it covered half my eye.

"Not to mention you're Paul's plus-one. That means you have an invitation," Danielle added.

"Yeah, maybe . . ." I pushed the hat back up on my head. "But Jamie's not my biggest fan." The menacing look she'd given me at Breana's party was still fresh in my memory.

"Believe me, you don't want to be her friend anyway," Danielle replied. "She's not . . . like you or me, let's say." She went to get something in the fridge on the other side of the room.

"*More salt!*" commanded Chef Sayle to an unsuspecting student. Breana and I laughed. Chef Sayle was the saltiest man on earth.

Mr. Harrison's class later that afternoon took place at the library. I found Jon at the back of a row of books, leaning against a shelf, his nose already stuck in a book. He looked surprisingly concentrated, mouthing the words he was reading, fingertips tapping on the paper.

"Hey, Jon, sorry I'm late."

His eyes shot up, and he closed the book and slid it into his bag.

"Where were you? We have to work on our project," he replied in annoyance, as if he'd been waiting for ages.

"I'm only two minutes late. Since when are you so obsessed with punctuality?"

He turned around and started pulling biographies of Malcolm X off the shelf and stacking them in a pile.

As he didn't seem interested in talking to me any further, I took out the notes we'd written up at his place and started looking them over.

"So, um . . ." Jon said, his back still to me. "You're moving in with him?"

"All signs point to yes."

He stiffened, and I fiddled with my papers. *He should be happy for me, right?*

"Let's get started," he said, tossing me a book with his usual I-hate-school-but-have-to-be-here look.

No "Congrats," no "I'm glad you can stay in America." Once again, Jon was acting completely indifferent.

"Well, don't get *too* excited," I huffed.

He responded with a sarcastic smile which suddenly bloomed into appreciation.

"Your hair's out of your face."

My cheeks flushed and I looked intently at the back cover of my book, pretending to be absorbed by the material. "Must be a coincidence," I mumbled.

"Mm, amazing coincidence." He grinned and clicked his tongue like he'd done in front of the Stones' place. And we got to work.

When the bell rang, I headed for Paul's car right away. I figured that he'd want to give me a ride after the intense lunch break we'd just shared. But I ran into Danielle on the way.

"Hi," she said, flashing me her signature smile. "Want to come shopping with me?"

Before I could reply, I felt an arm wrap around my shoulder. I didn't have to turn around to know it was Paul. His fresh marine scent was as familiar as home to me, and whenever he touched me, I felt at ease.

"Good idea, Danielle," Paul put in. "You can get something for Jamie's Halloween party tomorrow," he told me, kissing the top of my head.

"I'm not invited." I absentmindedly brushed my fingers over the hair on his arms.

I felt his breath on my earlobe as he leaned down and said, "You're my date, so you are. Don't worry about Jamie, okay?"

"See? Just what we said." Danielle motioned for me to follow her. "Shall we?"

I turned to Paul. "You want to join us?" This would be my first time hanging out with just Danielle, and I was worried that I'd turn into my awkward self without him.

"I can't, unfortunately."

"What are you doing?" I asked the question too quickly and tripped over my words.

"Nothing special." Paul looked over my shoulder at Danielle.

"Girl, you coming?" she called.

"Have fun on your girls day out." Paul gave me a quick peck on the lips and walked away.

What was that about? I trailed after Danielle to her black jeep. The knot in the pit of my stomach reminded me that Mrs. Stone would freak out when I didn't come home right after school and start cleaning. But I didn't care anymore. I'd be gone soon anyway. *Hopefully.*

"What do you think?" asked Danielle, coming out of the dressing room in a sparkly blue fairy costume. She looked like an angel with her golden hair and blue eyes that matched the color of the dress.

"You have to ask? You look flawless!"

"It's bought then." She laughed. "Have you found anything?"

I sighed and turned to my options again. Skeleton, vampire, zombie, bride . . .

"I don't know! There's too much to choose from and I suck at making decisions." I picked up some cat ears and a tail. "I think I'll just go as a cat."

"You have a ton of super scary and gorgeous costumes to choose from, and you go with the cat?" Danielle gestured at the admittedly uninspired outfit, almost offended.

"I think it's the safest option, and right now I think it's good . . . Ugh, I don't know." I chucked the costume back on the clothes rack in frustration and pressed my hands over my face.

"Hold on there, girl. Is this really only about a costume?"

My stomach lurched as I realized that she was right. This wasn't about the costume at all. Everything with Paul was happening at full speed and I was terrified of the inevitable collapse. How could I make the right decision if I couldn't even pick a Halloween costume? What if I fell in love with him but he got bored of me? *What if?*

"I'm too young to move in with someone," I blurted out. There was something in my eye, an eyelash, and I rubbed at it to get it out.

"Girl. You either start dating or you stay close friends. What's the big deal?" Danielle shrugged. My eyes teared up, and I wasn't sure if it was because the lash or that my emotions were overwhelming me.

"What if I fall hard for him and then go back to Germany with a broken heart?" I pulled my lower lip between my teeth.

Danielle sighed. She put her hands on both my shoulders and looked at me resolutely.

"And what if you have the time of your life?"

Her words hit me like a revelation. I was overthinking again.

"It's scary, I know," Danielle went on. "But isn't it also the only option you have left?" She wiped away a tear on my cheek. "Because let's be real here, you moving to another town isn't up for discussion anymore."

Yet again, she'd managed to make me smile. *Gosh, Danielle, you really have the talent of cheering people up.*

"So which costume do you *really* want?" She turned back to the rack and flipped through the costumes.

I looked around the store and spotted a sexy doctor costume on the other side of the room: periwinkle blue scrubs with a sassy cut-out top, little shorts and a stethoscope. Something my past self wouldn't have even dared to look at.

"I've always been a huge fan of *Grey's Anatomy*," I said, pointing at the costume. Danielle tilted her chin at it for a moment, then gave me an approving nod.

Costumes in hand, we lined up at the cash register. "You know what the best thing is about shopping?" Danielle asked.

"A large black coffee?" I replied with a yawn. All this shopping had drained me.

"You understand me, girl. Except that I'm getting a chocolate-chip caramel frappe."

We burst out laughing.

Chapter 18

The Brain and the Heart

DANIELLE TOOK MY HAND AND LED THE WAY THROUGH THE food court and into a coffee shop. It was a quiet space with muffled voices. Only the sound of a barista grinding coffee beans tickled my ear. Almost all the tables were taken up by students studying for exams or working on their next novel. I loved the atmosphere, the smell of coffee and sweets, the typing on laptops, how everyone was engrossed in their own world. As I scanned the shop, my gaze stopped to rest on a guy standing at the end of the queue.

"Hey, isn't that Marcos over there? From Bre's party?" I pointed in his direction and Danielle followed my gaze. He was typing something on his phone, deep in his thoughts.

Danielle nodded. "Let's go say hi." Creeping up behind him, she yelled "Boo!" and jumped at him like a lunatic.

Marcos let out a yell and dropped his phone. People stared at us, annoyed that we'd interrupted the peace, but quickly turned back to their work.

"Ah fuck, Danielle! Why do you always need to scare me?" Marcos reached for his phone, and I breathed out in relief when I saw that it wasn't cracked. Danielle laughed with pleasure at shaking him up.

"I will get my juicy revenge. Mark my words," Marcos threatened with a smile that revealed dimples on his unshaved cheeks.

"Bring it on," Danielle replied.

"Oh . . . !" The melodic voice behind me surprised and thrilled me once again. Kiki, the girl Jon had made out with at Breana's party, was giving me a look that was far less pleasant than her voice. "I wouldn't have expected to see you here," she said before looking behind me as if searching for someone.

"Why?" I asked. Seeing a high school student at a coffee shop didn't exactly seem surprising to me.

"Um . . . don't you have a crazy host mother or something?" She raised her shoulders. "Oh, hey, Marcos."

"Oh, I almost forgot! Your host mother crashed the party." Marcos started laughing, and I picked at my fingertips in embarrassment.

"Hey!" Marcos touched my arm. "Don't get me wrong, I don't blame you. It was actually fun running away from the house."

I let out a snort.

"Anyway, I don't have much time, Marcos." Kiki pointed at the time on her phone.

"Well, I assume I'll see you at Jamie's," he said, nodding at the costumes peeking out of our bags. He rushed after Kiki, who was already out of sight.

"Well . . . that was odd," Danielle said musingly. She opened the windows of the jeep to let the fresh air in and pulled out of the parking lot.

"You mean the way Kiki talked to me?" I asked, making sure we were on the same page.

"Duh! I mean, I get it. You're new, which is why she thinks that Jon could be after you, but seriously, she should just give up on him."

I sipped at my hot coffee and set it down again, carefully cradling it on my lap. I'd noticed that Jon acted differently with Kiki than with other girls, but wasn't she just another hookup in the end?

"What are you talking about?"

"Oh, right, I forgot that you're new to the group." Danielle cleared her throat, gearing up to sprinkle gossip through the empty streets of Boonville.

"Basically, Jon and Kiki are on and off every other week. Jon always breaks up with her when she starts getting"—in a stage whisper—"too close. But only a couple days later"—then in a shout—"*bam*! He comes crawling back."

"Does that mean Jon cheated on Kiki when he hooked up with Breana?" I swallowed. Was Jon taken all this time without my knowing it?

"Oh, no. They were on a *break*"—in air quotes—"for the last couple weeks."

I gave a sigh of relief.

"At Breana's party," Danielle went on, "Kiki was willing to give him another chance. But then Breana told her the truth. Gosh, you should've seen the slap Kiki gave her!" Danielle stopped at a red light and looked at me. "Wait, where were you when that happened?"

I knew exactly where I was—talking to Jon. I mumbled something vague in reply. Why had he never mentioned that Kiki was more to him than a random hookup?

"Anyway, Kiki and Jon fought again of course, but for the first time he hasn't tried to get her back yet. Normally she gets a message from him a couple days later, but this time . . . nothing."

The light turned green and Danielle's focus shifted back to the street. I leaned back into my seat, letting the wind stream through the open window and mess up my hair.

Danielle kept at it like a well-oiled gossip machine. "I told her to just let it go. Jon isn't the relationship type and never will be. But she has this crazy theory that it has something to do with you."

"With me?!" I screeched, spilling some of the hot coffee on my lap. Quickly I got out the napkins we'd brought with us and cleaned myself up.

"You're lucky it didn't get on the seats!" Danielle glared at me, but her eyes twinkled mischievously.

I sighed and ran my fingers through my tangled hair, making sure it wasn't hanging over my face.

"Emily?" Danielle said, her voice softer now. I turned to meet her worried gaze. "Jon is like fire. Please make sure you don't get burned."

"I want Paul . . . only Paul. Don't worry." But I knew exactly why she'd said it.

Danielle dropped me off at the Stones' house before it got dark. I rushed through my chores, then sneaked up into my room as quietly as I could. There was no sign of Mrs. Stone, yet I still felt tense. I closed the door and slid down its back, something I hadn't done since Breana first asked me to hang out the night everything started. My arms curled tightly around my legs, I rested my chin on my knees. *Jon is fire, I can't get burned.* I smacked my palm against my head for allowing Jon into it. A place only Paul should be.

I jumped when my phone vibrated. A message from Paul.

I can't wait to fall asleep with you in my arms

His flirty message flooded my chest with warmth. "He's the one for me," I whispered to myself, casting thoughts of Jon away and composing my reply.

I can't wait either :)

I snore when I sleep

I don't think your parents will let us sleep in the same bed . . .
Who says I'm sleeping in the same bed with you? ;)

I changed into my pajamas and crawled under the blanket, imagining Paul's broad arms wrapped around me and pulling me against his chest, snuggling his face in my neck. As my heart hammered in my chest, my phone screen lit up again.

Don't break my heart, Babycakes

Why do I feel like you're going to break mine?

I turned on my alarm and put my phone on the nightstand. The situation was twisted but I had no other choice. Staying with the Stone family wasn't an option anymore, even if Madison and I were on better terms now. I went back to picturing Paul and me cuddling, and with a smile on my face, drifted off to sleep.

"My parents called your area rep," Paul announced as he walked me to the Stones' front door. He'd driven me to their place after school. "Someone's coming over tomorrow to meet them and see the room they prepared for you. After that . . ." He gave me a wide, impatient smile. "I guess it won't be long till you can move in with us."

"I can't wait either." It was true—I was so ready to get out of this house. I was still scared, but with each passing day I got more and more used to the thought of living with him.

Paul's smile faded slowly. "I think we need to talk . . ."

I knew it was coming—the conversation I'd been avoiding right from the beginning. My time for decision-making had run out. But was my brain ready to give up its rule to my heart?

Chapter 19

Stalling For Time

"WHAT ARE WE IN YOUR EYES?" PAUL ASKED. His smile was a little crooked, his jaw a little stiff. Obviously he wasn't used to conversations like this, and neither was I.

I stared down at my dirty Chucks and took a deep breath in, debating what to answer. My heart, crushed in my chest, begged me to say that I was falling for him—but my lips couldn't form the words. I moved close to Paul and latched my arms around his neck, brushing my fingers against a wisp of hair. He reached up and took one of my hands in his.

"I don't know yet what we are," I replied finally, "but please, let's not ruin it with a talk." I gave Paul a smile I hoped was convincing.

I was stalling . . . I needed more time to really get to know the person behind those heart-shaped lips, those eyes that made me glow every time they settled on mine. It was so effortlessly exciting. There was no need to put a name to the sensation we felt when we touched, hugged . . . kissed.

I pressed my lips to his mouth for extra emphasis. His lips parted to let my tongue collide with his, and his sweet taste took over my senses. He grabbed my face with his hands to kiss me even harder, and I closed my eyes, letting him contain me in the best possible way.

But I knew we couldn't stand like this for long. What kind of relationship Mrs. Stone had with her neighbors, I didn't know. Prying eyes behind curtains might see me making out with a boy in the driveway and report the news. I pushed my hands against Paul's chest to get some distance and broke off the kiss.

He gulped down a breath. "You're really making it hard for me to let you go into that house right now."

"Soon we'll have all the time in the world," I replied, giving him one last brief and innocent kiss.

Reluctantly, I pulled my arms away from his body, got out my keys and slipped inside. I'd avoided the conversation, but a nagging feeling in the pit in my stomach wouldn't let me off easy about it.

Danielle came over a couple hours later and we dressed up in our costumes. To my surprise, the sexy doctor getup fit perfectly. The shorts hugged my thighs, making my legs look longer, and the top was just snug enough over my chest for my small boobs to fill it out. I grabbed a hair tie, but the thought of wearing such a revealing top without hiding behind my hair made me pause.

"Can I do your hair?" Danielle asked, already plugging in a curling iron.

"Um . . ." I pressed my lips together. It depended on what she'd do with it.

"I want to go to cosmetology school! Don't worry, I know what I'm doing." She clicked her tongue like Jon did, and I smiled.

"Okay, but I want to keep it down." I brushed my fingers through my hair.

"Duh! That beautiful hair needs to be shown off. I've been wanting to do something with it ever since I first saw you!" Danielle came over and inspected my split ends. "And if you like, I can give it a trim too."

Thankful that I was finally getting a haircut, I sneaked into the bathroom and got scissors.

"So you and Timo have been together for four years?"

Danielle came a little too close to my ear with the curling iron, and I squealed.

"Oops, sorry." She let the lock of hair fall from the iron. "Yep, and I already know he's the man I want to marry someday."

"How do you know?" The thought of it terrified me. *I mean, how do you decide that you've found your perfect match?*

"I just trust my gut." She put down the curler and finished off with a cloud of hairspray. "Okay, I'm done!"

I jumped up and rushed over to the mirror. Danielle hadn't only snipped off the ends—she'd created shorter layers in front that framed my face. I studied my new look and my reflection studied me back. I couldn't hide my chest with my hair anymore. There I was for the world to see. I looked . . . confident.

"I love it!" I covered my mouth with my hands, and like a little kid, ran into her arms.

"Are you even allowed to go out tonight or are we gonna have a Breana 2.0 situation?" Danielle quipped as we prowled to the car she'd parked around the corner to keep her presence discreet. The night she'd been locked in the Stones' house was an event she didn't intend to repeat.

"Mr. Stone said I don't have to follow the rules anymore. Plus, I'm moving out soon anyway." I threw myself onto the passenger seat. I wasn't sure if my talk with Mr. Stone was enough, but I was too scared to ask the dragon personally.

The ride to Jamie's place in Danielle's jeep was like out of a teen movie. We sang our favorite songs at the top of our lungs. We laughed, we gossiped, and a fifteen-minute car ride felt like it only took two. I could tell that this was the beginning of a deep-rooted friendship. In my head, I thanked Danielle for putting up with my long-drawn-out thawing process.

As we came into view of Jamie's place, my jaw dropped to my chest. I'd figured she was rich since she wore expensive clothes and had perfectly done nails and hair, but *damn*. This wasn't a mere house—it was a villa. Multiple stories of castle-like stone walls, a balcony right out of *Romeo and Juliet*. And the place was decorated to the nines with polished orange pumpkins, sinister skeletons and spider webs. A bouncy castle in the front yard generated shouts and whoops, and a queue led up to a photo booth. Breana had been right—it looked like the entire school was invited.

Danielle seemed unimpressed by the extravagance as she gestured for me to follow her inside. I guess she was used to Jamie's parties already. We climbed up to the porch and into the villa.

We found ourselves in a dark hallway faintly lit by a flickering light-bulb above. A funeral dirge thrummed in my ears. Chills rippled through my body as oversized, unblinking eyes stared at me from every angle—dolls dressed in white bib dresses. Something grabbed my hand—it was Danielle, squeezing it so tightly, I could feel the blood being cut off.

"Okay, this is not cool, I hate dolls!" she whispered and hid her face in my neck. I was about to reassure her when—

"*Boo!*"

"Ahhh!" Danielle and I jumped back and clung to each other as a clap of thunder echoed through the hall.

"Told you I'd pay you back," said a voice. Emerald-green eyes emerged from the gloom. Marcos.

"I hate you!" Danielle yelled and ran down the hall and through a door. I called after her, but she slammed the door behind her.

Marcos turned to me sheepishly, an awkward smile on his face.

"Sorry, I didn't mean to scare you too. It was just such a perfect chance to get even with Danielle."

"I think you just declared war." I giggled as more thunder rumbled in the hall. "Danielle nearly peed her pants."

Marcos' face relaxed. "I did, didn't I. I should get her some adult diapers then."

He laughed and I joined in, scrambling to think up a reply. I settled for pointing at the door after Danielle and raising my eyebrows.

"Yeah, I'll come with you," Marcos said. "I don't want to be alone with all these creepy dolls!"

We stepped inside the next room and I blinked a few times as my eyes adapted to the brighter lights. I couldn't believe what I was seeing. The decoration I'd glimpsed so far was already impressive, but this space that may once have been a living room was now a bona fide dance club. Colored spotlights washed the masses of people in lush purple and electric green. There was a buffet, a chocolate fountain, and a witches' cauldron that served as an ice bucket for drinks. More pumpkins and skeletons rounded out the ambience. Marcos tapped me on the shoulder and signaled that he'd spotted Danielle standing near the drinks. He turned the other way and disappeared in the crowd, and I walked over to her.

"Hey girl, are you okay?" I had to talk a couple notches louder than usual.

"Except for the fact that I almost died of fright, I'm already planning my revenge," she yelled in my ear, leaving a harsh pulsing in my eardrums.

"Figured," I shouted back, a little quieter than her.

Danielle offered me a beer, but I declined. I wasn't dumb enough to tempt fate again. I scanned the room. In one corner sat Jamie, legs crossed on a small couch, dressed up as a slutty version of Superwoman. She gave me a death glare and I quickly looked away.

On the couch next to her was Paul. Astonishingly, he was in scrubs too—only his were drizzled with fake blood. He even had a stethoscope looped around his neck. When our eyes met, he waved at me, and my heart instantly responded by thumping in my chest.

To hide the silly grin forming on my face, I continued sweeping my gaze over the room and spotted the devil side of Kiki near the witches' cauldron. She gave what looked like an apologetic smile. *Did Danielle tell her that I'm only interested in Paul?*

And far behind Kiki . . . Jon. He had on a plain white shirt spattered with blood with his leather jacket over top. At least he'd made an attempt at dressing up. The second our gazes crossed, he turned to Brandon-slash-scary-Mario and started discussing something with him.

"Gosh, you're like the girl at parties in movies everyone stares at," Danielle said with a laugh. A second glance around the room confirmed her statement. Paul, Jamie, Kiki and lots of people I didn't even know had their eyes glued on me. I rubbed my temple awkwardly. I really didn't like being the center of attention. Paul waved at me again, so I excused myself and made my way over to him even as I felt Jamie's eyes boring holes into my back.

"Hey, Paul." I sat down in his lap, molding my body to his. He cradled the small of my back with his hand and I felt my muscles loosen. I was with him now. I could breathe again.

"You look sexy as a doctor," he said, giving me his usual soft welcome kiss on the cheek.

"One might say we decided to get matching costumes." I giggled, gesturing at his scrubs. "Or did Danielle tell you what I was going as?"

"Danielle? Nope. Don't doubt destiny." Paul playfully raised his eyebrows and I bit back a smile, glad I hadn't gone with the cat ears.

A whole group of people came over to us: Kiki, Jon and Brandon, Hannah, Danielle and Breana, Marcos and his friend Leni. They pulled up chairs and sat in a circle around the couch.

Noting my confused facial expression, Kiki explained, "It's time for our tradition—truth or dare, Halloween edition."

"I don't get why we keep playing this. We're too old for this shit," Jon complained, and Kiki shot him an angry look.

The rest of the group fell silent. The chill in the air was undeniable— *they're still not on good terms.* Breana was making herself small behind Danielle, probably aware that she'd contributed to the tension between the two.

After a time, Brandon asked, "Want to join us, German?"

"Sure, but I can't drink because, um ... Mrs. Stone." I chewed on the inside of my cheek, feeling like a buzzkill.

Jamie didn't let the opportunity slip. "If you can't drink, why are you even here?"

"Jamie, c'mon. No need to act bitchy," Hannah said, her frown wrinkling her freckled forehead. Hannah was always so sweet to me.

"So . . ." Danielle peered at each face before stopping at Marcos. "Marcos! Truth or dare?"

"Knowing you, the safest option is truth." Marcos laughed, leaning back into a cushion.

"So. Which girl out of this group would you like to kiss the most?" Danielle tossed her hair, looking proud of her question. No matter what Marcos answered, it could only turn awkward now, and from his wide-eyed look, it was clear that he knew it.

"This is your revenge for me scaring you, isn't it?" Marcos pressed his fingers to his temples and looked at Danielle through his fingers.

"Oh, this is only the beginning," Danielle teased. "So?"

Marcos looked at each girl in turn, his expression neutral.

"Ugh, I don't know. You're all so great," he said, turning his red cup over and over in his hands.

"Not impressed by that excuse, dude," Breana said, sounding amused. But I couldn't shake the thought that she wanted him to consider her too.

"Okay, fine . . ." Marcos took a swig of his drink. "Emily," he said into his cup.

A murmur ran through the group as all eyes landed on me. Paul laid an arm around my shoulder protectively. I looked up at him, just as confused as the others.

"But only because I know what the rest of you have all done with your dirty mouths," Marcos added, saving the situation. Giggles erupted around the group. I didn't laugh, myself, but my tense muscles relaxed, and Paul's grip on my shoulder loosened too.

"All right, if no one minds, I'll continue?" Paul piped up, and a couple people nodded.

"So, um . . ." He rubbed the back of his head. *Is he about to lie?* "Brandon, I dare you to kiss Hannah." The words sounded practiced.

Brandon gave an embarrassed smile. I bet he'd asked Paul to do him this favor. This game was fixed.

"Oh, no way!" Hannah screeched in protest.

"What?" Brandon's eyes shifted in panic.

"Last time I had to kiss you, you made a show of it and said I drooled in your mouth," Hannah said indignantly.

"When?!"

"Seventh grade. You embarrassed me!"

Jamie stood up. "God, if Hannah doesn't want to . . ."

She leaned down over Brandon and pressed her mouth on his. Brandon tensed up, and Hannah snorted. It was only a little smudge of a kiss, but the disappointment in Brandon's eyes made it clear that he'd been waiting for this chance to kiss Hannah for a long time now.

Jamie dropped herself back down on the couch with a pleased look on her face, not realizing what she'd done. She shot Paul a see-what-you're-missing-out-on type of look—or maybe I read too much into it. Either way, I snuggled deeper in his arms.

"Easy," Jamie scoffed. "I don't get why you were so childish about it, Han." But her eyes were still on Paul. "So, as I volunteered, it's my turn, and I get to pick whether it's a truth or a dare," she went on. "House rules." She looked at Brandon for confirmation, and he nodded.

Paul caught my eye. I smiled with the thought that soon I'd be seeing these ocean eyes whenever I wanted to. *There's nothing better in the world to look at.*

I pulled my gaze away from Paul and watched Jamie preening as she looked around the circle. Then her eyes landed on me.

"Emily, I dare you to make out with Jon."

Chapter 20

Two Sides of a Shield

"**W**HA—" I INHALED MY OWN SPIT AND STARTED coughing. Paul jumped up in rage, me slipping off his lap, and people gasped around us. I huddled behind him on the couch, feeling the trap tighten around us. Cocking my head to the right, I saw Jon roll his eyes.

"Fuck, Jamie! What is your problem?" Paul shouted, taking a step toward her, his broad shoulders heaving. The party lights danced on Jamie's face, illuminating her scornful smile.

"My problem? It's just a game," she chirped, matching his step forward.

"Oh don't shit me! You're mad. I get that. But don't pull Emily into this!" Paul's fists were clenched. I doubted he'd hurt her, but it made me insecure that I couldn't see his face.

"Chill, man. What's the big deal?" Leni shrugged like he was waiting for some action.

Jon was concentrating on his beer bottle, ripping off the label. I tried to make eye contact with him in the hope that he'd intervene, but he just rubbed his cheek, smudging fake blood on the edge of his lip.

"You act like Emily's your girlfriend or something," Jamie taunted. "It's just a kiss, who cares?"

Paul snorted like a bull. "Emily's moving in with me! I'm serious about her!"

We were all left speechless. All except for Jamie.

"She—you gotta be kidding me! First you cheat on me with her, and then she moves in with you after just a few weeks? Fuck you, Paul!"

You know those scenes in movies where the big disaster happens in slow motion while the main character drifts away, paralyzed? That's how I felt in this moment. Frozen, unable to move or speak, the music suddenly muffled against my ears. *You cheat on me with her . . . You cheat on me with her . . .*

The sound of Jamie's hand smacking against Paul's cheek woke me from my stupor.

"You're a monster!" she spat, a tear tracking through her pristine makeup.

I still couldn't see Paul's face, but his shoulders were slumped now. Jamie stumbled past him toward me, bumping against him on the way.

My vision was blurry. I was on the edge of losing it too. I bit my lower lip hard, willing myself not to cry. The taste of iron spread through my mouth.

Jamie hovered above me, tears coursing down her face.

"You can't trust him!" she cried out. Then she shot Paul one last disgusted look before storming out of the room.

Even though Jamie treated me worse than gum under her shoe, I felt sorry for her. Paul hadn't only kissed me—he'd replaced her with me. My lungs tightened against my attempts to fill them with oxygen. Jamie hated me for a damn good reason.

The others were silent, waiting for Paul or me to react.

Jon's noisy swallow of beer catapulted Paul into action. He dropped down next to me on the couch and grabbed my hands. I looked away. He begged me to listen to him, pulling softly at my fingers.

"We weren't in love anymore ..."

As if that would make it any better. I turned to stare at him. My stomach twisted into a knot.

"That doesn't mean you were broken up." My lower lip trembled as I formed the words.

"Emily, you have to believe me when I say that it was over for me, for months," he said, super-fast. But I couldn't believe him. The silence of the people around us was too heavy for his words to be true.

I slowly got off the couch. The edges of my vision were turning black. I had to get out of here before the first tear fell. Everybody heard what happened. Everybody knew I was the girl who caused another girl's heartbreak. Paul had made me *the slut*. I made for the door to the hall, feeling their eyes stab at my back.

In the comforting solitude of the hall, I leaned against the wall for support. The dolls suddenly seemed less creepy than what had just happened in the other room. Why hadn't Danielle or Breana mentioned Paul's history with Jamie to me? I thought they were my friends, but they'd left me in the dark.

"Emily ... please look at me."

I spun around. Paul had followed me here without my even noticing. Carefully, he inched toward me as if he was worried I'd sprint away like a scared rabbit.

He'd come into my life like a hurricane, and now everything was destroyed.

"Did you ever say the three words?" I said, my voice strained.

Paul froze. "*I love you?* Yeah ... We dated for two years but it's been forever since I said it last and—"

"I didn't mean *those* words!"

The thought of Paul loving another girl made me feel not only betrayed, but jealous too—at least, I was pretty sure the disgusting feeling in my stomach was what jealousy felt like.

"Did you say *we are over* before you kissed me?"

Paul looked at me with his big blue puppy dog eyes. For the first time, they didn't make me smile. Now they made me shiver.

"I—" Paul gulped. "I didn't."

There, he'd admitted it. Everything that happened with him felt like a movie, too good to be true. Which was accurate because after all . . . it wasn't true. *This is reality, not some TV series.*

"I need some air."

"I'll come with you—"

"No!" I screamed at the top of my lungs. I'd found my voice again. Good thing we were the only people in this dark hallway. "I thought I could trust you, but you were playing a game this whole time!"

I pushed him away roughly, my palms against his chest, even though for a second my heart wanted to pull him in.

"It wasn't a game to me, Emily."

My face burned. I turned away to signal that we were done here.

"I didn't realize what was happening before it was too late . . ." Paul continued.

But he did.

I whirled around. "I don't want to hear it, okay? You used me to get out of your relationship! Was it because you needed comfort? Or just a nasty rebound? Do you know how disgusted I feel with myself right now?" All my pent-up anger was exploding out of me.

"Do you seriously think that I planned this?" Paul yelled, motioning between him and me. "Fuck, I didn't mean to hurt Jamie like that! You just came into my life and you . . ." His voice went from a lion's roar to a mouse's squeak.

"I what?" I demanded, my face still scalding.

"You . . . you showed me that I wasn't happy with Jamie! That my life was a freaking joke, that there's more to relationships than physical attraction!"

I backed up against the wall as he came closer and closer. My head was spinning from his confession, reeling through every conversation, every kiss, every touch we'd shared. How protected I felt when he held my hair when I was sick, how safe when we snuggled under the blanket, how playful when he showed me how to tackle. Our eyes locked and he reached out and softly brushed his hand over my hair.

"I didn't know what it's really like to care about someone until I met you," he whispered, so quietly that I wasn't sure if I'd heard him right. His breath tickled my cheeks.

I looked straight into his eyes. The pupils were a deep, dark black, rimmed with blue. But no matter how much I wanted to believe him, I couldn't. I wasn't that special—not a girl who opened someone's eyes to love. *That isn't me.* I said nothing. I tried to wriggle away from him and his eyes teared up.

"Please, be with me." Paul grabbed my hand but I shook it off. He betrayed me, lied to me. *And who says if he did this to Jamie, he wouldn't do it to me one day too?* I shoved him away and made for the front door.

"Please . . . don't leave me standing here like this."

My feet slowed.

"I want to be with you, Emily."

"I don't want to get into a relationship while I'm here." I said it because I knew it would make him leave me alone.

Thankful for the dim lights, I yanked the door open and went outside without giving Paul a last look. The first tear had fallen. My heart felt like it had been shattered into a million pieces. Paul wasn't the guy I thought he was after all.

Barely an hour had passed since Danielle and I went in Jamie's place. But during this time, all the people around the bouncy castle and the photo booth had disappeared into the house. Nobody was out here. Maybe because of the neighbors? To avoid attracting the police? *Who knows.* But it was in my favor because now I could sit on the porch steps in peace.

I leaned my head against the wooden railing, looking up at the clear night sky to keep the tears from escaping my eyes. What Paul and I used to have, it was so great. I thought he'd be my first. The first guy I really made out with, the first guy I'd sleep with . . . he was the first guy who touched my heart.

I heard footsteps behind me. Probably Danielle or Breana. They must have decided to come after me. But the shadow that fell over me was too tall. I craned my neck and looked up into chocolate brown eyes. Eyes with a fire that was about to go out. Jon's eyes.

"Hey, Little German," he said, a neutral statement. I looked back up at the sky. I couldn't deal with his insults right now.

"What are you doing here, Jon?" I murmured. I put my hands to my face and wiped away the tears.

He pulled his hand out of his pocket and held up a pack of Newports.

"Just having a smoke."

He sat down on the steps next to me, took out a cigarette, lit it. Nipping a little on it as he inhaled. The smoke curled in the air.

"Can . . . can I have one too?" I asked after a couple of seconds.

"Haven't I told you that you're better than that?" he growled.

I twisted around to look at him head on. "I'm not better than any of you!"

I took the pack out of his hands. My fingers brushed his for a second—they were ice cold. He looked at me sharply, but then reached into the pack and pulled one out. He placed it between my parted lips and struck his lighter. I sucked in the smoke of my very first cigarette.

I didn't know why I was doing this, but in this exact second, I wanted to punish myself—for being naive, for saying those words to Paul. A sting went through my chest and I started coughing. But then I took another hit and another . . . until I was coughing less. My lungs hurt but I pushed through it. The nicotine sped through my veins and my muscles relaxed.

Tipping my head back, I looked at the stars in this dark night. *So exhausted . . .*

I leaned my head on Jon's shoulder and he tensed up, but neither of us moved away. I needed his comfort right now . . . even when he was the last person I should get it from.

Chapter 21

Fix Me

"**A**REN'T YOU FREEZING?" JON ASKED AFTER A WHILE. I could feel his muscles contracting under my temple.

"No, the opposite actually."

My heart was still pumping like crazy, and with all this adrenaline and guilt rushing through my veins, I hadn't even noticed the cold. Suddenly Jon lifted his arm and offered me his chest.

"You got goosebumps all over you," he pointed out, his face suddenly innocent in his concern.

I snuggled my face into his chest and let him rub my upper arm. The goosebumps spiked as his hand dragged over them. He ran his fingers through my hair and gently untangled a knot. His smoky smell that in such a short time had become so familiar, yet so strange and forbidden, calmed me down. When our eyes connected, he tilted his head up at the night sky.

"Jon, when I told you I was moving in with Pau—him, were you upset about it?"

He didn't jerk away. Maybe he'd been expecting the question.

"Haven't you learned by now that I'm not a sentimental guy, Little German?"

I drew in a sharp breath. "Yeah, but . . ."

Jon stood up suddenly and offered me his hand. I took it and he lifted me off the ground like I was as light as a feather. I came up so fast that he had to grab my waist so I wouldn't fall forward. His grip wasn't firm enough to hurt, but it wasn't loose either. The nicotine spreading through my body was making me slightly dizzy. He didn't let go as I straightened up.

"But if it makes you happy, I'm gonna say it," he said quietly, his eyes focused on mine. "I'm glad you're staying."

My phone rang. My cheeks were burning. Jon let go of me and gestured for me to pick up the call.

"Hello?"

"You have to come home, asap!" screamed Madison on the other end of the line.

"Why?" I gasped, my heartbeat speeding up again. I pressed the phone against my ear.

"My mom found out about the party! And she doesn't approve!"

A blipping sound—Madison had hung up. Once again, I was in huge trouble.

"I need to go back to the Stones!" I said urgently, thrusting my phone back into my purse.

Jon looked at me, thunderstruck, but I didn't have the time to explain. I sprinted off down the street through the last minutes of October, not daring to look back. The moment Jon and I just had shared . . . it was dangerous.

After five minutes of running, the thought occurred to me that it would've been smarter to ask somebody for a ride. This was taking a lot longer than my ride with Danielle. I almost crashed into a group of little kids dressed up as ghosts, witches and dolls. I was glad it was Halloween, or I would've looked like a crazy person. I slowed to a stop and pressed my hands against my knees, catching my breath.

A car honked behind me. I turned and saw Jon's black BMW. Once again, I was a deer in his spotlights. Exposed and vulnerable in his presence. Jon pulled up beside me and the window slid open.

"C'mon, get in."

I stood stiff. "Didn't you drink tonight?"

"I had one brew, I'm fine." He opened the door to the passenger seat. "I thought you were in a hurry?"

I pushed my hands over my face. Looking to Jon for comfort was wrong. So why did I feel so relieved when I saw him? I gave a small nod and got in. As soon as my door was closed, Jon hit the gas, making me scooch deeper in the black leather of the seat. We drove in silence, and for the first time, I didn't mind it. I rested my head against the cold surface of the window, trying to not think about the cross-examination awaiting me at the Stone house. For a change, Jon didn't have the usual rap music on. A CD was playing "Fix Me" by Coldplay. I instantly recognized it; it was one of my favorite songs. To calm my nerves, I whispered along to the lyrics.

"And I will try to fix you . . ." I poured myself into each word.

Jon looked at me and his sharp mouth curved into a smile. He shook his head no with a snort of laughter, but I ignored him.

"If you never try, you'll never know . . ."

And eventually he joined in, sort of.

"Just what you're worth . . ." His voice was soft, dark. It was more like talking than singing, but I appreciated the effort.

"Lights will guide you home . . ."

We sang louder and louder until we fully lost ourselves in the music.

"And I will try to fix you."

As the last bars of the song died away, I saw that the ride was over already. One side of my heart was squeezed tight, yet the other was beating like crazy.

"Such a good song," I said as the car came to a full stop. "I didn't think you'd be into this type of music."

Jon shrugged. "I don't want to limit myself."

I sighed, enjoying the singing of the crickets outside before giving myself over to the tornado at the Stones'.

"Thanks for the drive." I turned to the door. I had to get away before—

"Wait—" Jon pulled at my arm. *Too late.* "Are you still moving in with Paul?" His voice was shaking slightly.

Good question . . . Will I?

"I don't know." My chest hurt as the words came out.

He swallowed harshly and put his hands back on the steering wheel. "He never looked at Jamie the way he looks at you. He really likes you, Little German." His words were meant to be supportive, but his voice sounded tired.

"He should've been honest with me then!" I scowled, unsure if it was Paul's actions or Jon vouching for him that made me feel so bitter.

For an eternity Jon and I just looked at each other. The fire in his eyes flickered like crazy. My heart was hammering against my chest.

"You're right, he should have . . ." he said through gritted teeth.

He was gripping the steering wheel so tightly that his knuckles were white. Without realizing what I was doing, I reached over to place my hand on his and stroked it with my thumb. His hold loosened. He moved his hands to my face and pulled me toward him, his fingers tangling in my hair. I grabbed onto his bloody shirt for support.

"What are you doing to me, Little German?" Jon whispered, his eyes shifting between my eyes and my lips. He rested his forehead on mine and shut his eyes. "You're his girl . . . you're off limits," he growled to himself.

Jon said out loud what I was supposed to be thinking too. But my anger at Paul outweighed my feelings for him right now.

That and the fact that the one I liked first saw me. Really saw me.

I skimmed my palm over Jon's stubbled jaw, losing myself in his dark chocolate eyes, shutting off my brain. His eyes opened and for a moment he just looked at me. Dazzled.

"Kiss me," I blurted out, craving for him to fix me.

I looked down, ready for rejection, but his lips crashed against mine fiercely, hungrily, as if he'd been yearning for this moment ever since we met. I gasped for air, and for a brief second I considered pushing him away, but instead I closed my eyes and let myself be engulfed by his fire. His lips, dry and hot, burned away my bitterness. My lips parted and our tongues danced along to the pulsing hum of the crickets in the quiet night. He tasted bitter, foreign. His motions were so different than Paul's—sharper, yet so strangely tantalizing. I bunched his shirt in my fist, pulling him in even closer. His hands wandered into my neck as he made the kiss last longer than possible. Adrenaline rushed through every vein of my body. I climbed into his lap and he drew me into him as our kisses got steamier. I curled my hips against him. Craving his touch, wanting to be his desire.

Jon broke off the kiss suddenly and looked at me, his hands cupping my face.

"Fuck, what are we doing here, Little German?" he said, studying me, licking his lip in longing.

Ignoring this very reasonable question, I was about to put my mouth on his again when Madison knocked hard against the car window.

"We need to get inside!" she commanded.

I jumped out of Jon's lap and gave him one last confused look before almost falling out of the car. I didn't know what to say so I mumbled lamely, "Thank you for the ride," and pushed the door shut. Jon gunned the engine and took off, tires squealing.

"You can't make out with a guy in front of the house when you're in trouble already, Emily!" Madison screeched in panic. She pulled my hand and led the way to the house. She was wearing a modest pirate costume and I suspected that she had added extra layers just before coming home.

"I told Mom that you're with me, so you're not in trouble," she explained, putting her key into the keyhole. "Tomorrow we're gonna talk about you having your tongue down Jon Denson's throat, all right?" She smiled, not condescending but curious, and turned the key.

In this moment I was getting sister vibes, and I was even a little sad to be leaving her. If I'd had Madison on my side right from the beginning, who knows—maybe staying with the Stones wouldn't have been that bad.

Quietly we rushed through the entranceway into the kitchen. I pushed—incompatible thoughts—to the back of my head. Mrs. Stone was sitting in her nightgown with a cup of tea placed in front of her. Her eyes were red and puffy and her hair unkempt. The only thing missing was a bucket of ice cream to complete the picture.

"Hey Mom, I'm sorry we're late. Every traffic light was against us," Madison said.

Mrs. Stone paid no attention to her words. "Madison, can you give Emily and I a minute?"

Madison mumbled something about sticking around, but for some reason I wasn't terrified anymore. No, the opposite. Seeing Mrs. Stone now, broken down as she was, almost made me feel sorry for her. I was curious to find out what this was about.

"It's okay, Madison," I told her.

Madison gave me a reassuring look before leaving the kitchen. Mrs. Stone gestured for me to sit down across from her.

"Would you like a cup of tea?" she asked like everything was normal.

"No thank you." I didn't want this talk to drag on longer than necessary.

"Emily, my husband told me that you're moving out on Sunday."

I jumped. "*Sunday?*"

I didn't know it would be that soon. I looked away and bit my lip. I should've been happy about the news, but now I didn't know what to think anymore. My future with Paul was uncertain and . . .

Wait, did I just make out with Jon Denson?

Chapter 22

Making Amends

MRS. STONE PUT A SUGAR CUBE IN HER CUP AND SWIRLED it around with a spoon. When she finished, she carefully placed the spoon back on her saucer.

"I wanted to talk to you about why you've decided to leave us." She cringed.

This was it. The talk I'd been fearing. The reason why Mrs. Stone and I had been steadfastly ignoring each other over the past week.

"So, why is it that you want to leave?"

My mind was divided. On the one hand, I wanted to give her a taste of her own medicine and lash out at her. But on the other hand, I was scared to do it, so I decided to sweeten what I really thought, like a sugar cube in Mrs. Stone's bitter herbal tea.

"You never treated me as part of this family, Mrs. Stone," I said evenly. "You made me clean the house or do gardening work all the time. I felt like your maid. And even though I did everything you asked, you didn't let me hang out with my friends."

Mrs. Stone stared hard at a spot on the ground like she was trying to keep herself from freaking out at me.

A warm feeling spread in my chest, so I kept going.

"You accused me of doing so many things. Things that are harmless."

Tears gathered in the corners of Mrs. Stone's eyes, spilled out noiselessly, and dropped to the ground. No grimaces, no whimpers, just tears.

Well, what did she expect? Was she so delusional? For two minutes she just sat there stiffly, tears dripping down her cheeks. Against my instincts, I tried to calm her down.

"I'm sorry, I didn't mean to be that harsh—"

"You're right, Emily," she interrupted, folding her arms over her chest. "I really didn't see you as a part of my family."

The sentence launched itself at me like a poison arrow. I looked down.

"When I read your application, I felt that you were the perfect fit for us . . . and then you got here, and you weren't what I expected." She was on a roll. "I mean, you're friends with boys, and you go out too often."

Yeah, I should probably star in a TV show about reckless teenagers; that's how bad I am. NOT!

"I was probably overwhelmed with the situation. You're not like Madison and I'm not used to that."

I suppressed a giggle. Madison and I had more in common than she could ever imagine. "I'm sorry that I'm not how you wanted me to be, but that's no excuse for treating me so badly."

I crossed my own arms. It was 1–1, we were even, and I wanted to come out of this conversation a winner. I wouldn't let her twist the truth.

Mrs. Stone pretended not to hear me. She dabbed at her eyes with a napkin.

"Could you give me another chance? I would really like to make it up to you." Her lips curved up into a fake smile, and mine did the opposite. "Spend the rest of the weekend with me and then you can decide if you still want to go."

I knew that the only way out of this conversation was to agree, so I nodded, said my goodnights and headed into my room. I'd think about tomorrow later.

As soon as I got there, I dropped down onto the bed face first without even undressing. The bedsprings groaned under the force of my weight. *Why did I kiss Jon?* I was just as bad as Paul. Even worse. I stuffed my face into a pillow and screamed into it.

I was awoken by a fist knocking at my door.

"Good morning, Emily! It's time to get up!" shouted a woman's voice. Mrs. Stone. I suddenly remembered that I'd accepted to spend the day with her.

I cracked my eyes open. It was still dark outside the window. My eyes were burning and my head pounded from exhaustion. It had to be early, way too early to get up on a Saturday. A glance at the clock confirmed it: *6:45 am.*

"I've made a lot of plans for today!" chirped Mrs. Stone. She sounded like she'd drunk six cups of coffee already.

"I'm coming," I said in a raspy voice.

I climbed out of the warm bed, still in my doctor costume. The air was cool on my skin. Quickly I put on a loose blue dress, brushed my hair and dabbed on concealer to hide the dark circles under my eyes. I hadn't slept much. My mind was preoccupied with so many things— well, two things. Paul . . . Jon.

I turned on my phone after having charged it overnight. Multiple messages from Paul popped up, but I didn't open them. I wasn't ready to think about everything that had happened yet. For now, I just needed to survive the day.

Down in the kitchen, Mrs. Stone was sitting at the table. Across from her was a large black coffee and a plate containing a cheese bagel.

"Good morning, Emily. You look very nice. I've made you breakfast." Mrs. Stone reported this like she'd learned it by heart.

"Um, thanks?"

She'd never made breakfast for me before. If she had, she would've known that I despise cheese.

"You look stunning in that dress, honey!" Mrs. Stone clapped her hands when I walked out of the dressing room in a beige-colored lace dress. It reached down to my knees, and peeking at the mirror, I saw that it made me look even shorter.

"Um, I'm not sure . . ." I mumbled, not wanting to dismiss her pick outright.

"Not sure?" Her eyes got so wide, I was concerned that her eyeballs might pop out. "This dress suits you so well!"

Suits the version of me you want me to be, maybe . . .

I grabbed the price tag to check how much it would cost to have this sit in the closet. "A hundred dollars?!" I looked up. "I'm sorry, but I can't afford this . . ."

She came over to me and adjusted the drape of the fabric. "You know what? It's on me. I just love you too much in this."

"I can't—"

Mrs. Stone placed a kiss on my cheek, almost hitting my nose.

"You're welcome. Just keep it on."

I didn't try to fight her. She was doing this to soothe her conscience, so she wouldn't feel bad about the abuse when I was gone. But there was no way that one day could make up for all those months of me being her own personal servant . . .

Around noon she asked me if I could teach her a German dish.

I suggested something stereotypical: bratwurst sausages with mashed potatoes and sauerkraut. We did our best to gather up all the ingredients at the grocery store and headed back home, where I desperately tried to teach her to cook. The easiest things stymied her. I could tell she wasn't used to holding any cooking implements.

After our meal of not-really-German-tasting burned food, we went to the movies. Mrs. Stone really was trying her best to make me feel comfortable, but I couldn't shake off the tense feeling I had around her. In the theater, I curled myself up in my seat as far away from her as possible, thankful for the interval of silence between us. It was a film about slavery. I tried hard not to see the irony in this.

My brain took advantage of the break to start functioning again. I quickly lost track of the plot of the movie as my mind migrated to Paul. Tears sprang to my eyes. I had broken my promise last night. I couldn't make any sense of why I did what I did—but I had to try and fix it.

After the movie ended, we idled outside the theater for a while. Streams of people passed by with empty popcorn buckets, giving each other their opinions on the film.

Mrs. Stone followed suit. "That was a really good movie," she gushed, still a little too excited.

"Yeah, it was fine," I said vaguely, trying to get a kernel of popcorn unstuck from between my teeth without her noticing.

I heard a woman's voice I didn't know that well yet but still recognized. "I think Paul might really like that girl," she was saying.

Paul's mom, Gena, was standing there with his dad. I perked up my ears.

"Nah, they're just friends," Henry said, waving his hand dismissively.

Noticing me, Gena gave me a friendly wave, and Henry turned to me with a grin.

"Excuse me for a moment," I said to Mrs. Stone, gesturing in their direction. "Those are my . . . um, new host parents." *Hopefully.* With that statement I confirmed that Mrs. Stone hadn't changed my mind about moving out tomorrow. I felt kind of bad for rubbing it in her face like this. She frowned but didn't stop me from walking over to them.

"Hey, you two," I greeted them shyly.

"Emily! It's so nice to see you," replied Gena. Henry presented me with a clownish bow, and I couldn't help but giggle.

"Are you excited to move in tomorrow?" Gena asked.

I'd anticipated this question. "Very!" I bit my lip. Excited—and nervous.

"We are so lucky to have you stay with us, Emily," said Henry, and as I nodded he pulled me into a hug.

My chest suddenly felt warm. These people who barely even knew me were so welcoming. And even though I hadn't moved in yet, I already felt like a member of their family. I needed to apologize to Paul and come clean about my feelings for him. It was time to take a risk.

I'm sorry, Jon, but last night was a mistake.

When Mrs. Stone finally took me back to her house, my entire body was sore from all the tension I'd accumulated from being with this woman. I was exhausted. I shut the door to my room behind me and sank down to the carpet, hugging my knees. *I survived today.*

I was wondering what to do next when I heard a soft knocking at my window. Paul was kneeling on the roof, his mouth in a straight line. His eyes were red and tired-looking, like he was still recovering from a hangover. A yellow leaf was stuck in his hair—he must have climbed up the tree. Our eyes locked and my body froze. His lips moved but I couldn't understand what he was saying. I cursed myself for not having thought things through more clearly. I still had no idea what I was supposed to say to him.

Paul spoke a little louder. "Emily?" The sound of it sent chills over my skin.

What I did last night wasn't like me at all. I just didn't know what to do next. I straightened my heels and got off the ground to open the window, unsure if I should tell him about Jon and me or not. The only thing I knew for certain: I wanted to fix things with him. I wanted him. The question was . . .

. . . *does he still want me too?*

Chapter 23

Him and I

"**T**HANK YOU." PAUL GAVE ME A TIRED SMILE AS HE CLIMBED through the open window.

Barely moving, I watched him dust himself off before closing the window behind him. My mind was racing, trying to come up with what to say or do next. I regretted telling him that I didn't want a relationship. He'd made a mistake, but I was the one playing games. At least, that's what he had to be thinking now?

Paul turned to me, shoulders hunched forward, hands in his pockets. He stayed by the window, maybe to block an exit so I wouldn't run away again.

"I saw your parents today!" I blurted out, too loud, a desperate attempt to stretch out my thinking time.

"My parents?" Paul looked confused.

"Yeah. I went to the movies with Mrs. Stone and they were there too."

"You went to the movies with Mrs. Stone?" Now he was more baffled than ever.

"It's a long story." *Wrong topic for now.* I shuffled over to the bed and sat down slowly. My time for thinking had run out. I placed my hands in my lap and looked down at them, waiting for Paul to say something, but he stayed mute.

"I think we should talk," he said finally.

"Uh-huh . . ."

I hated that Paul was in distress because of me. I heard his footsteps treading over to me, and my bed squeaked as he sat down. I looked up cautiously.

"Um, we have to whisper though. I've still got to survive tonight." I pointed at the door.

Paul nodded and gave me a smile. The dimples I so adored creased at the corners of his mouth. Just seeing his smile again made my muscles relax, and I remembered to breathe again.

But then his expression shattered.

"Do you still want to move in with me, Emily?" He rubbed at his thumbnail.

"I . . ." I drew in a breath. "Of course I still want to move in with you." Now that he'd asked me this question personally, my heart and my brain were united in their decision.

Paul's eyes lit up, shone like the sun. He clasped his arms around me and I sighed in relief as I felt his touch. He still wanted me to move in too!

"I'm so sorry, Paul!" I burst into sobs against his chest.

Suddenly, I knew why I'd avoided thinking about last night. I felt guilty. Ashamed about my words to him . . . disgusted for kissing his best friend. I did that . . . not Paul, not Jon. Just me.

"You're what?!" said Paul, startled. "No, I'm the one who's supposed to be sorry, Babycakes!" He cupped my face with his broad hands. I rested my cheek in his palm and closed my eyes. His touch was so comforting, so reassuring . . . It felt like home.

"I should have told you what happened with Jamie. I don't know what I was thinking, keeping this from you." Paul's voice was shaky.

I tilted my head back up and our noses brushed together. I soaked in the moment. Then I opened my eyes. Worry was etched in his gaze.

You have to tell him about the kiss, you have to! screamed my brain, but my heart feared the consequences. Losing him would mean losing a part of myself. Because I'd already given Paul a piece of my heart. There was no coming back from this.

He said, "There's something you should know—"

"Stop!" I placed my index finger on his lips. "Let's start over. Today. Right now. A fresh start."

If we started from scratch now, it wouldn't matter what happened last night. We hadn't been dating, we'd never promised each other anything. What mattered was what would happen from now on.

"I think you need to hear—" Paul began, but I shushed him.

"Please . . . I don't want to hear it." I pressed my lips to his, inhaling his ocean smell, his sweet, sweet taste. "I want this to work more than anything."

Only him and I. No one else. Not Jon, not Jamie.

"I want to fall asleep in your embrace—" I kissed him once.

"Wake up to the sight of you in the morning—" and again, tasting the salt of my tears on his lips.

"And get to know your every layer. Good and bad." This time I kept my mouth on his a little longer before pulling away. My lips tingled.

"I'm ready, Paul."

He stroked my cheek quietly for an awfully long moment.

"Took you long enough," he teased.

Our tongues collided. I was done being afraid. I wanted to live—I wanted him to be mine. I lay back on my elbow and guided him farther onto the bed.

"Shouldn't we be careful? Mrs. Stone?" Paul looked at the door.

"I don't care." I grabbed his shirt and pulled him closer to me.

Accepting my invitation, Paul moved over me, sliding his body against mine. My head pressed back into a pillow as a feeling of ecstasy flushed through my veins. I was contained. Contained by his kisses on my lips, his fingers smoothing my bare skin, his breath tickling against my neck. I had to feel that he wanted me. I wanted him to know how much I needed him.

He broke the kiss and started gently sucking the skin beneath my earlobe. I moaned, overwhelmed by the magnetism between us. I had never understood why everyone was always talking about sex. I wasn't waiting for it to happen . . . but right now, my instincts were to feel him, to have him as close to me as humanly possible.

Paul peppered kissed over the sensitive skin on my collarbone, then farther down to the neckline of my dress. His hands were finding a path beneath the bottom of my dress, caressing my thighs. I tugged his hair with my fingers, pulling delicately at the roots. His head moved up and our eyes connected. I let out a soft breath. My vision was slightly blurred, as if I was drunk. Intoxicated by him. Intoxicated by desire—a feeling that was new to me. My entire body quivered as Paul glided his hand up, over my stomach, under my dress, and drew little circles around my belly button. Then he ran his fingers along the top of my panties and I arched my back, asking for more.

"Could it be that you've never done this before?" he whispered.

I swallowed and looked to the side, embarrassed about my inexperience.

"Hey, don't look away. We don't have to go further." He moved up to meet my face again and stroked my cheek with his thumb.

"I didn't want you to stop," I murmured between panting breaths.

My words made his eyes glow.

"You sure?" he asked, giving me another electrifying kiss, then another.

"I'm sure."

Paul kept his face next to mine as he slowly wandered his hand down to my panties again. He slipped his fingers under the waistband and I closed my eyes, tilting my head to the side on the pillow, welcoming his touch. One finger glided over my clit and my legs twitched. It was such an unusual feeling, but unusual in the best possible way. He rubbed slow circles and I let out a moan.

"Shhh," Paul whispered in my ear before kissing my neck again. I pulled in my bottom lip and pressed it against my teeth to keep any more sounds from escaping my throat. Paul went faster. I was getting wet. It felt marvelous.

"Can you, um . . . go in with one of your fingers?" I asked shyly, wanting more but afraid it could hurt. Paul kissed me in response before scooching down a little ways to get a better angle. His other hand rested on my belly. I grabbed it and squeezed as tightly as I could, closing my eyes again. He parted my labia and slowly, gently, deeply, pressed his index finger inside of me. I bit my lip as a slight sting flashed through me and my body adapted to this new sensation.

"Does it hurt?" He stilled his hand and looked at me for reassurance.

"A little."

He pulled his finger out.

"Not much though, keep going, please." I smiled at Paul and he put his finger back in, not going as deep this time. Slowly he moved it in and out. The stinging sensation was replaced by a burning heat deep down in my stomach. He gently picked up the pace, rubbing me with his thumb. A couple more seconds—I felt a hot rush ripple through my entire body and I bit down into the pillow, experiencing my very first orgasm.

When I woke up the next morning, there was no sign of Paul. For a terrifying second, I thought it had all been a dream. But I could still see the imprint of his body in the sheets. I'd fallen asleep in his arms last night. I scrambled for my phone and found what I was looking for.

I'm sorry I couldn't stay . . . but in a couple hours we'll have all the time in the world ;)

With a gasp, I checked the clock: 10:30 am. Mrs. Stone told me she'd drive me to the Shields' house for noon, and I hadn't even started packing. Quicker than lightning I ran to the closet and got my suitcase out of the very back. I didn't want to stay here a second longer than necessary. Even more, I wanted to be back in Paul's embrace. I threw my clothes haphazardly in the suitcase, something I would've never done back in the days, but right now I didn't have time for tidiness. Twenty minutes was all it took, a perk of being an exchange student—you don't have much stuff to pack.

But a glance in the mirror made me realize that I'd forgotten something. My skin was blotchy and my hair a greasy mess. I still had time to make myself look pretty for Paul. I grabbed what I needed back out of the suitcase and applied a bunch of concealer, plus a shiny lip gloss. No time for a shower, so I put my hair up in a messy bun. Dressed in a sweet but not too casual Sunday outfit, I headed down the stairs with my suitcase, grinning widely. I didn't bother looking back at the room I'd never called mine anyway.

At precisely 11:58, the entire Stone family was lined up in the hall.

"We wanted to give you a proper goodbye," Mrs. Stone said tremulously.

My smile was premature . . . it wasn't over yet.

I held on tight to the handle of my suitcase, looking into their expectant faces. Crocodile tears were running down Mrs. Stone's face, but Mr. Stone was standing there rigidly, as if uncomfortable about how I'd gotten discharged. The only one who sincerely looked upset was Madison. She wasn't crying or anything, but the way she was fiddling with her hands said it all.

Mr. Stone went first, taking a step toward me and giving me a rather stiff hug.

"I hope you'll be more comfortable with your new host family, Emily," he said quietly.

"Thank you."

As Mr. Stone walked out of the hall toward his office, my mind drifted back to the talk we'd had in there. Were he and Mrs. Stone truly happy together, or were they only going through the motions to keep up the facade of a perfect family?

"See you at school, I guess." Madison shrugged. She chose the stairs as her escape.

"Yeah," I called after her. I didn't blame her for such a blunt good-bye. If it had been my decision, I wouldn't be making a big deal out of it either.

I shifted in the passenger seat awkwardly, feeling the weight of Mrs. Stone's heavy silence. The tears weren't flowing anymore, but that didn't stop her from sniffing dramatically. I'd apologized for leaving for the fifth time now. I was counting the seconds in my head until I could get out of this car.

My phone vibrated and I took it out, grateful for the distraction. It was a message from Madison.

I still want to hear every detail about that kiss with Jon ;)

I smiled and let out a breath. Of course she still wanted to hear about it. If there was something I'd learned about Madison, it's that she was curious as hell. How ironic that we'd become friends just when I was leaving.

"How about you come over every Sunday for dinner and a movie?" Mrs. Stone said suddenly. My phone dropped onto the floor. "We can stay in touch and have a nice chat," she chirped as if this was the best idea ever.

"I, um . . . yeah." I reached down for my phone.

"Wonderful! I'll text you!" she screeched, super-duper excited, and I tried to hide my astonishment with a crooked smile. This woman really didn't know when it was time to give up.

Once we got to the Shields' house, Mrs. Stone scooted over to me by the car door and clamped her arms around me, extorting me to return the hug. For what felt like ages, she clung to me. I was disgusted by her fake affection. Deep down, I wanted to scream at her, blame her for all the cruelty she'd put me through in the past three months. I wanted closure. But even though I'd come a ways in finding confidence for myself, telling her all that—*it's simply not who I am.*

When Mrs. Stone finally released me from her claws, I spied the finish line. She overtook me on the walkway to the door and rang the doorbell herself. *Three . . . Two . . . One.*

Chapter 24

Moving In

ND THERE HE WAS—PAUL SHIELDS. WEARING THE brightest smile I'd ever seen, showing off his pearl-white teeth. He seemed to forget his hand on the doorknob as he gazed at me and my suitcase. My heart leaped in elation.

Paul's dimples disappeared when he took in the sight of Mrs. Stone's stern face. He grabbed my suitcase in one hand and guided me inside with the other, his palm on the small of my back, protecting me from my own personal nightmare.

Mrs. Stone gave him a look of disdain before striking out again. "See you on Sunday!" she sang out extra loud before promenading down the path to her car. There was no hint of remorse in her voice. She'd won the game and made me look like the bad guy.

"Sunday?" Paul looked at me, eyebrows furrowed.

"She asked me if I'd come over every Sunday and I couldn't say no," I said miserably.

Paul's face turned hard. He let go of my waist and jogged down the path after Mrs. Stone. When he was about three meters away, he shouted at her, "Emily isn't ever coming over to your place again!"

"Excuse me?" Mrs. Stone turned around with her arms crossed over her chest, a superior look on her face. I stayed still in the doorframe, holding my breath.

"You heard right. Learn how to deal with your own issues and don't force her to make up for your mistakes!"

Paul flipped her off and strode back to the house. A giant grin bloomed over my cheeks. He'd given me the closure I so desperately needed. He shut the door and I finally snuggled in his embrace. I was home now.

Our hug was interrupted by Henry coming down the staircase and calling out, "Emily! Welcome to our humble home! Tell me, what's your favorite snack?"

I quickly stepped out of Paul's arms and turned to his dad.

"Um, I'm a big fan of cookie dough." I'd had it once in Culinary Arts. It was the definition of delicious, a huge sugar bomb.

"Gotcha!" He grabbed some keys off a table near the door and headed out.

I turned back to Paul. "Where's your dad going?"

"To the grocery store, honey." Gena was standing at the top of the stairs. "There's a football game on TV this afternoon and we always get our favorite snacks, so he's getting yours."

"That wouldn't have been necessary!" I protested.

"Oh, it is, Emily," said Paul. My name sounded strange coming from him—I'd gotten so used to being called Babycakes. "And if you don't mind," Paul went on, "I'll tag along with him because I'm suddenly craving apple pie." He stroked my cheek and followed his dad outside.

Gena laughed at the baffled look on my face. "I told Paul to go with Henry so we could have some girl time. C'mon, I'll show you your room." She gestured for me to come up the stairs.

It was the first door to the left, a mid-sized room painted in slate blue. A single bed flanked the wall in one corner with a fluffy red comforter that looked brand new. Across from it was an old wooden writing desk with a view overlooking the street. Shelves on the walls were filled with books of every genre. It was simple, yet just right for me.

"This was Henry's old office," Gena said. "I hope you don't mind the desk and all the books."

"This is perfect!" I hugged her tightly and she returned my affection, laughing. "I still can't believe you let me move in," I told her. "Thank you."

"Oh, honey, please don't thank us. We're glad we can help."

I gave her another squeeze. I'd only met her a couple times, and she'd done all of this for me already.

"Hey, Mom, where are the snacks?" came a male voice behind us. I turned and saw a boy standing in the doorframe who was tall enough to make me feel like a midget in comparison. Yet his round baby face gave away that he was only around thirteen or fourteen years old. His shoulder-length red hair was scraggly and matted, like he'd tried to make himself dreadlocks but failed. When he saw me, he burst into a loud kind of horselaugh.

"Dad will be back from the grocery store soon, you'll get your snacks. Don't worry, Zack."

The boy rolled his eyes impatiently, and Gena did the introductions.

"Emily, this is Zack, Paul's little brother. Zack, this is Emily, our new host daughter."

"Oh!" I exclaimed way too loud.

Paul and Zack didn't look like siblings at all. At times like these, what I was doing seemed crazy. I'd moved in with a guy who I didn't even know had a brother. *Why has he never mentioned him before?*

"What's up," Zack said, shrugging his shoulders.

I couldn't tell if he was curious to see me or if he'd just come in here to ask for snacks. I greeted him with a little wave, but he turned around and left the room.

"He doesn't like making small talk," Gena explained.

"He didn't look happy about me being here."

"Oh, honey, he's excited about it. He just needs some time to adjust."

I gave Gena a slight nod. I'd need time to get used to living with two teenage guys too.

"You should probably know that he has ADHD," Gena continued. "Attention deficit hyperactivity disorder."

"Thanks for letting me know."

In my first ten minutes with the Shields, I already knew more about them than I'd learned from three months with the Stones.

"Oh, and there's no need to unpack your whole suitcase. We're going to Oklahoma for Thanksgiving to visit our family, lovely!"

My jaw dropped. She'd called me lovely, just like my mom always did.

"Guys, we're back!" called Henry from downstairs. "Let's watch some football!"

A cute room, cookie dough and a trip to Oklahoma. I loved it here already.

We spent the afternoon watching the game and eating junk food. I still didn't get the rules, but watching the Shields yell when a player made a mistake helped me understand at least a little. Henry kept offering me nachos while Gena asked me about German words she'd heard before.

"What does *Schadenfreude* mean?" she asked.

"Oh, I know a German word. *Doppeeelgaanger!*" Henry put in, making the word sound silly with his heavy American accent.

"Doppelgänger!" My cheeks were starting to hurt from all the laughing we were doing. I relaxed into the couch. I was free. I'd escaped. And nothing was holding me back anymore.

After dinner, I went up to my new room with a full stomach and a head brimming with happy thoughts. I felt so blessed that Paul had come into my life. I sifted through my suitcase to find my pajamas. So far, the adventure I'd come to America for had been more like prison, but this was about to change. I still had a full six months and twenty-eight days left to make the best of it. I pulled down the window shade and took off my shirt and pants.

"Hey . . ." I heard Paul say as the door creaked open.

"Ahh, don't look, I'm not dressed!" I screeched, but Paul had already swung the door wide open and come in.

"Oh, sorry!" He spun around and shut the door, then covered his eyes with his hands.

I suddenly felt silly for being so modest, considering what we'd done last night. But no guy had ever seen me so exposed, and I definitely didn't want my first time to be in childish pink panties with a red bow. When Paul would see me in my underwear, I wanted to wear something pretty and be prepared for it. Keeping my braw on, I threw a loose black shirt over my head and pulled on some sweats.

"I'm changed now," I whispered. I was still used to keeping quiet at the Stones.'

Paul turned around, his cheeks flushed. He ran his tongue over his upper lip, scanning my body as if I was still in my underwear. "How come you look that good even in sweats?"

I grinned and pretended like it took all my focus to rearrange the bun on top of my head.

"Want to come down to my room to hang out?" he asked. "The walls are thin here . . ."

I didn't need any coaxing. I gathered up everything I needed for the night and followed him downstairs.

His room looked exactly the same as the first night I'd been there aside from some new chalk drawings on the walls, illuminated by the moon through the window—dogs and leaves and words. Right above the bed in white capitals was written: *BABYCAKES*. My heart skipped a beat. I walked over to the wall and skimmed my fingers around the words.

Paul pointed at the left side of the bed. "It's your space . . . if you like." I smiled in agreement and he added, "You can draw something on the walls too."

He threw me a piece of yellow chalk and I caught it with both hands. I felt his eyes on me as I picked an empty spot on the wall across the bed and drew a circle.

"A sunset?" he asked after a moment.

"Yeah. When the world is covered in golden light, everything looks so peaceful," I said, not interrupting my artistic moment.

When I was done, I gave my sunset one last critical look. It basically looked like a sunny-side up egg. I frowned.

"I think it's perfect." Paul came up behind me and gave me a kiss on the shoulder, just above the neckline of my shirt.

"No it's not, it's—"

I lost my voice mid-sentence when I turned around.

Paul was wearing nothing but sweats, granting me the sight of his bare torso. And I was pleased.

Chapter 25

Different Order

PAUL GAVE ME AN IMPISH LOOK, AS IF HE'D BEEN PREPARING this ruse over the last few minutes. His ocean-blue eyes sent a thrill down my body, past my silly pink panties and into my toes. Memories of last night tickled my mind, and I suddenly wanted nothing more than to feel his skin on mine again. My eyes skimmed his muscular torso and lingered there.

Leaning toward me, he pressed a hand to the wall above my shoulder, making me cozy up against it.

"I shall never erase this gorgeous sunset from my wall, Babycakes," Paul declared, gallantly ignoring my drooling.

"Oh please, it's so ugly!" I laughed and whacked my hand against his chest as an excuse to touch it.

"This right here is real art!" he joked, sweeping his hand at my drawing. Then more seriously: "And it's by you, that's all that matters." He moved his face closer to mine. His breath, to my surprise, smelled like peppermint. So fresh and—

"Hold on! Did you think you could seduce me into making out with you?" I pushed him away with my palms, giggling.

"Yup." Paul shrugged, giving me a mischievous smile.

"Now you're for sure not getting any tonight," I said teasingly, showing him that I wasn't one of those easy girls.

"No complaints," he replied nonchalantly.

The reverse psychology worked. I pouted at him, craving his kisses.

He grazed my arm with his fingertips and I shut my eyes for a moment, inhaling deeply. My body longed to explore once again the intense rush he'd given me last night. I peeked down at his v-line, and he accepted my unspoken invitation by grabbing my wrists and pulling me closer to him.

"Emily, I don't want you for your kisses, I want you for the person you are."

His gaze dropped to my mouth and I bit my lower lip, my heart doing triple time. He crashed his lips onto mine and my entire body sang with pleasure. Paul awakened all my senses, awakened all of me, body and soul. I couldn't wait for every moment we'd spend together. Because with him, I wasn't a boring little girl anymore—I was a woman, confident, resilient, even beautiful. The opposite of how I usually described myself.

Still kissing, we stumbled over to the bed and dropped onto it, laughing at the tangle of our limbs. We weren't officially together, yet we already lived with each other. We were following a different order than the usual. But I wasn't afraid of the speed at which Paul and I were hurtling toward each other anymore. I embraced our fate with open arms.

Except for one thing.

"Wait . . ." I mumbled in between kisses. "What about your parents?"

I hated taking my lips off him, but this question had been burning in my chest ever since Paul flirted with me at his family's taco dinner. I couldn't go on ignoring it. If his parents didn't approve of me . . . I didn't know what to do then.

"What about them?" Paul shrugged, stroking my cheek and giving me another sweet kiss on the mouth.

"Um, won't they care . . . about us?"

I eased myself off his body. Paul sighed and stretched out on the bed, crossing his arms above his head. Moonlight from the window shone on his bare skin, making it incredibly hard to keep my focus.

"I don't want to ask them yet." He scratched his head and glanced at the door.

"You want to sneak around?" I peeked up at him to get a better read on his face.

"I just think we should wait a couple days before dropping this bomb right after you got here." He softly caressed the back of my head.

I nodded. He was right. It was too soon. I didn't want to risk having to move out again already.

Yet I felt kind of guilty as I dragged a pillow under my head and nestled myself against Paul. Gena and Henry had bought a new bed just for me and I wasn't using it. *Oops.* But this—right here—it felt too good to deny. After last night, I didn't want to sleep alone anymore. I'd had a taste of this serenity, and now it was impossible to resist. Whenever I looked into Paul's eyes, a warm, buoyant feeling spread in my chest, like I was floating a few centimeters off the ground. Everything seemed possible with him by my side. I sighed with contentment as he tucked a strand of hair behind my ear and squinted at me with his irresistible smile.

"Paul? Can I ask you something else?" I whispered into his chest, tracing small circles onto it with my finger.

"Anything you want," he replied.

"Why are you helping me so much? Why are you acting like some kind of knight in shining armor, saving me from the evil dragon?"

I still couldn't understand why he'd chosen me to turn his life upside down. *I mean . . . it's just me.*

Paul took some time to reply. For a moment, I just listened to the beating of his heart.

"Why so poetic?" he asked finally, chuckling.

"Why not?" I said defensively.

"I like the way you talk. Especially how you compare me to a knight."

"Paul, you didn't answer my question."

"Emily, I like you . . . a lot. Remember?"

His dramatic pauses were driving me nuts. I rolled onto my side to get a better look at him, pressing my elbow into the sheets and resting my head on my palm.

"I have this urge to make you happy," Paul went on. "I can't explain it, but whenever you smile, I just instantly feel good."

His words made my heart surge with elation. I put my head on his chest, feeling the heat radiating from it, and wrapped my arms around him tightly. He pulled me in even closer and started petting my hair again. I felt . . . safe. I might not be in my own country here, but in Paul's embrace, I'd found my second home.

"Thank you. Paul, you truly are wonderful," I said with burning cheeks.

We stayed silent for a while. I had almost drifted off to sleep when Paul suddenly piped up.

"Can I ask *you* something now?"

"Sure." I rubbed my eyes.

"What's going on—between you and Jon?"

My hand froze. For a moment, I didn't dare move or even breathe. It sounded like he'd been waiting all day to ask me this.

"We, um . . ." I faltered. *This isn't good.*

"I just noticed the way you look at each other sometimes, and you seem closer lately and—you know what, forget about it, okay?" He raked his fingers through his hair.

I lifted my head off his chest and saw panic in his tired eyes.

"I'm yours, okay? Yours only," I whispered, desperate for him to be-lieve me.

The way Jon kissed me, held me, talked to me . . . it still jangled somewhere in the back corridors of my brain. But I'd sworn to myself never to let Jon invade my mind again. I wouldn't pay attention to the weird feelings I got when he was around, how he confused me, challenged me. *It can't matter anymore.* Paul was everything I'd ever wished for. He was the one who made me happy. *Jon . . . he just pisses me off.*

Paul was studying my face wordlessly. I suddenly had the urge to show him how much he meant to me. To prove that he was the only one I wanted to give my fragile heart to.

"Can you, um . . . guide me?" I asked, moving my hand down beneath his navel and resting it on the waistband of his sweatpants.

"Are you sure you want to do this?" Paul said with a gasp. His eyes were sparkling with excitement, yet he was trying not to push me. He was so adorable.

"I want to return the favor you did for me last night . . ." I pulled at my lower lip with my thumb, embarrassed. Every time I talked about something sexual I felt tongue-tied, and my lack of experience irked me.

"Just because I did it, you don't have to do it too."

Those words made me want to do it even more. I had to know if I could make him feel the way he'd made me feel too.

"I want this. I just need a little help . . ."

Paul gave me another kiss before starting the lesson.

"Here." He gently picked up my hand. It felt small in his. He put it down on the crotch of his pants and curled my fingers around his length. I pressed my fingers down a bit and felt how hard it was. I'd thought it would be softer at first.

"Just by looking at you I'm ready, babe," he said, seeing the surprise on my face.

"Oh!" I breathed, letting his words sink in. The way he'd called me babe instead of Babycakes made my head spin. I had never been someone's babe. But even though it sounded kind of foreign, it made me feel desired. Not a little girl—a woman.

I started squeezing around the fabric of his pants and he groaned slightly. I tried to lift the waistband over his boner but struggled with it, so he helped me out with a little chuckle. I peeked at his penis as if taking part in a science project. I'd never seen one before, except in the nude coed saunas I always went to with my mom in Germany. But those were only old men's, and I avoided looking at them at any cost. This one right here . . . it was real, and I wanted to look. Cautiously I ran my fingers over the tip and Paul shuddered.

"You need to put your fingers around it."

He smiled at me, and suddenly I threw my hesitation to the wind. He was here to help me, to guide me, and I knew he wouldn't judge me for my first time. I wrapped my fingers around it and squeezed.

"Not so tight," Paul said with a whimper, and I quickly loosened my grip a little.

I figured I needed to move my hand up and down, so I did it instinctively. Paul pressed his head back into the pillow and moaned. I looked up at him as I kept going. The way he was letting loose in front of me made my heart race. I bit my lip, trying to hold back a smile.

"Fuck, if you keep looking at me like that, I'm gonna come in no time."

Paul winced but kept his eyes locked with mine.

And within another minute, he came entirely undone in front of me. I was proud of myself for satisfying him in my first try.

We settled back into the sheets. Paul was absolutely perfect. The ideal boyfriend I'd always dreamed about. A guy who could've easily been cast as the love interest in one of my favorite romance movies. I'd found him, and I had to make sure not to let anything get in the way. *I've got to talk to Jon about never mentioning that kiss to Paul.*

Chapter 26

Trouble in Paradise

THE NEXT MORNING, I WOKE UP TO PAUL LIGHTLY SNORING IN
my ear, the heat of his body blanketing mine. He looked so cute
and precious while he was sleeping. I stroked his hair for a bit
before carefully pulling myself out of his embrace. He made a little noise
of protest when we broke contact. But I needed to get to my own room
so his parents wouldn't be suspicious about us.

I sneaked up the stairs into my official room and got ready for the
day. I chose a green wool dress that wasn't too short, but short enough to
highlight my legs. Then I decided to straighten my hair. It was still pretty
early and I had nothing else to do anyway. I almost burned my ear with
the iron, but the sight of myself in the mirror more than made up for it. I
looked happy and well rested. My cheeks were glowing. I'd slept like a baby
next to Paul. Feeling way too styled up for a school day, I passed on makeup.

Around seven, I headed down into the kitchen and found Gena standing by the stove. The smell of cinnamon rushed into my nostrils, giving
me an instant appetite.

"Hi, Gena!" I said when she turned around.

"Good morning, lovely! I made cinnamon rolls," she announced with a smile.

"They look amazing! But you didn't have to go to all that trouble."

"Oh, honey, if there's something I don't mind doing, it's making food for my kids." She walked over to the kitchen table and picked up her bag. Gena was definitely the polar opposite of Mrs. Stone.

"Zack, we need to go!" she called in the direction of the staircase.

Moments later, Zack slumped in, looking exhausted.

"Do I have to go?" he whined, giving an exaggerated yawn.

"You ask me that every morning, you know the answer."

Gena bustled to the front door. Zack rolled his eyes and trudged after her, not giving me a single glance. I had to find a way to connect with him so I wouldn't be treated like a ghost.

"Goodbye, Emily, have a nice day," said Gena right as I took a bite of piping hot cinnamon roll.

I swallowed. "Thanks, you too."

The second the door shut, Paul came up the steps out of the basement. He'd showered and looked refreshed in a dark blue shirt with a white stripe on its pocket and faded jeans.

"Long time no see, Babycakes." He twirled me in closer by the waist and planted a soft good morning kiss on my mouth.

"Mmm . . . cinnamon." He licked his lips and went for the roll in my hand with his teeth.

"This one's mine!" I protested, jerking my roll away from him.

He chuckled and grabbed his own off the counter. His eyes rolled up in a dramatic expression of pleasure as he chewed in slow motion, and I cracked up. I poured out two cups of coffee. Freshly brewed. I'd officially arrived in paradise.

Paul looked me up and down. "You look beautiful, Babycakes," he said.

I smiled over the edge of my coffee cup. Meeting Paul had boosted my self-esteem, and yet my cheeks still flushed whenever he complimented me.

My mom's words suddenly popped in my head. *Find a man who makes you feel comfortable in your own skin, beautiful and worthy. Not a man who makes you question whether you're good enough.* Paul seemed like the definition of the kind of man she approved of. I had to remember to call her later today to let her know that the move had gone smoothly.

After having injected enough caffeine in my blood, I climbed into Paul's grey Fiat and we headed for school. To my surprise, we stopped to pick up Brandon a few minutes into the drive.

"What's up, German?" Brandon greeted me with his usual friendliness, not questioning my presence in the passenger seat.

The guys started chatting about some football game and my mind drifted as I looked out the window. The city I'd so despised at first was decked out in glorious fall colors, glowing like it was on fire.

We passed by the Stones' and I felt Paul hit the gas to make the house go by as quickly as possible. I giggled and got out my phone. I had texts from Danielle and Breana asking me what it was like to live with a hot guy.

When Paul slowed to a stop again a little later, I looked up, confused. We were parked in front of Jon's house. *Shoot!* I dropped my phone in my lap. *Why is Paul everyone's freaking cab driver?!* I'd wanted to talk to Jon before he saw Paul again.

"Man, do you know if he's even up yet?" Brandon called from the back seat.

"Nope, which is why I'm going in," replied Paul. He got out of the car and flashed me a melt-worthy smile before shutting the door.

Brandon stepped outside and lit a square. I didn't want one myself but got out too so I wouldn't be alone with my paranoid thoughts. I scanned the windows of Jon's house, hoping to catch a glimpse of Paul, praying Jon wouldn't tell him what happened Friday night.

"You nervous or something?" Brandon sucked at his cig, looking at me with a bemused expression.

"I, um . . . I just don't want to be late for class," I mumbled.

"Yeah, well, you can say goodbye to that." Brandon snickered, exhaling smoke. "Jon is never on time. I don't understand why Paul keeps driving him to school all the time if he's never ready anyway."

I shrugged. "He's a good friend."

Brandon nodded in agreement and invited me to watch funny clips on his phone.

A couple funny cat videos later, Paul came out of the house, looking pissed, Jon tailing behind him. Paul jerked his hand at Jon to move his butt.

Did Jon tell him?

We all got in, and to my undying relief, Paul put his hand on my thigh with a smile.

"I'm sorry, Babycakes, we'll probably be late."

"It's okay."

I bit my lip nervously as Paul got the car into gear. I sneaked a peek at Jon through the rearview mirror. He looked like he'd just woken up from a rough night. His hair was sticking out in all directions, and the dark circles he normally had under his eyes were even more defined. His shirt was rumpled and tucked into only one side of his jeans.

"Morning," he muttered when he caught me looking at him. Cold and hard. We were back to how it used to be . . . thankfully. *Right?*

"Seriously, I can't always give you a lift if you don't actually set your alarm," Paul complained as he pulled out of the driveway.

"Sorry, man. Slept bad" was all Jon mumbled into his five-day beard. He shot me an accusing look, as if it was all my fault.

Paul stepped on it. He was a confident driver. The way he effortlessly manipulated the steering wheel, picked up speed or let up a little . . . he practically became one with his car. *Gosh, he's so attractive.* He was going about twenty miles over the speed limit, but it didn't bother me—I was used to fast driving on Germany's Autobahn, which, in some parts, doesn't even have a speed limit. I actually missed getting sucked into the seat from the velocity.

Paul managed to get us to school with time to spare. As we walked down one of the main hallways, still packed a few minutes before classes started, I felt a lot of eyes on us, tracking between the three guys and me.

"Why are people staring at us?" I asked Paul in a low voice.

Jon beat him to it. "Because you're surrounded by three dudes, Little German."

"I wasn't talking to you, Jon." I gritted my teeth. *Why is he being such an ass this morning?*

"Whatever." He turned down an adjacent hall, weaving through the mass of people with ease. It was like everyone was stepping aside to make way for him. He was clearly respected by his fellow students.

I picked pieces of lint off my dress, trying to gather my thoughts. Jon was acting like our kiss had never happened. I should have been happy about it, but his behavior annoyed me. I thought we were past the grumpiness, but nope. We were back at square one.

"You ready for your US History presentation?" Brandon asked me, pulling me out of my thoughts.

"My *what?*"

"Today's presentation day," he said, quirking an eyebrow.

"Today?!" I gasped. I hadn't even looked at our project since Jon and I worked on it last. Brandon shrugged. *I'm so gonna screw it up . . .*

The school bell rang and Paul gave me an instinctive kiss on the cheek. "I'm sure you're gonna do great." He headed off and I lost sight of him in the throngs of people. If only I'd gotten a class with him.

I stared at my more-or-less completed English test and it stared right back at me. Commas . . . Just like in German, English has plenty of grammar rules. Too bad they aren't the same. My teacher collected the test and I knew I'd probably failed, but she wouldn't be harsh with the grading. In the last essay I'd handed in, she barely highlighted any mistakes, just commented on the content. My school in Germany didn't even care about my grades at Boonville High. They wouldn't accept any credits from an exchange school—that simply wasn't how it worked, they said. I would have to repeat my year when I returned.

In Math, the teacher was going so fast that I eventually gave up trying to follow her and went over my presentation notes instead.

When US History rolled around, I pored over my notes one last time as I headed for class, desperate to stick the essential facts to my memory. Eyes glued to my sheets, I walked right into Jon's hard chest at the door and the papers went flying.

"Sorry." He shrugged and bent down to pick up the sheets. When he gave them to me, my hand grazed his and our eyes met. A shiver traveled over my skin as flashbacks of Friday night surfaced in my mind. How he'd cupped my face, how he'd licked my lips.

Jon shook his head with a snort and turned on his heel.

"Jon, wait! Can we, um, talk?" I chewed on the inside of my cheek. *This has to be done.*

"No." His voice was as sharp as a knife. He walked into the classroom, leaving me standing there with panic in my heart.

Chapter 27

Back To Square One

"I CAN'T WAIT TO HEAR YOUR PRESENTATIONS," SAID MR. Harrison, seated in the first row with a pen and paper in front of him. Hannah and Brandon were up first. I shifted back and forth in my chair, waiting to get this over with.

"We chose John F. Kennedy," Brandon began. "He was the 35th president of the United States, serving from January 1961 until he was assassinated . . ."

I tried to follow their words and soak up new pieces of information, but my brain was cramped with thoughts of Paul and what he would do if Jon told him about the kiss. I was so stupid, I felt sick. Paul deserved to hear the truth right away . . . *What was I thinking?* I was falling so hard for him that I'd neglected common sense. I'd let my heart rule, and now I was a complete mess. And even worse—a liar.

"I hate this!" I said to myself. Quietly, but not quiet enough. Gasps echoed around the classroom. Hannah swallowed the end of her sentence and stared at me, her eyes wide.

"What do you mean, Emily?"

"Um, I meant—I hate that JFK got shot!" I blurted, thankful that Jon had told me this once while we were studying.

Mr. Harrison turned around with a sigh. "Emily, I'm glad to hear that our history touches you so deeply, but please let your classmates finish before you share your thoughts."

"Sorry . . ."

I turned to look at Jon. He was picking at his fingertips, his jaw set.

As the presentations trickled by, I slowly began to hope that there wouldn't be time for me and Jon to present today.

But that scenario didn't happen. I found myself standing at the board with him.

Jon kicked things off. "We based our project on Malcolm X because we think he's one of the most influential African Americans in history." His voice was cool and composed, like he could do this in his sleep. There wasn't even a hint of nervousness to him. He kept on talking while he jotted down keywords on the whiteboard. The class was hanging on his every word.

When we'd practiced, I was the one in charge of writing down the keywords while he talked, and he'd given me cute little winks as signals. But now, during the real thing, he hadn't even looked at me once. He'd made me invisible, a useless accessory to his speech . . . and yet again, he was making my blood boil.

"Little German!"

Jon barked my name like he'd said it for the third time. "Stop daydreaming about me and talk about Malcolm X's childhood," he quipped, making the whole class laugh.

I spun around and grabbed a whiteboard marker, taking a short moment to swallow down my tears. My voice shaking, I started my part, messing up dates and facts, and misspelling words I knew by heart.

The school bell hadn't even finished ringing when Jon was up and headed for the door. But I was ready for this. I sprinted after him and out of the classroom while the others were still at their desks.

"I'm not taking no as an answer!" I snapped.

Jon froze and turned around, his expression contemptuous.

"Fine."

He grabbed my arm and pulled me down the hall and into a storage closet. The room was small and cramped, leaving just a tight space between us. I closed the door, shrouding us in near-darkness. I could just make out the bored look on Jon's face. I looked down at my shoes, regretting my demand. But he was the one teaching me to speak my mind, and I wouldn't flake out now.

With only a few centimeters between us, I remembered Jon's smoky flavor on my tongue. Paralyzed, I looked up and searched his nearly black eyes for their usual fire, but it was absent.

"So? I thought you wanted to talk."

"I, um . . . yes." I bit down on my lip until I tasted iron. "About the kiss."

Jon sighed and looked up at the ceiling, the muscles in his neck tensing.

"I didn't say a word about it to Paul if that's what you're worried about." His voice was taut with scorn. "And I'm not planning to do so, ever. I'm not stupid, Little German."

My jaw dropped. "You're not?" *He isn't going to use this chance to get rid of me?*

"Fuck no!" His tone was so hard, it almost scared me. "Paul is my best friend, and I fucking regret kissing you. Okay?"

His words sent a sting to my heart and radiated there.

"Oh . . ." I looked down, flustered, biting my bottom lip again. The way he looked at me with disgust—it was worse than his usual annoying way.

"That's all?" He lifted a shoulder.

"I guess."

"Good." He threw me a fake half-smile, then elbowed past me and out of the closet, closing the door behind him and leaving me alone in the darkness.

I sat down on a ladder in the back of the closet, my legs wobbly, and pressed my palms against my knees, trying to calm my breathing. Ten deep breaths weren't enough to get my nerves under control.

"This is wrong, you can't let him affect you like this . . ." I whispered to myself, trying to convince my body that it didn't need to tremble and my heart that Jon was bad news.

Three weeks passed in which life treated me to no further drama. I did my best to focus more on school again. Paul helped me improve my grammar and spelling. He was so patient with me and never complained when I made, yet again, the same mistakes.

Every night I sneaked down to his room and we did what we already had done to each other countless times. Each touch was a rush, potent with the energy we shared, leaving me electrified. I wasn't ready to go further yet, and even though Paul was being patient, I could tell that it drove him nuts not to do more with our bodies. Understandably—he was used to the entire package already. I apologized but he told me not to feel sorry, that I was worth the wait.

On Wednesdays, Paul arranged for Danielle to give me a ride back from school, and he'd come home later that night. When I asked him about it, he said he was getting some bro time in with Jon. It still made me nervous when they hung out just the two of them. I didn't trust Jon in his vow that he would never tell Paul our secret.

Zack still barely acknowledged me. But one time when we were both in the kitchen, he smiled at me after he opened the fridge. Henry joked that it was because there was more food in there now that I'd moved in.

Danielle, Breana and I grew closer, though. Our joking around during Culinary got upgraded to sleepovers and shopping marathons. Getting slushies at Target became our tradition. We always did "princess parking," as Danielle called it, which basically meant getting the closest parking space possible, no matter how tricky it was to squeeze into. Clothes and beauty products were way cheaper here than in Germany, which resulted in spending all my pocket money for the entire month in one afternoon. With each passing day, I was able to be a little more myself around Danielle and Breana, and for the first time in my life, I felt like I finally had real friends.

On weekends we often ended up at Hannah's backyard bonfires, hanging out with Paul and his friends. All my clothes smelled like smoke, but I didn't mind. Gazing into the flickering flames had the same calming effect on me as sunsets.

Tonight was one of those nights. Paul passed me a half-smoked joint and I took a light drag. Smoking pot was something that the entire group, or as they called themselves, "the fam," did. I was so out of my comfort zone—I never would've pictured myself doing this back in Germany. I didn't feel like the same person anymore.

"Jon, what are you doing for Thanksgiving?" asked Paul.

"Just the usual, man." Jon shrugged, not bothering to look up from the fire.

"What's the usual?" I asked.

"Nothing special," he mumbled.

I'd sort of hoped that Jon would make fun of my curiosity, but nothing. I missed his teasing and how he called me Little German. Disappointed, I passed the joint to Breana, who happily accepted it.

To my pleasant surprise, Jamie wasn't showing up to the bonfires at all. No one mentioned it, but I assumed it was because of my being here. I could tell that the fam was still a little skeptical about me being new to the group, though Kiki was nice to me again since she'd found out that Paul and I were serious. One night, the two of us had walked down the hill from the bonfire to sit by the lake that fringed Hannah's backyard. Kiki had assured me, "You're a part of Paul, so you're a part of us." Yet I didn't see her and Jon hooking up. I didn't see Jon around any girls at all. He just looked more and more exhausted with each passing weekend.

"It's getting to be about that time of night. You ready to go?"

Paul offered me his hand and I took it, my heart aflutter. He was the perfect boyfriend.

"Enjoy your Thanksgiving break, man," Paul said to Jon, and the two of them bumped fists and slapped backs.

"Bye, Jon," I hazarded to say when they'd stepped away.

Paul looked at Jon expectantly. After a pause, Jon muttered, "Uh, yeah . . . bye."

But Paul wasn't satisfied. He coaxed Jon into giving me a hug. I wished a hole in the ground would open up and make me disappear. If Paul had known what happened between Jon and I, he never would have set it up.

Chapter 28

Thankful

"**I**T'S GOING TO BE A COZY RIDE."

Henry gave a hearty laugh as I wedged my backpack into the already full load in the trunk. We were about to drive to his parents' place for the Thanksgiving break.

I claimed a window seat in the back and Paul scooched into the middle spot, leaving just enough room for Zack. Gena gave me a tired smile from the passenger seat. It was clear that she needed this break more than any of us.

Henry eased into the driver's seat. "Next destination, Oklahoma!"

I didn't say anything to the Shields about it, but I would've much rather spent the break in Boonville. I was still just starting to get to know Paul's parents, and now I'd be meeting his grandparents and every other family member he had. The thought of it made my stomach twist into a knot of apprehension.

Paul spread a blanket over our laps. Peeking at me out of the corner of his eye, he found my hand under the blanket and enfolded it in his.

I wanted to pull away at first—his parents still didn't know about us, after all. But feeling his calming touch on my palm, I simply couldn't.

Henry started singing along to country music while Gena flipped through a book on antiques and Zack played games on his phone, studiously ignoring the rest of us. Paul and I kept squeezing each other's hands as we talked with his dad about random things like nature, his work as a professor and his cooking goals.

We stopped at a restaurant for lunch. "These are the best ribs in the country," Henry announced, and he was right. They were deliciously smoky and savory. "Oh, by the way! My family is Native American," he said between bites, his voice proud. "We belong to the Kiowa tribe." That perked me up a bit. I was curious to be introduced to this culture, which I knew absolutely nothing about.

After a three-hour nap, I woke to Paul gently shaking my shoulders. We'd arrived. The others were already carrying their stuff to the front door of a pretty house.

"Ready to meet more of my family members?" Paul checked to make sure his parents were occupied with their luggage, then gave me a quick kiss on the cheek.

I rubbed my eyes and nodded. I wasn't ready at all, but I didn't want him to know that. We gathered our things and locked up before following them inside.

From the entryway, I could already see evidence of Paul's Native heritage. The rustic interior was decorated with handicrafts made of carved, painted wood, beaded leather and long, delicate feathers. I was enveloped with the smell of woodsmoke, a cozy, welcoming fragrance that reminded me of my own grandparents' house, and I noticed a fireplace that had recently been used.

An elderly woman came to greet us. "Do I have a grandchild I've forgotten about? I mean, I know I've gotten old, but that old?" she joked. She shuffled toward me and placed a gentle palm on my cheek.

"That's our exchange student, Emily, Ma," Henry said. "We wanted to surprise you."

"That is indeed a pleasant surprise! I'm Grandma Pauline," she told me.

Paul's grandmother was a curvy woman with pale skin and short white hair. Though she was all dressed up in black, she had the air of a lady with a big heart. I smiled shyly and looked down at my hands, but Grandma Pauline tucked me into a hug, making my anxiety vanish.

"Welcome to the family," called a man with a gravelly voice, entering the front hall. "I'm Robert. Paul's grandpa."

Robert was in casual khakis and a violet button-down. He looked a lot like Henry, though with streaks of grey in his hair. All three of the men in Paul's family shared the same nose and eyebrows—and the same charming dimples.

"Thank you. I'm Emily." I bit my lip and looked at Paul, unsure of what to say next.

"C'mon, honey," said Grandma Pauline. "Let's go to the kitchen and meet the others!"

She took hold of my arm and gently pulled me along with her. Paul lifted his shoulders like he was wishing me luck.

When night fell, Zack claimed the living room couch, leaving me with no other option than to share the bed in the guest room with Paul. Considering that I'd been sleeping in the same bed with him for weeks now, I didn't mind in the least.

I took advantage of a wooden partition in the guest room to discreetly change into my pajamas. Even though Paul and I had been plenty intimate, it still felt weird to undress in front of him.

"Grandma Pauline likes you a lot!" Paul exclaimed from the bed. "They all like you, actually."

I peeked around the corner of the partition and raised an eyebrow. "How do you know? You were busy stuffing yourself with cookies on the couch with Zack." I threw my shirt at him and it landed right on top of his face.

He pulled it off with a grin. "She wouldn't have stayed with you in the kitchen for hours if she didn't like you."

He threw the shirt back at me and I caught it, giggling. "Well, I like her too. She's lovely."

I put on my pajamas, this time leaving off my bra, then crawled under the blanket with Paul to nuzzle into his embrace. I felt like I'd been hit by a truck, even though all I'd done was sit around all day.

Paul brushed my hair back with his fingertips and placed a kiss on my hairline, and I let out a little sound of pleasure.

"Thank you for coming with us," he said in a hushed voice. His breath in my ear tickled a little.

"Of course I came here with you."

"You could've stayed in Boonville, but you were down to meet my entire family. Believe me, I'm a little freaked too. This is all happening pretty fast."

So he'd noticed the miles per hour too.

"I feel like I'm in a movie," I admitted, lifting my head to give him a kiss. "A darn good one."

Paul ran his fingers through my hair and tugged at the tips. His lips found their way to my neck, and he kissed me more ardently. Pretty soon, he was hovering over me and I was arching my back in expectation.

"You know, this house has some pretty thick walls." Paul looked up at me with an eyebrow cocked.

My first instinct was to protest, but as he started stroking my inner thighs, I abandoned myself to his caresses.

Paul was my prince charming, my protector, my companion, and suddenly, I wanted to go further with him. To give him more of my heart, of myself. To feel him in every layer there was to me. Even though we were at his grandparents' place, it felt right. I couldn't wait any longer.

Paul started rubbing me in a familiar motion, but I shook my head and took hold of his shoulders to push him down my body. He didn't complain, moving lower until he'd reached my hips. He licked his lips and pulled down the sexiest panties I owned—black with a little lace on the sides. Danielle and Breana had tried to convince me to get something more revealing, but I didn't see myself wearing a leopard-print G-string.

Paul parted my legs, and I closed my eyes and rested my head into the pillow. He took his sweet time, first touching me with just his fingers, making me moan with pleasure. Then he dipped his tongue down and a shudder ran through my legs. It felt different—softer, warmer . . . more intense. I rolled my head back into the pillow as he lapped little circles with his tongue. Quickly I came to that delicious release . . . coursing through me, pure bliss.

The next morning, I was in the kitchen getting a cup of coffee when Paul's uncle Leo came in, surprising me. As we had our coffee, he peppered me with questions about Germany. It turned out that he was a documentary filmmaker who shared my interest in learning about other cultures.

After we'd drained our cups, we moved to the living room, where Paul's aunt Claire sat on the couch, doing a little girl's hair. The girl peeked at me cautiously before darting over to Zack, and when I waved at her, she ran away. "Megan is seven, and she's a little shy with new people," her mother explained.

After the first bit of chit-chat, Paul came up next to me with a smile. I cocked my head at him and saw a proud look in his eye—proud, maybe, that I was there with his family, talking to them so casually.

"Go away!" Zack shouted as Megan, having crept back into the room, tried to poke at his tangled mess of hair. Paul and I laughed and Megan took this as encouragement to annoy her cousin further. Zack sighed extra dramatically.

Around noon we all ended up in the kitchen, and I helped Grandma Pauline and Gena with the cooking. Today was Thanksgiving, after all. I chopped vegetables to go into the stuffing for a turkey that was—impossibly—five times as big as my face. All those hours of cutting technique in Culinary paid off. I'd finished in no time.

Paul wandered in with a giant bowl of potatoes he'd peeled in the living room. "Can I have a beer?" he asked.

Henry nodded his approval. "Sure."

Zack's head popped in the doorframe. "Oh, can I get one too?" He'd clearly been listening in. Henry and Leo laughed out loud.

"You're fourteen, bud," Leo said. "Another two years and you might get one too." He patted Zack on the shoulder.

"Beer isn't even that tasty anyway," I added in consolation, but he acted like he hadn't heard me.

Grabbing his beer, Paul beckoned for me to come to the living room with him, where someone had put on Native American music. Paul's grandpa started doing a traditional dance. At first it just looked like a lot of fun, but as everyone joined in, I saw how lovely it was. So connected.

Grandpa Robert suddenly ran up to me and grabbed my hand to pull me to the dance floor, aka the middle of the living room. I screeched little "no"s, panicking about having to let loose in front of them, but he ignored me and started twirling my arms from left to right, almost making me fly through the living room. I burst out laughing and decided to not care about how I looked. I waved my arms, jumped up and down and shook my head until my hair looked like a bird's nest. Grandpa Robert guided me toward Paul, who took over the lead, and by the end of the song, I was crying with laughter.

When Grandma Pauline invited us to the dinner table later on, I couldn't believe my eyes. "Wow, this is so much food!" I gasped.

"Yeah, it's a real feast," said Paul.

Everyone took turns sharing what they were thankful for, a Thanksgiving tradition. Mostly, it was family—appreciation for being able to gather together in good health.

"I'm thankful for the food," Zack cracked, making everyone laugh.

"Well, I'm thankful for Emily being here today," Gena said. My cheeks burned.

"We're glad to call you part of our family now," Henry chipped in, which didn't help any in getting my face back to a normal color again.

"I'm thankful you took me in. I still can't put into words how much it means to me." These people were so *good*, I still couldn't understand how I could possibly deserve them.

Paul's grandpa stood up, pulling a white and purple bundle from under the table.

"To make it official, here's your own Native American blanket," he said to me, holding it up high. It was beautiful, with an intricate pattern of tapered pink rectangles, fringed with purple yarn. It looked hand-made, unique ... *and it's for me.*

I noticed that my mouth had dropped open. I quickly closed it and shook my head slowly, trying to work through the shock. Grandpa Robert gestured for me to come closer, so I got up and let him wrap me in it.

"You look like a burrito," Zack said, throwing me what was maybe his first real smile.

Everyone started clapping, and Paul looked at me in awe. I was a part of them now. Part of their little tribe. And I couldn't be more thankful for that.

Henry suggested I take the blanket off again for dinner, and we ate and ate and ate for what seemed like minutes but extended well into the evening. Eventually I had to open the first stud of my pants. I hid it behind my sweater, a little embarrassed. I'd never eaten that much food in my entire life, but as Paul explained, it's what you're supposed to do at Thanksgiving. I reminded him that it was about being grateful for the blessings of the harvest, but he waved me off with a grin.

"Basically, it's about family and being together." He helped himself to more turkey.

How can he still eat? I giggled into my sleeve and he gave me a wink.

As we kept on chatting and nibbling at our plates, I accepted a glass of red wine. Henry joked that since I was German and drinking at sixteen was legal for me, the twenty-one rule didn't apply. I only drank a little though. I didn't want to disgrace myself in front of Paul's entire family, no matter how comfortable I felt with them.

Paul suddenly raised his glass and clinked it with a spoon. He laughed when the lively chatter died down and everyone turned to look at him.

"Damn, that actually worked. Always meant to do it since I saw it in the movies."

He laughed again, a little drunk, and the others joined in. But before they could return to their conversations, Paul cleared his throat.

"Actually, there's something I wanted to say."

The room went silent again. Paul gave me an intense look and I held my breath. Even Megan, playing with dolls on the other side of the room, put them down to see what was happening.

"You know we took Emily in because she was living with a terrible host family . . . but that's not the whole truth of why I suggested it to you, Mom and Dad," Paul said earnestly, looking directly at them. Confusion showed in their eyes.

My heart sank. I shook my head vehemently at Paul.

It's too soon!

Chapter 29

The Storm

"I T'S OKAY. I'VE GOT A GOOD FEELING ABOUT THIS."

Paul gave me a reassuring nod and grabbed my hand, but it did nothing to quell the panic rising within me.

Addressing his parents, he went on, "I *like* Emily . . . fuck—no, I have strong feelings for her."

"Language, young man!" his grandpa chided from his end of the table.

"You—why now?!" I whispered frantically, looking from Paul to his parents. This was surely not the right moment to come clean about everything to them.

"No, it's time for them to hear the truth! I don't want to hide what we have anymore, I want to make it official." Paul took a deep breath and intertwined his fingers with mine.

"I'm in love with you, Emily."

He beamed at me, making the dimples show on his cheeks.

I couldn't move, couldn't even breathe as Paul's words sank in. In front of everyone . . . his entire family . . . in love with me? Little me? A boring, quiet girl who couldn't even love herself?

Grandma Pauline was the first to react. "I knew it!" she cried, almost pitching the wine out of her glass as she thrust her hands in the air. "I'm going to have such beautiful great-grandchildren!"

I swallowed down my saliva with difficulty, seeing Henry blink at us blankly and Gena give me a stern look.

Then the charade was up. Gena cracked up over her wine glass. "You thought we didn't know?"

"We knew the second we met you, Emily!" Henry said, joining in the laughter.

Gena gave her husband a pointed look. "You mean that your wonderful wife knew! You were blind to it until the night we saw Emily at the movies, Henry."

She nudged his side and he dropped his chin in mock defeat. Then he picked up her hand and kissed it as a peace offering. They seriously were couple goals.

"Emily, you can relax!" Gena snorted, seeing that I was still holding my breath.

My eyes twitched over to Paul, who was giving me his most adorable grin.

"Oh yes, let's see a kiss!" Grandma Pauline screeched way too loud.

Her enthusiasm was contagious. All around the table, people picked up their cutlery and tapped their glasses like Paul had done before his speech, aside from Zack who pretended to gag. Paul's face lit up even brighter than when he'd seen me on his doorstep on move-in day. He raised his shoulders in a *why-not* kind of way.

I wasn't sure if I was more embarrassed or excited. I pressed down all the fear and my chest flared up with heat. Kissing Paul in front of his family was a strange new idea. Yet the thought of tasting those beautiful lips whenever I wanted to—it uncaged me. Nothing would stand between us being together. Well, nothing but the distance between Germany and America.

Paul took my hand and pulled me into a standing position beside him. He stroked my flaming cheek, then softly placed his mouth on mine. It was a beautiful kiss, a little shy on both sides with his entire family watching us, but our first kiss as a real couple—as something substantial that existed only in togetherness, that was lacking when we were apart.

Apart . . . I had exactly six months and four days left to be with Paul. Six months to figure out if this relationship had an expiration date or not . . . I already feared saying goodbye at the airport.

Zack interrupted the moment with a loud burp, shifting the group's attention onto him.

"Oh, Zack . . ." Gena sighed while everyone else laughed.

"All right everyone," Paul's grandpa said, "it's time for our yearly family photo!" He stood up and beckoned us outside.

With our bellies full and our cheeks glowing from the wine and merriment, we all trooped into the backyard. I offered to take the picture, but everyone insisted that I be in it too, which led to less-than-perfect photos with the self-timer. Yet those spontaneous shots of our unprepared, laughing faces captured the moment better than any photographer could.

"You could have warned me, you know?" I nudged Paul before putting a kiss on his cheek. We were still in the backyard, sitting on a stone bench after everyone else had gone back into the house.

"I didn't know what I was doing until it was happening," he confessed, leaning in to meet my lips. A breeze blew a few strands of my hair onto his face and I pushed them off.

As he pulled away from the kiss, the reality settled into my stomach. We were *officially* together now. I tucked my hair behind my ears to keep it from blowing about and looked at Paul apprehensively. "I think what we're doing here is crazy."

"What are you talking about?" he asked, a crease appearing between his eyebrows.

"You know, you still haven't told me what your missing link is . . . Or why you dropped out of football. I feel like there are so many things I still don't know about you."

"I really thought you'd forget about that." He chuckled.

"Hey! I was drunk, yes, but I listen to what you say!" I crossed my arms and pouted.

"Oh yes you do!" he crooned, pinching my cheek like I was a little kid. But then his gaze drifted to the sky behind me and his mouth dropped open. "Oh, shit!"

I tilted my head to see what he was so shocked about. The clouds in the distance had turned a deep, dark grey-blue and were gathering into a large mass low on the horizon. The wind whipping my hair around my face heralded a drastic change in the weather.

I shrugged, disappointed that the subject had gotten changed yet again. "We should head back inside."

"Go inside? Hell nah, we're going out!" Paul grabbed my hand and ran into the living room, pulling me behind him. Everyone was lolling on couches, rubbing their bellies.

"Paul, what are you—" I started.

But he didn't stop. "Dad, can I get the car keys? There's a storm coming!"

Henry threw him his keychain, and literally seconds later, I found myself in the passenger seat while Paul started the car.

"Paul, what on earth?" I protested, trying to catch my breath from the running. "The storm could be dangerous, we shouldn't go out right now!"

"Do you trust me, Babycakes?" He placed his hand on my thigh and looked at me intently, eyebrows raised.

I pinched the bridge of my nose. "Of course I do, but—"

"Then sit back and relax. We're going storm hunting!"

I stared at him as he pulled out of the driveway. *Storm hunting?!*

"Paul! It's dangerous!"

"Yeah, but it's nature. It's fascinating, Babycakes—what Mother Earth is capable of." Paul's eyes sparkled as he rambled on about the science of storm clouds and updrafts and wind shear.

"Okay . . ." I ventured a smile, my heart warming from his excitement.

Rain started beating down on the car and Paul flipped on the windshield wipers to swing back and forth like mad.

"Oklahoma is known for its tornadoes," he said. "Dad and I always go storm hunting when we visit. Must be destiny that there'd be one today!"

Destiny?

We drove down empty streets through the veil of rain until Paul pulled over near the summit of a hill. Sitting in the car, we had a perfect view of the slowly turning mass of dark blue clouds on the horizon. We watched, thankfully from a safe distance, as a funnel of cloud emerged at the bottom of the mass and gradually spiraled down, then hit the ground at full force. I suddenly understood why Paul was so fascinated by tornadoes. The gyration was hypnotizing. The sky looked surreal, almost magical.

"This . . . this right here is the reason I dropped out of football." Paul's voice sounded unsteady as he swept his arm at the horizon, not breaking eye contact with the twister.

"Storms?" I looked at him, confused.

"Nature. How it all works." He cocked his head and rubbed the base of his neck. "I know it's silly, but it's my passion . . ."

The reason for Paul's secrecy suddenly dawned on me. He thought that people wouldn't understand.

"It's not silly!" I took his hand. "Why would you say that?"

With a squeeze of my fingers, he inhaled, then slowly let out his breath. "Everyone was always talking about how great I am at football. That I should go pro and make a living from it." He paused to gaze at the storm. "But seriously, I hated it. I wanted more—something that actually has meaning in this world. Something that isn't just for entertainment."

"Paul, I think it's wonderful," I said softly. My chest warmed in sympathy, witnessing him burn for something like this.

"I . . . I think it's stupid. It's not like I'm gonna find a cure for global warming or anything. And it's a tough field to get into." His eyes turned dark and he pulled his hand away from mine to wipe his face. "I was worried that you'd be disappointed. It's nothing to do with fame or money . . . not like football."

It pained me to hear that he didn't think what he loved would satisfy me. I wasn't the only one with insecurities. Paul had his own list to explore, just like me.

"I tried talking to Jamie about it this one time . . . She brushed it off like it was nothing." He stared straight ahead at the storm. But I could tell by how he swallowed hard, as if there was something stuck in his throat, that her reaction had hurt him.

"I'm sorry she did that . . ." The thought of Jamie bringing him down made me ball my hand into a fist.

Paul cocked his head at me again. "You were actually the reason why I dropped out of football."

"What?"

"Yeah. You coming here . . . I thought it was so brave of you to leave your home behind. It was an eye-opener. I need to go for what I really want." He gave a sigh. "Being scared isn't an excuse not to at least try to save the world."

"All I did was join an exchange program. I can't take any credit for this. It's all you, Paul. Not me."

"No, you inspire me . . . You make me want to be the best version of myself. And I'm grateful for that. So, for a couple of weeks now, I've been taking an environmental science class at a college on Wednesday nights."

My cheeks started to burn. He wasn't hanging out with Jon at all, then. I couldn't believe that I'd had such an influence on his life path.

Paul put his hand on his door handle and lifted an eyebrow invitingly. "You ready?"

I didn't hesitate. He'd invited me into his world and revealed who he really was. And that made me fall for him even harder.

"I am."

We jumped out of the car and into the pouring rain. Paul ran around the car to my door so I could take shelter under his jacket, but instead, I turned my face up to greet the rain and let the wind in my back push me all the way up to the top of the hill with its force.

When he caught up with me, Paul wrapped his arms around my waist from behind and twirled me around. Just like the first time we'd hung out in his room just the two of us—but now, I knew he wouldn't drop me. I was his and he was mine, and we brought out the best in each other. We were connected. Two souls, good apart, but together, unstoppable.

He let me down to the ground and I turned and jumped back into his arms. The rain tickled our skin, but we didn't have eyes for the storm anymore, just for each other. Entirely soaked now, we kissed like it was the end of the world.

Paul pulled away to look at me, his eyes more serious now. He cupped my cheeks and leaned his forehead against mine. I could feel his breath on my skin.

"I love you, Emily Klein."

"I love you, Paul Shields." It came out as clear as a bell.

Paul lifted me up again and I wrapped my legs around his sculpted torso. My heart was beating as hard as the rain drumming down on us. I pressed my lips to his, not afraid anymore, but overjoyed at how wonderful life could be. Paul was my Reason #3.

Chapter 30

Jumpsuits and Zombies

THE NEXT DAY, PAUL AND HIS DAD TOOK ME OUT FOR SOME Black Friday shopping. They weren't exactly enthusiastic about it, but Gena and Grandma Pauline insisted that I experience the madness.

The deals in the stores were extreme—and so were the crowds fighting over them. Poor shop clerks. This had to be the most stressful day of the year for them. I wasn't keen on the idea of squabbling with strangers over a stupid pair of jeans, so I sought out the less busy corners instead. When I saw the price tags, I cursed myself for having already spent my allowance for the month.

"What do you think?" Paul held up a teal-colored jumpsuit with lace trimmings. It had a plunging neckline, too much for my little boobs for sure.

"I'm not sure." I scowled and turned away, uncomfortable about being here with an empty wallet. I should have mentioned it earlier. I didn't want Paul to think that I expected him to pay for me. I really didn't—I'd just forgotten that I was broke.

"Really? I think it was made just for you. C'mon!"

Paul squeezed my shoulders and led me to the women's change-room. Though the ground was littered with discarded clothes, there was no one in there. Maybe the customers were in such a rush to snap up the deals that they didn't bother trying things on. I was still reluctant, but when Paul said, "Just try it on . . . for me, please?" I had to give in. I'd do anything to see him happy.

To my surprise, he sneaked into a stall with me and closed the curtains behind him. But he kept his gaze fixed on the fabric. He was such a gentleman.

I stripped out of my tight jeans and lifted my sweater over my head. But as I went to pick up the jumpsuit, I froze in midair. I didn't want Paul to look away anymore. I wanted him to see me. *Really see me.*

"Turn around," I instructed.

I was allowing him to see me in my underwear for the first time ever—in a changeroom at Macy's, no less. I rubbed my palms together awkwardly, instantly regretting the impulse. My body was way too out of shape. I was thin, yes, but I wasn't fit, and I could tell that the Thanksgiving food had done nothing to flatter my belly.

Paul turned around to face me and his eyes widened before roaming up and down my exposed body. He darted out his tongue to wet his lips.

"I know I said I would never eat again after yesterday, but wow . . . I just want to eat you up right now."

If my body could have collapsed in on itself out of sheer embarrassment, it would have. I turned to the mirror so I wouldn't have to look at him directly.

"Hot damn!" He whistled, and I relaxed a bit.

"What?" I grinned nervously.

"Your, uh . . ." He gestured at my butt. "Your ass is . . . mmm."

The heat in my cheeks skyrocketed. I quickly turned to face him again in an attempt to hide my butt. It was one of the only parts of my body that was round and feminine. I had my mom to thank for it. I did outright thank her once, because I actually liked this butt of mine, disproportionately curvy as it was.

And I had Paul to thank for making me feel so good about myself, helping me accept the way I am.

Paul crouched down and lifted me into his arms, bridal style, before hungrily pressing his lips to mine. I could feel his hand cradling my butt. A hot, throbbing feeling pulsed between my legs. Paul ignited me, made me forget common sense in this public place. My mind wandered to what the two of us could possibly do in here—and as if he was reading my dirty thoughts, his hand slid down between my thighs.

Suddenly, I heard Henry's voice on the other side of the curtain. "Emily, are you in there?"

"Oh my gosh!" I screeched. Paul brought his index finger to his lips and I clapped my hands over my mouth.

"Um, yes! I need a couple more minutes!" I called out, hoping that this would convince Paul's dad to walk away again. He might have approved of us, but I didn't want to give him a taste of how far we were going already.

"Alright, have you seen Paul?"

Paul waved his hands at me vigorously, urging me not to give him away.

"Um, I don't know. Maybe he's in the fishing aisle?"

"We're at a clothing store!" Paul whispered in my ear, and I gasped as his lips brushed my earlobe.

"Gotcha!" said Henry, and we knew we'd been caught.

Once the footsteps had faded away, Paul asked me, "Hey, how did you know I like to fish?"

"I saw the pictures in the living room." I smiled at him, still in his arms.

"As soon as we get home, I'm going to tell you every detail about me. No more secrets—I'm gonna be an open book." Paul gave me one last kiss before letting me down onto my feet.

Guilt suddenly washed over me. No more secrets . . . I needed to tell him about that kiss with Jon.

"So, you gonna try this on now?" Paul held up the jumpsuit.

"I don't have any money with me!" I admitted, covering my face with my hands.

"Who said you were going to pay?" He scowled and passed it to me.

I protested plenty, but when I saw the look on his face after I'd put it on, I knew the battle was impossible to win. To my surprise, the fabric nestled perfectly against my weird proportions. I kind of *owned it* in this jumpsuit. Paul was right. It was made for me—the *new* me.

The car ride back to Boonville on Saturday was less lively than the one on our way out. Over the last three days we'd all eaten way too much, making us drowsy and quiet. It wasn't long before I gave in to my extended food coma.

By the time we got home, I felt well rested from all the sleep I'd gotten in the car. I emptied my backpack in my room and got everything back in order before changing into the jumpsuit Paul had bought me yesterday. I wove my hair into a quick fishtail braid and applied mascara and rose lipstick. I wanted to catch that spellbound look on Paul again, the one that crossed his face when he'd seen me in my underwear.

I headed down to the living room and saw, to no great surprise, Zack sprawled on the couch playing Zombieland, a bag of potato chips and a bottle of Dr. Pepper on the coffee table in front of him.

"Hey, Zack." I sat down next to him.

"What's up?" He was busy driving a knife into a zombie brain. His eyes didn't leave the screen as he took a potato chip out of the bag. I scooted over a bit closer and tucked my legs to my chest.

"Sooo . . . you like playing video games?"

"As you can see." Zack was now mashing buttons like crazy. "Fuck!" he shouted as a zombie bit him in the arm.

First category—the curse-like-crazy Americans.

"I hate playing on my own though. I need backup." Zack swore again and threw his controller on the coffee table, where it bumped against the one that was already lying there.

This was my chance to get closer to him, the first chance I'd had since moving in. "I can be your backup."

He turned his head to give me a deeply skeptical look. I noticed a tiny brown spot in one of his blue eyes. "I'm good," he said, picking up his controller again and scrolling through the menu at top speed.

I grabbed the other controller from the table and hit the multi-player option.

"What are you doing?" Zack complained.

"Just one game. And if I'm shitty I'll never ask again." I smiled at him.

He growled and shrugged his shoulders but accepted the deal. I suddenly appreciated how my big brother Lucas had always made me play video games with him. I handled myself pretty decent in Zombieland.

"You know what's really cool? If you pin them against the wall with the garbage can lid before you use the machete . . ."

And finally, Zack was talking to me. Mostly about how to kill zombies in the best possible way—but talking nonetheless.

When the round was up, Zack tossed his controller down and leaned back into the couch, downing his glass of Dr. Pepper. "Never thought you'd be that good," he admitted, wiping his mouth with his shirtsleeve.

"So there'll be another round?" I asked, lifting an eyebrow.

He grinned. "Zombie-slaughtering will be our thing." He offered me some of his chips, which I accepted like they were my prize.

"I understand why Paul likes you, I guess," Zack said, looking at me through his glass.

My cheeks flushed with warmth. "I really like him too." And now that I had Zack's approval, the final barrier was down between me and the Shields.

Once we'd slayed the next round of zombies, I went down to the basement to see if Paul wanted to watch a movie with me. After being surrounded by his entire family for so long, I wanted him all to myself for a night.

"Hey, Paul." I opened the door to the basement expectantly.

"Yeah, I'll be there," Paul said into his phone before hanging up to look at me. "Wow!" He gasped as he raked his eyes over my body. "You'd never know that you just spent six damn hours in a car. You look hot."

Every compliment from Paul made my heart sing. The way they came out so smooth from his lips . . . I couldn't hear them often enough.

He threw his phone on the bed and sauntered over to me, undressing me with his eyes.

"Thank you." I pointed at his phone. "Who was that?"

"Jon. He wants to hang out. Want to join?"

"With just you and him?" I asked cautiously, picturing the awkward scenario.

"Nah, we'll pick him up and go to Hannah's. She's having another bonfire at her place tonight." He stroked my arm gently.

"Okay." I looked down at his chest and placed my palms there, absently playing with a curl of chest hair that peeked out the collar of his shirt.

"We don't have to go . . . if you'd prefer stay in?" Paul lifted my chin to make me look at him.

"No, it's fine!"

I had no right to claim Paul all for myself. He had friends, and he hadn't seen them in a while. I didn't want to be the type of girl who put her boyfriend's friendships on the back burner. And after all, we'd still have all of Sunday left to hang out together.

But if I'd known what was waiting for me at Hannah's, I probably would have chosen differently.

Because after that night, nothing was the same.

Chapter 31

Sunset

"I'LL BET YOU ANYTHING JON DOESN'T WANT ME COMING inside his place," I pointed out, reluctantly undoing my seatbelt.

Paul got out of the Fiat. "I'm not leaving you in the car like a dog," he replied. "Plus, if you don't help me get him out of there, we'll both have grey hair by the time he's ready."

I sighed in defeat and joined Paul on the driveway. The neatly trimmed bushes in Jon's front yard had lost all their leaves by now. I grabbed Paul's hand and followed him to the front door. He didn't even knock—we just let ourselves in. A man who had to be Jon's father was there, having a sandwich. He looked like an older version of his son, right down to the sharp lips and the fire in his eyes.

Paul waved. "What's up, Tim?"

Jon's dad raised his hand in greeting as he chewed, seemingly unaffected by our sudden intrusion. It was probably normal for Jon's friends to come in and out of the house like this.

Letting go of my hand, Paul walked down the stairs to the basement and I trailed behind. He pushed the door open, again without any preliminaries, and went straight into Jon's room. I kept my distance in the safety of Paul's shadow.

"Hey, man, get out of bed," Paul said. "We want to get to Hannah's!"

The first thing I saw was Jon's naked shoulder. He was facing away from us, propped up on his elbows in bed. He turned around when he heard Paul's voice.

"Fuck, man, I thought you'd give me twenty minutes longer!" He scowled at the sight of me.

"I did, man." Paul snorted as he realized what was behind Jon—or more precisely, who. A woman's head had popped up from under the covers, revealing glossy black hair, pale skin and cherry-red lips—Kiki.

"I guess we forgot the time." She giggled, not at all embarrassed about being half-naked in front of us.

Great, just great.

Paul didn't seem too surprised at the sight of her. He looked at me with an amused smirk—but it vanished when he saw my face.

"Are you okay, Emily?"

I caught a glimpse of myself in a mirror across from me. My face was as white as the paint on the wall, and my eyes were shiny, like I was about to cry. My stomach twisted into a knot. Quickly, I rubbed at the corner of my eye, pretending to have an eyelash caught in it. All I wanted was to get out of here.

What is going on with me?

"Emily, talk to me . . ." Paul said, wincing.

I hadn't even realized that he was holding me by the shoulders until he was shaking them. I nodded vaguely when I saw how worried his eyes looked. He ran his hand over my cheek gently.

"Hey, man," he called to Jon, "we're gonna wait outside." Then to Kiki: "Make sure he gets his ass in gear." She nodded, and Paul pulled me up the stairs. I glanced over my shoulder as we left the room and saw Jon's paralyzed look.

"What was that about?" Paul said urgently the second we were back on the front lawn. He placed his palms on my shoulders and stared at me, his eyebrows drawn up in worry. I sucked in little puffs of air and rubbed my hands up and down over the teal fabric of my jumpsuit, trying to catch my breath.

"I don't know . . . maybe all the food I had . . ."

My heart was racing and I willed it to slow down, but Paul's concerned expression made it go even faster. He looked at the house then back at me again, and his face grew somber.

I kind of crumpled onto the ground and pulled my knees up to bury my face in my lap, cowering like an idiot. Paul kneeled down in front of me and put his hands around my shoulder blades, keeping me steady. I grasped at his shirt and swallowed down the lump in my throat, leaving a burning, stabbing feeling in my chest.

"Do what I do," he instructed. He took a deep breath in, and I copied him. A deep breath out, and I did that too.

In and out, in and out.

Slowly, my breathing calmed and my heartbeat slowed down. I got back to my feet.

"Thank you, Paul . . . I really don't know what happened."

I latched my arms around his waist and felt his body tense up for a brief moment, but then he put his hands behind my neck and pulled me close.

"It's okay, Emily," he whispered, a little gloomy, as if he knew what this was about. I didn't dare ask though. I was embarrassed and sorry enough as it was already.

Can it be possible to be in love with two people at the same time?

One thing was for sure. I had to learn not to get a panic attack around my boyfriend's best friend.

The drive to Hannah's in Paul's Fiat wasn't chatty. We just listened to loud music. The smell of the green apple air freshener had faded away by now. From my spot in the passenger seat, I watched the little cardboard apple swinging gently back and forth, avoiding any glances in the direction of Kiki or Jon.

Hannah's front yard was cloaked in a bed of leaves. Kiki and Jon went on ahead, walking around the house and through a shrieking gate to the backyard. After I'd grabbed my jacket out of the trunk, Paul and I followed behind. I concentrated on the lake down the steps ahead of us, glittering in the golden light of the sun that was low on the horizon.

We met up with the fam, who were gathered around a bonfire. Not everyone was there, only Breana, Leni, Hannah and Brandon. Breana and Leni seemed a little closer than the last time I'd seen them together. It took Breana a minute to pull her eyes off him and realize that we were there. I smiled to myself, glad to see her find a guy who returned her interest. She deserved someone who made her happy.

A few people I'd never seen before came out of Hannah's house and joined us around the fire. They didn't bother introducing themselves— one of them just gave Paul a slight nod as Paul added a log to stoke the fire.

Hannah walked around in a circle, passing out cans of Budweiser. I hated to admit it, but over time, I'd gotten more or less used to the shitty taste of the beer around here. Still, I sipped at it slowly instead of gulping it down like the others. As I moved my can away from my mouth, I caught Jon looking at me through the flickering flames. He quickly looked away, then eyed Paul in a hard way I'd never seen him use with his best friend before. Jon's hand was pressed tightly around his can, so that it crumpled in a little. *What's his problem?*

Brandon got up and went over to Paul. "Hey, man, can you come with me for a second?" he asked, rubbing his neck. Brandon's eyes briefly landed on Hannah, and I gathered what this was about.

"Sure, dude," replied Paul.

Brandon went ahead down the steps to the lake, his shoulders hunched forward, and Paul leaned down to give me a sweet kiss on the cheek. "Will you be okay if—"

"Yes, go! It's different this time." I winked at him and he laughed.

"Meet me down at the lake in ten," he said. "The sunset here is incredible."

I heard Jon snort, but Paul didn't seem to notice as he leaped lightly down the steps after Brandon. *He really is a great friend.*

The chit-chat went on for a while. Brews got downed. Faces grew pinker in the light of the fire. Then Breana and Leni got up at the same time. "We're gonna go get drinks," Breana announced to the group, giggling under her sleeve. They weren't even trying to be subtle, as Leni's hand was firmly planted on her butt as they walked away.

"Hannah," Kiki said in her lilting voice, "are you aware that Brandon and Paul are talking about you?" She drew a heart in the air with her fingers.

"Of course I know," Hannah replied. "But Brandon's got to man up and talk to me. I'm not gonna make the first move." She shrugged and took a sip of her beer. "I want a man who can admit his feelings to me, you know?"

"You're gonna wait long then," Jon said, rolling his eyes.

"I've got time." Hannah preened, and Kiki giggled.

I suddenly realized that I hadn't said anything since Paul left. I tried to come up with something fascinating to add to the conversation so I wouldn't look like a lost puppy someone had left behind.

"I like how confident you are about Brandon" is all I could manage. I took a casual sip of my beer, as if it hadn't just taken all my courage to voice this out loud.

But my statement was buried under the shriek of the gate as Marcos entered the backyard. He greeted the fam with a "Whassuuup?"

Hannah jumped up. "Marcoooos!"

I curled back in my seat awkwardly. I was part of the group, but whenever Paul, Breana and Danielle weren't around, I still felt like a bit of an outsider.

I stood up to give Marcos a brief hug, then took my chance and made my way toward the lake. I could feel Jon's eyes on me, but I didn't turn around to call him out on it. Hannah had a solid point. If someone couldn't muster up the courage to talk to you, why do the work for them?

Though—there was still a little hollow in my chest, begging for closure. I wanted things with Jon to go back to normal, even if normal meant him annoying the crap out of me again. Not this. Not this constant nervousness whenever he happened to look my way.

I got down to the dock and Paul immediately dropped a half-smoked cigarette on the ground and stamped it out. It seemed that he and Brandon were done talking.

Brandon came up to me. "Congratulations on finally being official," he said, giving me an approving pat on the shoulder. Then he took the steps two at a time back up the hill.

"Why do you always stop smoking the second I'm around?" I asked Paul, walking up to him somewhat apprehensively.

He reached out and cupped my cheeks in his hands. The last of the sun draped him in a rich golden-orange light and his blue eyes seemed even clearer. That was all it took to make everything else fade away. My heartbeat sped up in a thrill that sent blood rushing into my cheeks and through my entire body. I was weightless—his gentle touch made it so.

"Because you're too lovely," he said.

"Too lovely?"

"Yeah, you feel with your whole heart. You're pure." His voice was soft. I saw the black of his pupils contract. "I don't want to be a bad influence."

"Just because you smoke doesn't mean I'll start smoking too." I playfully traced his lips with my fingers.

"But you taste it on me when you kiss me." Our lips got closer. "I intoxicate you when I have nicotine in my mouth."

"Maybe I don't mind being intoxicated by you?"

My hands reached for his neck and pulled him in. And then we kissed.

Paul had already left his mark on me. He showed me what it was like to be one hundred percent invested in someone. The thing I had with Michael was nothing compared to this. I hadn't even met Michael's parents. And with Paul . . . I was already part of his family, even though we'd only met two months ago.

Two months. That's all it took for him to turn my world upside down, to make me breathe in his smell like oxygen. I was lost in him. Lost in his warmth, lost in his soul.

I pulled back, missing his lips as soon as they were off mine. "Paul?"

"Yes, my lovely one?" he said.

It brought my heart to the edge of exploding.

"I love you so much."

Footsteps scuffled down the stairs. "Hey, guys!" Kiki called. "Want to join in a round of beer pong?"

Paul ignored this, his gaze rapt on mine. "Not as much as I love you."

"Um, guys?"

Paul gave me a deep kiss before turning to Kiki. "I'm in, but I'm playing with Emily." The wash of gold from the setting sun had faded now, darkening the features of the landscape. Kiki agreed and went back up the stairs.

"I've never played beer pong before!" I said, a little insecure.

"About time you learned. How long have you been in America? Almost four months?" Paul teased.

"Yeah, but most of that time I was locked in, remember?" I crossed my arms over my chest.

"True, but now you're free and you're with me. It's time I showed you what it's like to be a real American teenager." He laughed and I had to join in. We walked hand in hand up the stairs as the last rays of the sun were extinguished.

Chapter 32

Bottoms Up

KIKI SKIPPED OVER TO A LARGE FOLDING TABLE UNDER THE back balcony of Hannah's house, and Paul and I followed. The table held a whole bunch of red cups, already filled with amber-yellow liquid. The balcony provided handy shelter from the weather, though the night sky was clear. All around the backyard were the silhouettes of a couple dozen new arrivals. The air was filled with muffled voices and laughter.

Paul pulled Hannah aside as she put out some snacks on a nearby patio table. "You're having a party tonight, Hannah?"

"Yeah, my parents are out of town, and I thought, why not?"

She went over a set of speakers and put on some rap music, cranking up the volume, and Paul sighed. *Is he not in the mood for a party?* I pulled my gaze away from all the people on the lawn I'd never seen before and touched his shoulder.

"Everything okay?"

"All good. I just thought we'd be a smaller group tonight."

Paul arranged our red cups in a triangle formation at one end of the table.

"Who are you playing with, Kiki?" Paul asked as he cleaned a white ping-pong ball in a cup of water.

"Jon," she answered, lining up her cups.

Kiki clapped as Jon came sauntering out the back door of Hannah's house. His brow knitted together when he realized that I was his opponent, but he quickly recovered, crossing over to Kiki's side of the table and leaning back against a cement post that was holding up the balcony. I focused determinedly on Paul's explanation of the game.

"Okay, so you gotta throw the ball into one of those red cups." Paul picked up the ping-pong ball and motioned a throw at the cups in front of Kiki. "If you get it in, they have to drink what's in it, and vice-versa."

"Oh, and keep your elbow away from the edge of the table while you're throwing," Kiki added importantly. "If it passes it, your throw doesn't count."

I nodded and watched Jon prepare his first throw. The ball flew through the air and landed neatly into the middle of one of our cups.

"This game's gonna be over fast," he said with a self-satisfied smirk. He slung an arm over Kiki's shoulder and she giggled. The superior look he gave me made my toes curl. I guess he wanted to see me fail. To prove that I'd never truly be part of their world. I grabbed the cup he'd scored in, took the ball out and downed its contents before Paul had the chance to object, Kiki cheering me on. The watered-down piss-like flavor went down sour.

"Someone's thirsty, huh?" Paul said. His eyes shifted from me to Jon, seeming to catch the tension hanging heavy in the air between us.

I washed the ball and narrowed my eyes at it. I was going to prove Jon wrong.

Cling. The ball hit the cement post instead. I was closer to hitting Jon's head than a stupid cup. The beer was definitely going straight to my head.

"Aw, it was your first try. The next one will be better!" Paul said encouragingly, squeezing my shoulder.

Jon snorted.

"Man, it's her very first time playing. Don't be an ass," Paul hissed at him between gritted teeth.

"I'm not the ass here," Jon shot back.

Paul just looked at him in confusion, then shook his head.

What is he talking about?

As the game went on, the color of the sky deepened to a velvety black. Only the moon—nearly full, the bonfire and a bunch of vanilla-scented candles shed light on the crowds of people laughing and drinking in the darkness. We had gathered an audience of people waiting for us to finish so it could be their turn.

I still hadn't scored a single time, and I was getting impatient with the game. I wanted to sink just one ball to show that I belonged here just as much as any American. I kept having to see Jon and Kiki jump into each other's arms and kiss whenever they scored. I always pretended like I was focused on something else. Then Paul and I had to drink down another cup. I wasn't seeing too straight anymore.

With his excellent aim, Paul managed to shore up our score. Each of the teams had just one cup left on the table, and I . . . I was hella tipsy.

When my turn rolled around again, Marcos called out to me, "Just let Paul throw."

"Fuck off, man!" Paul gave him a light shove and handed me the ping-pong ball. Marcos laughed out loud and looked at me in an *I-didn't-mean-it-like-that* kind of way.

I just knew it was my turn to get it in. "This is the one!" I proclaimed, holding the ball up in the air. Then I belched and Paul burst out laughing.

"I know it is, Babycakes," he said, kissing my hand for luck.

I squinted through my blurry vision, stumbling a little as I tried to focus on my target.

"Little German, just give up," Jon mocked. "Hitting the last one's the hardest and—"

Beer splashed right in Jon's face. I had finally landed the ball in a cup. And not just any cup—the *final* cup.

"I did it?!" I watched the ball, paralyzed, as it drifted in small circles on the surface of the beer.

"*Yesss!*" Paul shouted. He lifted me up to spin me around in a circle, and we both whooped and laughed to the point of tears of joy.

"Congratulations, guys!" Kiki cheered.

"I can't believe it, I finally scored!" I jumped up and down, then latched my arms around Paul's neck and gave him a laugh-kiss. "Take that, Jon!" I crowed, pointing at him. "You should change my nickname to Little American." A huge grin was plastered on my face.

He rolled his eyes and mumbled something, then skulked away through the crowd.

"*Little American?* Oh, darling, you will never be one of us."

The blood froze in my veins as I heard the voice that made my heart tighten with jealousy. Jamie. She gave me the once-over, then arched an eyebrow at me.

"I've got to say, I'm surprised to see that you're . . . with him." Her voice was sharp enough to cut right through me.

I bit my lip and fingered the sides of my jumpsuit. I'd forgiven Paul for cheating on Jamie with me, but getting reminded of it still stung.

Paul wrapped his arm around my shoulders and started walking, taking me away from her poison darts.

Once we were a safe distance away, he leaned his head against mine. "Just ignore her, okay?" he said in a low voice.

I turned toward him and leaned into his chest to inhale his ocean smell. True to form, it soothed my nerves like it always did. Paul was mine now. Whatever happened in the past lay in the past.

We looked back at the party and spied Jamie in the beer pong crowd. She'd already moved on to chatting with Marcos, kissing his ping-pong ball for good luck. When she caught us staring, she winked at Paul provocatively and threw back her head, her boobs jiggling as she laughed.

Paul snorted. "Let's go back to the bonfire," he suggested. I took his hand and he led the way.

We were about to sit down when my phone vibrated in my jacket pocket. It was a call from my mother. It had to be like five in the morning for her, so why was she calling?

I held up the phone. "It's my mom, I think it's important." Paul nodded.

"Hello?" I said, skirting around the groups of people, hoping to find someplace quiet down at the lake to talk to her.

"My lovely one—I was worried!" She was practically screaming into my ear.

Accidentally missing a step, I almost dropped my phone. I fumbled for it and managed to catch it before it hit the ground. My clumsiness—the blurriness of my vision—I was drunk. My mother would not be pleased about this after I'd almost gotten sent back to Germany for drinking.

I took a deep, calming breath and tried to focus on the conversation. "Sorry—there was a distraction. You're worried? Why?"

"You promised to let me know how Thanksgiving went. I've been waiting for your calls for two days!—Ah, I'm sorry . . . I want you to enjoy your time there, but I miss you so much," she said, her voice breaking at the edges.

I felt terrible for forgetting to call her. "Oh, Mom . . . I miss you too."

I emerged at the lakefront, where I spotted a certain black leather jacket I so hated—yet admired. Jon was sitting at the edge of the dock, dangling his feet just centimeters above the surface of the water. Next to him was a red cup, half-full of a dark-colored liquid. He looked up at me shortly as he snapped the lid shut on what looked like a pill bottle.

"Oh . . ." I gasped as he quickly slipped the bottle into his pocket and took a gulp of the stuff in his cup. From the way he swallowed it down with a grimace, I guessed that it was stronger than beer.

"Um, Mom? I promise to call you tomorrow, but I'm at a party right now." I heard my mother sigh at the slur in my voice. But I hung up before she could reply. It was shitty of me to shut her out like this, but I didn't want Jon to witness how I was still a little girl who tried to please her mom.

"You didn't have to hang up," Jon said, his speech slower and louder than usual. "I don't care what you talk to your parents about."

"Are you sure you should be taking your medication with alcohol?" I blurted out, eyeing the little bulge the plastic container made in his pocket.

Jon shrugged. "It's not medication." He looked up at the night sky, no longer paying me any attention.

I sighed. That was the thing about Jon and I . . . We couldn't just have a civil conversation like normal people. Talking to him was always a fight. And I was tired of it. I tried to do the right thing by going back up the steps again.

"Why did you get a panic attack in my room?" Jon asked suddenly, so quiet that I could barely make out the words.

My body went rigid. I slowly turned around and looked at the back of him.

"I . . . I didn't have a panic attack. I just felt sick." I bit my lower lip and took a slow, measured breath through my teeth.

Jon unfolded himself from the dock and staggered toward me with a grim look on his face.

"I know what a panic attack looks like, Little German. You definitely had one." He studied me with his chocolate-brown eyes. They were bloodshot, and he looked exhausted . . .

Is he speaking from experience?

"I . . ." I didn't know what to say. I forced myself to look away from him and watch my shoes as I wiggled my toes inside of them. I needed a distraction.

"Why have you been ignoring me?" I asked, catching his eye again.

"I haven't been ignoring you." Jon shifted a shoulder.

"Yes, you have. Either you glare at me or you treat me like a freaking ghost." The alcohol was making me belligerent.

"Fuck, are you seriously gonna make me talk about this again? I thought we'd already settled everything in that storage room." Jon turned back to the lake.

It was true—we *had* decided to forget about it. But why couldn't I?—The memory of his smoky flavor still haunted me. I stepped next to him and both of us stared out at the water.

"I never really thanked you properly for that," I said hesitantly.

Jon turned his head to look at me. "For what?"

I perked an ear, making sure Paul hadn't followed me down here, then let out the breath I was holding. The music from the party was so loud, no one would be able to hear us anyway.

"For not telling Paul that you and I kissed. I wasn't sure if you meant it when you said you would keep it to yourself." *Why did I feel the need to say that?*

"You found out about Jamie, huh?" Jon said, his voice full of pity.

"Jamie? You were there when she told everyone that Paul cheated on her with me . . ."

I gasped, realizing that Jon meant something else. "What else happened?"

"Fuck, forget what I said," he growled.

"No, tell me!" I almost shouted, feeling my heart smash against my ribs in fear.

"Little German . . . it doesn't matter." He looked at me with dark eyes. One of them twitched a couple times. "Just forget about it, okay?"

"No," I said, strong and clear. Finally putting into action what he'd taught me. "Tell me, Jon, or I swear . . . I'll tell Paul we kissed." I sounded composed, but the words were borne of desperation.

Jon sighed and whispered little *fucks* to himself. I stared him down fiercely.

"Fine," he said finally. "He slept with Jamie at Halloween."

And with that truth, my world turned upside down.

Chapter 33

Not Fair

MY HEART SEEMED TO HAVE BEEN PUNCTURED.

Paul slept with Jamie.

The lump in my throat was so big, swallowing down my own spit was painful. Within seconds tears were running down my cheeks. I buried my face in my hands and sank down onto the dock. My knees wouldn't hold me up anymore.

"Kiki told me this morning. Jamie told her." Jon sighed and ran his hands over his face.

"Paul didn't even tell *you,* his best friend?" I said, startled. My sadness suddenly transformed into anger. I might have kissed Jon, but Paul had done something much worse.

"No." Jon's hands were clenched into tight fists.

He helped me to my feet and gently took hold of my shoulders. My skin prickled at his touch. "I don't like seeing you like this," he said. He reached up and wiped away the tears on my cheeks, then brushed back a strand of hair that had come loose from my fishtail braid and tucked it behind my ear. He stumbled backwards a bit, seeming to lose his balance.

"Jon, what type of pills did you take?" I asked. Anything to avoid the image of Paul and Jamie between the sheets.

"Don't play all innocent with me, Emily. I know you know it."

My chest heated up with a small, secret joy. Jon wasn't putting me in the naive-little-girl box. And for the first time, he'd called me Emily.

I gave him a rueful smile. "Xanax?"

"Correct." He grabbed his cup off the dock and knocked back the rest of its contents before throwing it back down.

Suddenly I saw something more to the angry guy in front of me. He kind of looked like a little kid who'd experienced a tremendous trauma. He was fighting a battle in his head, and surrendering to pills to help him out.

"Jon . . ." I took his hand and gave it a small squeeze. His muscles tensed.

"You didn't deserve to have him do this to you," he said obstinately, directing the conversation back to Paul. "He *had* you. He should've . . ." He trailed off.

"He should've what?"

"He had the chance to go after you at Halloween, but he didn't."

"But you were there, so I wasn't alone."

"But I shouldn't have been there, okay!" he yelled.

Jon let go of my hand and started pacing down the length of the dock, looking like he was fighting against his thoughts. I watched him, perplexed, as he passed me once, twice, a third time. Then he stopped in his tracks.

He spun toward me, his face screwed up.

"I liked you first, fuck!"

"You . . . what?!"

"Yes, I fucking liked you first. And he knew! I told him about you right after I first saw you in US History! I was the one who got Breana to invite you to hang out that night! It was all me. Not him!"

Jon's confession whipped me like a rope. I felt his words tighten around my throat. *Is it a lie or the truth?* Either way, he had no right to tell me this now. It was too late.

"You"—thrusting my finger at him—"were hooking up with Breana that night!"

Jon pressed his hands to his face and groaned with rage. He marched up to me, stopping only when we were nose-to-nose.

"You know why I hooked up with her? Because you made him smile. Fuck, I was trying to be *altruistic*. He hadn't been that happy in months, and I . . ."

His eyes shifted to my lips and he stumbled back. For a moment I was afraid that he'd fall into the water.

Jon growled like a wolf who'd been denied his sheep. "And I knew he'd be better for you than I would!" He clenched his fists. "Because I'm a fuck-up!"

"You can't be serious right now, Jon!" I yelled back at the top of my lungs, balling my own fists. My head was pounding. I didn't know what to think at all anymore. "You can't come around after all these months and suddenly say that you want me! This is not fair!" Hot tears streamed down my cheeks. I was full-on sobbing.

"Not fair?" Jon's expression turned suspicious. "Why is it not fair?"

He stepped toward me again, though not as close. I tried not to look at him, not to unstopper everything that had been on my mind. I couldn't. It wouldn't be fair to Paul. Or to me. Or Jon. Anyone.

"Tell me, Little German! What is not fair!" Jon grabbed my shoulders and shook them. I whimpered little "no"s to the side, but he took my jaw and directed it straight at him. Then his expression broke.

"Tell me . . . I'm begging you," he whispered. "Please, I need you to say it."

My heart ached from his words. The flames in his eyes flickered to life as if he'd just awakened.

"Jon . . . I can't."

He let his thumb brush over my lips. "Yes, you can. You have to."

He pulled me in close to his chest. I could feel his heart thump under his leather jacket. "Please. You've got to remember it again."

"Remember what?"

Skipping back over all these months of Jon mocking me and ignoring me in turn, back to that fateful night, I realized the truth in his words. They made sense. Everything made sense. Breana had barely said two words to me, and then suddenly she wanted to hang out? The way Jon got all flirty with me in the car at first? How his attitude toward me had changed just like that . . .

And all of a sudden—

I remember . . .

Breana and Paul had gone outside, so it was just Jon and me in the room. Everything was like a blur. I was taking swigs of the rum bottle Jon had stolen. He wanted the bottle and I was making him sweat for it.

Jon said something to the effect of "Give me that bottle, Little German" and I told him to come and get it, jumping up on the couch with it.

He grabbed me by my waist and spun me around, and I screamed and bit into his hand.

"Fuck, Little German!" He let me drop onto the ground, and I giggled.

"That's what happens when you mess with me." I looked up at him dreamily from the carpet. I remember seeing four eyes on him, and thought it was hilarious.

Jon kneeled down and hovered over me. "You never been this drunk before, have you?"

I shook my head no. In Germany, I mostly stuck to beer.

"God, you're too good for me, Emily." He bit his lip, his eyes fixed on mine.

"That's *Little German* to you!" I reminded him, brandishing the bottle. *Did I really admit that I like the nickname?*

"Fine, I'll only call you Little German from now on then. Deal?" He grinned at me.

"Deal."

Our smiles faded away as we simply stared at each other. There was something about his eyes that magnified me. He brought his face down closer to mine.

"Are you going to kiss me now?" I blurted.

"If you want me to, then I will."

"I don't know . . . I haven't kissed many people yet. I might be bad."

"*Bad?*" Jon laughed out loud and stroked my cheek gently.

I wasn't holding back a single one of my cards, and I wasn't the slightest bit embarrassed about it. *Damn you, alcohol.*

"Yeah . . . and if you kiss me, you need to promise not to break my heart." I poked Jon's nose with my finger playfully. "You have to give me lots of hugs, and rides after school. Oh, and you need to make Reason #3 come true!"

"Reason #3?"

"Yes. It's from the pro side of my list for doing the study abroad program," I explained proudly.

"Mind elaborating what #3 is?"

"Making me believe in love again, duh." I giggled.

Jon's eyes widened in shock. But I didn't realize the meaning of my words back then.

"Those are big demands for just one little kiss, Little German." He gave me a weary smile.

"Too many? Fine, you don't have to give me rides after school." I batted my eyelashes. *Gosh, I'm like a little kid.*

"I'm not sure if I'm the person who can give you all of that."

"Hmm . . . why not?"

Jon's voice turned quiet. "Because I don't believe in love myself." For an endless moment, we just stared at each other again.

"That's tricky then," I said.

I rolled away from him and kept rolling just for the fun of it, taking the bottle along with me. Then I crashed into a different pair of legs. They wobbled and Paul fell on top of me. To my luck, he managed to catch himself on his hands right before he would've smashed into me. He slipped down to an elbow, so that his face was only a few centimeters away from mine.

"Oh, you're back, rude boy!" I laughed.

"Rude boy?" Paul lifted an eyebrow. And then he laughed too, and it was whole-hearted, so full of joy and energy.

"Yeah, you were rude to me in the car. You're my rude boy," I said confidently, not at all minding the feeling of his body pressed against mine.

Out of the corner of my eye, I caught a glimpse of Jon. His happy expression had vanished, and so had the conversation we'd just shared. Breana was behind him, looking upset.

"You okay, Bre?" I asked.

"Um . . . yeah. You should stop drinking, though." She pointed at the bottle that was still in my hand.

Paul grabbed it from me. "I agree! I want you to remember how you made me fall for you," he said with a mischievous grin.

I remember how I thought he meant falling *on* me at first. *Oh, English and your many confusing prepositions.*

"I promise I will not forget this moment," I said as seriously as I could muster. Then I dived into his ocean eyes.

"I'm gonna go lie down," Jon muttered.

"I'll join you . . ." Breana said, and then, it was only Paul and I.

But here, it was Jon who was with me, standing at the edge of the dock right in front of me, giving me pleading eyes. I took a deep breath in and let it out slowly, playing back the memory in my mind. Realizing that

I could have ended up on the couch with Jon instead of Paul. That Jon had kept his distance from me because he thought he couldn't give me what I longed for.

"You wanted to kiss me?" I whispered.

Jon's eyes sparked up. "At first . . . but when Paul walked in, I knew he was the better choice to make you believe in #3. I couldn't." He heaved a sigh.

I bit my lip and looked down at my hands, flustered. I couldn't believe I had told Jon all this about me back then.

"Please . . ." Jon pulled my chin up again. "I need to hear you say it." And I knew exactly what he was talking about. "I need to know if I made a mistake or not," he went on urgently.

I inhaled, filling up my dizzy head with oxygen. "Why? It wouldn't make any difference. You're with Kiki and I'm . . . with Paul."

I didn't want to say what Jon wanted me to say. I couldn't. Because saying it out loud would make it real. It would change everything.

Jon's eyes darkened. "Can't you just do what makes you happy for once?" he snapped.

My mind went back to when he'd chewed me out in front of his house for being a people-pleaser. But now, I didn't like how he was trying to mess with my mind.

"I *am* happy!" I fired back. "Paul makes me happy! He doesn't criticize me like you do. He respects me. He treats me like . . . like I'm the only girl in the world!" I shoved him away.

"If you're so happy with him, why have you never told him about our kiss then?" Jon stepped toward me again. "Why didn't you come clean about it the second you saw him? You weren't dating. He wouldn't have had the right to be pissed at you."

My jaw dropped. I could feel my heart pounding angrily against my chest.

"I didn't want him to be mad at you! You're best friends—"

"Bullshit!" Jon interrupted. "That kiss meant something to you. *That's* why you were afraid to tell him about it! Because"—his voice growing softer with every word—"it was more than a random hookup . . ." Jon cupped my cheeks in his hands again.

"Please, Jon . . . I can't." Tears were running down my face. The truth in his words cut right into my heart.

I had granted him permission to approach me when I didn't walk back up those steps from the lake. I'd let him confuse me like this. He wasn't the one playing games—I was. Right from the beginning, without even noticing it.

"Yes, you can," Jon whispered, his lips only a hair's breadth from mine.

And then he kissed me.

Chapter 34

Drowning

BEFORE I COULD OBJECT, THE BURNING TOUCH OF JON'S LIPS against mine ignited me. Ignited my heart, shutting down my brain. I gripped his jacket to push him away, but for just a second, I couldn't. I could only respond to this kiss, ablaze with emotion.

Then my brain switched on again. *I can't do this . . . not like this.* I forced my lips away from his.

"Jon, no . . ."

"You fucking asshole!"

Paul's voice reverberated through all of my senses. I jumped away from Jon with guilty lips. Paul was standing on the last step, panting, looking at me like the world had fallen out from under his feet. I thought I might be paralyzed. I sucked in all the air around me, hoping for the universe to hand me the right words to say, but the universe gave nothing away.

Then Paul launched himself at Jon in a fury. I screamed as they flew through the air and landed in the water with a loud splash. Running to the edge of the dock, I kneeled down, and silence hit me briefly, the two boys vanished under the worked-up surface of the lake. Then I cried out their names, and their heads crashed through the surface again. They went at each other immediately.

"She's one girl you were supposed to stay away from! You fucking asshole!" Paul roared.

He landed a punch square on Jon's nose. Blood sprayed into the water. But Jon barely even flinched at the pain.

"You betrayed her with Jamie! She deserved better!" he roared back.

His punch hit Paul's jaw so hard, I was afraid it might have cracked. Paul jerked toward me. When he saw my expression, his face fell.

"You know?" he croaked, and I looked down at my lap. I couldn't stand seeing the desperation written all over his face.

"Emily . . . please look at me. I wanted to tell you, but you insisted that we start over that night."

But I couldn't bring myself to look at him. I curled up into a ball and wrapped my arms around myself as tears blurred my vision.

The sounds of grunts and water splashing warned me that Paul and Jon were still in a rage. I blinked back my tears. They were trying to push each other beneath the surface. I screamed for them to stop but they ignored me.

Jon snarled, "You were supposed to treat her better than I would!"

"That gives you no right to kiss her!" Paul bellowed.

I was seeing a side of Paul I could have never imagined, even in my wildest dreams. A vein on his forehead was pulsing, and his face was contorted . . . He was in pain.

More and more punches fell. Blood mixed with water on their faces. I looked up the stairs, vainly searching for anyone who could possibly help, but the loud music effectively drowned out the screaming, and the others were all just faraway shadows.

So I jumped into the water. The cold engulfed my body, making me tremble violently. I swam up to Jon and Paul and wedged my way in between them. It worked; they stopped going at each other's throats.

"Fuck, Emily! Why on earth did you jump in!" Paul yelled at me.

"Because I'm the person you should be mad at, okay?" I cried out. "Jon and I kissed. At Halloween. That's why I wanted to start from scratch."

I had to say it. It was no longer a secret worth keeping.

Jon kicked himself away from Paul, anticipating the next punch, but Paul only looked at me in pain.

"I know, Emily . . . I saw it."

What?!

"You followed me outside Jamie's house?" I gasped, unintentionally swallowing some water and coughing it out. My arms were getting heavy. I tried not to drown in the mess I'd made. Paul followed me . . . That meant he was fighting for me right from the beginning.

"Yes. I was so mad at the both of you, and . . ." Paul took a ragged breath, and his face hardened. "When I got back to the party, Jamie was there. I was so messed up after seeing you guys kiss," he said, his expression tight.

My heart sank. For a moment, my legs forgot to kick to keep myself afloat. Watching Paul say this so bitterly was infinitely worse than anything I could've ever imagined. It made my heart crack.

"Why didn't you say anything?" I shoved water at him in frustration.

"Fuck, isn't that clear? Because I fell in love with you right from the beginning!" He pounded his fist into the lake and dark water erupted around him. "I knew it already. But I was afraid you wanted *him*." He shot a disgusted look at Jon. "I thought if I just pretended like nothing ever happened between the two of you, you'd eventually forget about it and be happy with me."

Jon kept silent. I could see his eyes frantically moving between Paul and me, apparently at a loss for what to do. And so was I.

"But apparently, I wasn't enough for you," Paul concluded.

"You *are* enough for me, Paul!" I cringed. The kiss . . . He was there . . . I just didn't see it.

"Then why did you let him kiss you again?" he growled.

I watched the reflection of the stars on the water, bobbing up and down uncertainly. The moon was there too, just short of a full circle, pale and wobbly on the black surface of the lake.

"I don't know . . ." I said, my voice small and shrill.

I had so many questions but no answers. I was lost, overwhelmed by the emotions thrashing inside me. Shivers kept running down my spine, from the cold, from the pain.

"Do you want to be with him, Emily?" Paul pressed.

"I . . ."

I wanted to speak, but sobs overtook my throat, smothering the words.

"Man, give her a second to breathe, you're suffocating her!" Jon interjected. "It's not just her fault. I made her admit it!"

"Admit what?" Paul spat.

No . . .

"Don't do this, Jon!" I cried out, so loud that my throat hurt.

"I'm sorry, but I have to." Jon gave me an apologetic look, then focused on Paul again.

"She liked me first too."

Time stopped.

The two boys stared at me. Paul and Jon. Jon and Paul.

Blood stained Paul's features, but it was his eyes that carried the most pain. Jon's were burning with the flickering flame that lived within them. These two boys who couldn't be more opposite had given me the adventure of a lifetime, spinning my world around so fast that I no longer knew which way was up. *Reason #1.*

One was my protector, saving me from my Nightmare, giving me a new home, helping me accept myself as I am. The other . . . my downfall. Exposing me as a people-pleaser, exciting me with the challenge of finding my voice again, of being confident. *Reason #2.* They both awakened me, shaped me, conquered my thoughts. They confused me, yet touched my soul. But I couldn't be with both . . .

"Is it true? Did you really like him first?" Paul's eyes bore down on mine.

"It . . ." A deep breath. "Yes."

Paul shook his head slowly. Then he swam back to the dock without another word.

Jon took a few strokes toward me and reached for my shoulder. "Are you okay?"

I flinched. "Leave me alone, Jon! You messed everything up!"

The words came out smooth, without a second thought. I swam as fast as I could after Paul, not looking back at the boy who made my head spin. Before coming here to the party tonight, I had everything I'd ever dreamed of. No matter what feelings I had for Jon . . . he was too late. My heart already belonged to Paul. And I couldn't let him walk away with it.

Paul had already reached the steps. I couldn't see his face. "Paul, wait!" I shouted. Grabbing hold of the edge of the dock, I tried desperately to haul myself up, but I slipped back into the lake. I wasn't strong enough. "Fuck!"

I tried it again, this time catching my jumpsuit—the one Paul had bought me—on a nail. The sound of ripping fabric echoed the splitting of my heart.

"Paul . . . please!" My lips were trembling.

He halted on the steps and ran a hand through his hair, looking up at the moon shining brightly down on us. My breath caught in my throat and I waited, tasting the salt of my tears on my lips. "Please . . ." I whispered, clutching at the edge of the dock with the last of my strength. Finally, he turned around, looking down at the ground as he walked toward me.

"Thank you . . ." I said in a shaky voice as he bent down and grabbed me under the arms to lift me out of the water. The second I was back on my feet, he wrapped his arms around me like he wouldn't ever let me go.

"I won't make the mistake of walking away again," he said. "I love you too much."

Reason #3.

And then we kissed, and the choppy waves of my inner world found peace. My list was complete. And Paul was my lovely one.

Acknowledgments

Studying abroad sounds exciting, right? Well, my sixteen-year-old self thought so too, and my year as a foreign exchange student changed my life. I met amazing people who shaped me into the person I am today—and who made this story possible. So a *huge* thank you to everyone who left their mark on my soul and inspired the characters in this book. Though *The Lovely One* is a work of fiction, it wouldn't have been the same without your impact.

This story was a big part of my life for a good while. After working on it for five years on Episode, an interactive reading app, I finally gathered the courage to publish it as a novel, a dream I thought I wasn't good enough to realize. What kept me from giving up were the people in my life who reminded me that I can follow my heart in everything I do, no matter how terrifying it seems.

So thank you to my wonderful family—my mother, my brother and my father—for believing in me and supporting me in my dream. To my friends Shanen Ricci and Kat Valentine for putting up with my overthinking and for kicking my butt when I wanted to quit. To my editor, Laura MacAulay, for giving me the best advice there is and always having faith in me even when I didn't. I couldn't have found an editor who gets my characters like she does. To Philip—words can't describe how much you've affected me and my writing. To my cats, Chino and Luna, for giving me cuddles when I felt like my writing was crap. And to coffee for giving me energy when I had to meet a deadline.

Some people are meant to appear in just a chapter of our lives and not the entire book, but that doesn't mean they don't influence the path we're on. I'll always carry **you** in my heart, no matter where my compass of life takes me.

I dedicate this book to all these lovely people, but especially to those who inspired Paul, Jon, Gena and Henry. One of the things I'm most thankful for is having met them. They helped me find myself, and they gave me an adventure I'll always think back on with a smile.

I wrote this book as a guide to things I would've loved to know before taking part in a study abroad program. If you're dreaming of trying it out too, I highly recommend it. Because I did manage to fulfill my own personal list. So what's yours?

About the Author

Naemi Tiana is best known for her interactive mobile stories *The Lovely One*, *Hot News*, *Bad Reputation*, and *Enemies with Benefits*. Her work has been featured multiple times on the award-winning reading app Episode, and she has garnered 36+ million reads. This is just the beginning of her journey as a writer. Naemi lives in Germany with her two cats and a family she loves deeply. Her path is guided by Shakespeare's words: "Love all, trust a few, do wrong to none."

Naemi's stories can be found on the apps Episode and Romance Fate. For more, check out @naemitiana.writes on Instagram.

Made in the USA
Monee, IL
25 October 2021